I0634873

# The House with a Secret Cellar

## by

## Kay Pritchett

*Mosey Frye Mysteries*

The Wild Rose Press, Inc.
PO Box 708
Adams Basin, NY 14410-0708
Visit us at www.thewildrosepress.com

Publishing History
First Edition, 2025
Trade Paperback ISBN 978-1-5092-6008-9
Digital ISBN 978-1-5092-6009-6

*Mosey Frye Mysteries*
Published in the United States of America

## Dedication

For my teachers, colleagues, and students, who have inspired and encouraged me along the way.

Chapter One

*Monday, January 4, 2010, 7:00 a.m.*
*Hembree Police Station*

Sergeant Springer lifted the lid on a box of fresh doughnuts and, with fingers wavering between the jam-filled and the caramel-iced, muttered under his breath, "Raspberry it is." He pulled out the plumpest of the jam-filled, but just as he was taking his first bite, the sound of a ringing phone interrupted his momentary indulgence. He sauntered over to Ms. Hill's desk and, quickly wiping his chin, picked up the receiver. "You've reached the Hembree Police Station. Sergeant Springer speaking."

"Sergeant Springer, remember me, Lauren Wilson?"

"Of course, I remember you." He chewed, then licked his fingers. "Not likely to forget you, ma'am. You're the new, uh—"

"—forensic psychologist."

"Of course, over at the college. So, ma'am, what can I do for you?"

"I ran out for a minute this morning, Sergeant, and just as I was returning home, a strange man came from behind the house."

As Springer sensed uneasiness in her voice, the peaceful morning atmosphere of the station

1

unexpectedly shifted to a state of alert. "Strange man, eh? Strange how?" He lowered his hefty frame into Ms. Hill's swivel chair and took a ballpoint from the pencil holder.

"I mean I didn't know him."

"Wouldn't have been a delivery man, I reckon?" He was hoping to ease her concern.

"I doubt it. He was coming from behind the house."

"Well, I don't know. Shall I drive over?"

"He's gone already. I'm calling from my car. I'd rather come to the station if you don't mind. Is Lieutenant Olivera around?"

"Not yet. He gets here about eight thirty." He glanced at the wall clock. It wasn't quite seven fifteen.

"I don't guess, well…" she stammered.

"What was that?"

"Do you suppose you could give him a call?"

"I sure could if it's urgent." He silently pleaded for an answer in the negative. Oh, man, he didn't want to wake up the chief. If he did, he'd be regrettin' it all day.

"Well, I'm not sure I'd say it's *urgent*. Pressing, maybe."

"Ma'am, is there something you're not telling me?"

"No, Sergeant."

"Well, come on over if you want. The chief might even beat you here." He hung up the receiver. "Dang it! A body can't finish a doughnut!" He pulled out his cell and sent a text to the chief. "I bet he won't get that," he mumbled. "I'd better call. Unlikely he's awake." He punched in Olivera's number. "Chief?"

"Springer…that you?"

"I texted you just now but thought maybe I oughta call. It's Lauren Wilson. She's got a problem at her house—not exactly sure what. Somebody was in her yard. Said it was *pressing*."

"Pressing?"

"That's what she said." Springer resumed his position at Ms. Hill's desk and, picking up a pen, doodled on her desk calendar. "She's on her way here now. I offered to drive over, but—"

"Somebody in her yard?" Olivera yawned. "Doesn't sound pressing to me."

"To me either, but—"

"You know who she is, don't you?"

"The new forensic psychologist." Springer knew who she was, all right, and his doodle on the desk calendar was starting to look a good bit like her. Turned-up nose, big round glasses, long hair parted down the middle…

"I heard that 'ugh,' Springer."

"Chief, I didn't say a word." And while it was true that he hadn't spoken out at that precise moment, it hardly made a differ'nce. His strong opinion of women sticking their noses into police business had already been made perfectly clear.

"You play nice. I imagine we'll be seeing a lot of Dr. Wilson."

"Ya think?" Springer added a jagged speech bubble and wrote "pressing" in caps followed by an exclamation point.

"I'll be there shortly. Put the coffee on."

"Sure thing, Chief." With a utility knife from the pencil holder, he cut around the doodle, then slipped it into his breast pocket.

A few minutes later when Wilson showed up, Springer had a pot of coffee going. "Have a seat, ma'am." He waved her in. "I been thinking." He emerged from the nook. "Reckon it was the man checking the water meter? My momma always gets spooked when the meter man comes around. You know, it's kinda weird looking out the window and seeing a man in your yard. You don't expect it. You think nobody's around, and then—"

"I have no clue, Sergeant, honestly." She completely shrugged off his offer to sit down. She just stood there fidgeting in her coat pockets, then pulled out a pack o' cigarettes. "No smoking in the station, Ms. Wilson."

"It's *Dr.* Wilson, actually." She crumpled up the empty pack and tossed it into the waste basket.

"I knew that. Sorry. Take a seat, Dr. Wilson." He motioned again toward the bench.

It hadn't been no more 'n a couple of weeks since her and Mosey Frye come in to sign their statements vis-à-vis the Sunny Banks case. But now, standing there in the entrance, she looked to him more like a fidgety teenager than a hoity-toity forensic psychologist. "When the chief gets here"—he squinted in the direction of the back lot—"just tell him what you know. That's all, Dr. Wilson."

"I won't let my imagination run away with me if that's what you're implying. I'll certainly tell him *what I know*."

Springer crossed his arms and took a step back.

"Sorry, I didn't mean to snap." She offered a small smile. "I suppose I'm feeling a little, well, off kilter."

"Sure you don't want to sit down?" He gestured toward the bench again. "Let me bring you somethin'—coffee, a cup o' water?"

"Yes, thanks. Coffee if you've got it made." She

headed toward the bench. "I had to forgo my usual morning cup. The utilities are still off." She looked away, then back. "Sorry, I didn't mean to whine."

Springer, just about to accept her apology and *play nice*, as per the chief's instructions, was interrupted by the sound of the back door opening. He glanced around and, yup, it was the chief coming in.

Chapter Two

After hastily getting dressed and driving to the station, Olivera pushed through the door at the back and made his way toward the front. Passing by the coffee nook, he waved to Springer, who responded with a friendly, "Morning, Chief." As he approached the front entrance, Wilson stood and came forward. He glanced at her, then Springer and from the puzzled look on Springer's face, deduced that something was amiss.

"I really am sorry, Lieutenant," she said.

He responded with a nod. "Let's go into the interview room." He guided her in. "Have a seat over there, please, Dr. Wilson." After hanging his hat on the hat rack in the corner, he settled into the captain's chair and pulled out his tablet and pen.

Wilson strolled to the end of the table and took a seat. "Like I said, Lieutenant, I *am* sorry."

Another apology, for God's sake… "You said it was pressing, did you?" He got up and motioned to Springer, who was watching through the glass panels.

"Yes, Chief?" Springer came to the door.

"Coffee…please." He turned to Wilson. "Care for coffee?"

She blinked in Springer's direction. "Your sergeant

6

offered me a cup, and yes, thank you, I would."

"Two cups." Olivera waved two fingers at Springer, then turned to Wilson. "So, I understand you decided on the Morris house. Or do they call it Morris House? On McAllister, isn't it?"

"Yes," she replied, absently toying with a button on her work shirt. Instead of meeting his gaze, she stared at a *naïf* oil of the old Tavernette hanging on the wall across from the door. "They seem to have a penchant here for calling a place *the so-and-so house*, don't they?" She snickered. "I find it rather quaint."

He chuckled. "Yeah, they do, and I guess I'm doing it, too, now."

She sat with her face angled toward the wall as she stared at the painting. He could see only a sliver of cheek and chin and the tip of a slightly upturned nose. Her face, barely visible behind a mane of dark reddish hair, seemed more youthful than he remembered. "That's the Tavernette." He glanced at the painting. "Recognize it?"

She looked his way for an instant. Her eyes, comely now, were a sort of blue-gray shade. Disregarding his question, she asked, "How long have you been here, Lieutenant?"

He stopped to think for a second. "Summer…2008. About a year and a half."

"I've been here, let's see, two weeks." She sighed and let go of the button. Her pale hands briefly touched the table before she withdrew them and dropped them in her lap.

Yes, it had been just about two weeks since he had met Wilson at the Tavernette and they'd sat chatting over a beer. She hadn't struck him then as jumpy—a tad reserved, maybe, but confident, composed, not at all

7

hesitant to share her impressions of Charles Ashby. As a forensic psychologist versed in profiling, she had deduced from one casual encounter that Ashby was probably narcissistic, perhaps even sociopathic. Impressive, he thought. Besides, given her interest in the case—and, of course, she would be interested since she'd been present at the discovery of the body—it seemed odd now that she'd sidestepped the subject entirely. Hadn't uttered a word about Ashby, the business at Sunny Banks…none of it. But, actually, come to think of it, neither had he. He raised his brow, shrugged, and casually flipped through his tablet for a clean page. "Exact address, Dr. Wilson?"

"My address?"

"Yes," he replied with a nod. "Your home address."

"It's 313 McAllister."

"Telephone number?"

"I don't have a land line." She opened her handbag and pulled out a card. "My contact information is here." She leaned forward and placed it on the table.

He stretched to pick it up. "That's a nice business card. The psychology department supply these?"

She nodded. "They had them for me when I arrived."

He tucked the card into the back of his tablet. "You think you're going to like it here? I mean, you've come from a much larger—"

"I know," she cut in. "It *is* a big change, but I think I'll be all right."

*All right.* Hmm. That was an interesting choice of words. Had she *not* been all right at her last job? "Where were you exactly before? I forget."

"Philadelphia. I had a post-doc—"

"Oh, that's right. I remember now. This is your first full-time job."

"Yes." She fiddled with the button again.

He sat back and crossed his arms over his chest. "And this incident. What happened?"

"Well—" She broke off, glancing at Springer, who'd come in with two mugs on a tray.

"Need anything else, Chief?" Springer placed the tray in front of Olivera, then picked up a mug and handed it to Wilson.

"I don't think so, Springer. That's all for now."

Springer left the room but not without a glance back at Wilson, which made Olivera wonder again what had transpired between the two of them. "Care for cream, sugar, Dr. Wilson?"

"Yes, cream, please, no sugar."

He pushed the tray in her direction. "Here, help yourself."

She poured in a scant dollop of cream, stirred, then tapped the spoon against the rim of the mug.

"Morris House…that's the last house on the street." He tore open two packs of sugar and emptied them into his mug.

"That's right."

He stirred and laid the spoon on the tray. "Kind of woodsy at the dead end, isn't it?"

"Yes, I ought to clear it out, cut back some of the undergrowth. Not the trees. There're some lovely old cottonwoods around back and a sweet gum. Mosey called it a sweet gum. I have no idea. I've never lived in a place like this before."

"You're not really a small-town girl, are you?" He bit his tongue for having called her a girl. In

Philadelphia, he imagined, women might take offense at being referred to as girls. "By the way, Dr. Wilson—" He cleared his throat. "—where was it you were when this...?" He didn't finish the question, thinking he'd leave it to her to describe the incident.

"In the front room."

He flipped to the page where he had jotted down the information from Springer's text. "I thought you were *outside*...in your car."

"I was, but that was later. I saw him the first time early this morning. I was in the front room. Mosey called it the master bedroom, but I've chosen an upstairs room for my bedroom. I think I'll turn the front room into a den of some sort or maybe a little library."

"You were in the front room, then, which faces—?"

"—McAllister."

"So, tell me, just what was it that—?"

"I heard a screeching sound," she cut in. "Like a bird, then a terrible cry, like a small animal."

"A small animal? You mean like a rabbit, a squirrel?"

"I don't know what it was, but it was an awful sound, like an animal in distress."

"And?"

"Well, that was what caught my attention...hearing the animal cry out like that."

"You were *where* when you heard this?"

"In the front room, like I said before. I was up on a little ladder cleaning the windows."

"Inside the house. You were *inside* the house, not outside."

She nodded.

After making a note, he proceeded. "Okay. So, what

time did you say it was?" He flipped back through his notes. "Sergeant Springer gave me to understand that it was at approximately a quarter past seven that—"

"No." She shook her head. "That was later. I saw him the first time, well, it must have been around six-thirty. But then, a little after that, I had to run to the Superette for paper towels. When I got back to the house, I saw him again."

"Okay, I think I understand. You were in the front room, cleaning the windows, earlier this morning, about six thirty."

"That's right. I know it seems strange, but I've got a lot to do and little time to do it in…before classes start. I'm trying to do everything I can."

"No need to explain, Dr. Wilson." He relaxed his face and softened his eyes. "It hasn't been so long, you know, since I was in *your* shoes, and I dare say, well, you couldn't do worse than I."

"How's that?" she asked with a half-smile.

"You should see my living room. Ha! Not a stick of furniture. Well, no, that's not true. I bought a floor lamp from Nadia Abboud. I suppose you're familiar with Abboud Antiques?"

"Yes," she nodded. "Mosey and I dropped by there when I was here before."

"Then you know the place. You can get anything you want. Furniture, dishes, what-nots." He cleared his throat, then gestured toward her mug. "Is the coffee okay? You haven't touched it."

"Oh, forgive me." She knotted her brow. "I guess I'm feeling a little out of sorts."

Maybe he should have responded with something a tad more affirming like, "Of course, you are," but he didn't. It was too blasted early in the morning, and he wasn't really feeling overly sympathetic. So he just sat there tapping his pen and repeated what she had said. "Out of sorts?"

She looked directly at him but didn't say anything.

He sipped his coffee and waited a moment longer for an explanation. "Out of sorts?"

She nodded, then, dropping her head, stared down at the table.

After a brief pause, he continued. "Give yourself some time. It takes some getting used to."

She glanced up, eyes narrowed. "What does?"

"Philadelphia to Hembree, Arkansas. It's a big change, wouldn't you say?"

"Yes." She nodded.

"I'm from southern California myself," he volunteered.

"Yes, I remember Mosey mentioning that."

"It's taken a while, but I'm getting used to it…finally." He twisted around in his chair and gazed through the plate glass window behind him. The sun was up now and was burning off the fog…some of it, but even so, he had a feeling it was going to be one of those gray Delta days…overcast and gloomy. "I've grown accustomed to the dreariness and the humidity, so thick you can cut it with a knife, as the locals like to say. But I still prefer a Santa Clara morning. I imagine I always will," he added wistfully. Twisting back around, he looked toward her end of the table. "What are mornings like in Philadelphia?"

"Oh, in winter, it's about like this. Gray, but much colder."

"You like cold weather?" he asked, carrying on with

the weather talk.

"Not particularly. Why? Do you?"

"Not at all." He chuckled and shook his head. This tactic, his shifting the conversation away from the matter at hand, seemed to be working. She was loosening up a bit, gradually turning back into the Lauren Wilson he remembered from the afternoon in mid-December when they'd chatted at the Tavernette—rather amicably, comfortably, he thought. But unlike then, she now seemed—what? Visibly distracted? Preoccupied with something that she didn't want to say? Clearly there was more to this foolish complaint of hers than met the eye. He glanced through the glass panels at Springer, who stood hunched over the box of doughnuts. Olivera nodded toward Wilson's mug. "Shall I get Sergeant Springer to warm that up for you?"

She responded with a slight jiggle of her head.

"No?"

"No, thanks."

"You sure?"

"You know what, Lieutenant?" she said, standing.

But before he could discover *what*, she fell like a plank flat on her back.

Chapter Three

*Monday, 8:00 a.m.*
*Mosey Frye's Bedroom*

Mosey and Robert were sleeping when the phone rang, piercing the early morning silence. She poked a hand out from under the covers and brought the receiver to her mouth. "Hello," she mumbled.

"That you, Ms. Frye?"

Hearing the lieutenant's voice, Mosey sat up in bed and switched on the light. "Yes, this is Mosey."

"Lieutenant Olivera here."

"Morning, Lieutenant."

"Sorry to call so early, uh—"

"Not a problem." She yawned as she rubbed her eyes. "What can I do for you?"

"I've got a situation here at the station. Lauren Wilson is here, and she isn't feeling well."

"Really?" She twisted around and put her feet on the floor. "What's the matter?"

"I'll fill you in when you get here. Oh, sorry, can you come pick her up?"

"Of course. I'll be right there." She put the phone down and shook Robert. "Robert, get up. Something's wrong with Lauren. Olivera wants me to pick her up...at the police station." Without waiting for a response, she slid off the four-poster and, snatching up her jeans,

14

headed to the bathroom.

"What the devil?" Robert moaned.

She answered in mumbles over the sound of trickling water.

"For Pete's sake, Mosey, take the toothbrush out of your mouth."

She peeked around the door. "Get up and come with me."

"Why?" He pulled the sheet over his head.

"You drive her home in the hatchback. I'll follow in her car, see?"

"All right," he grumbled.

"Get your clothes on."

He slipped into his running pants and sat back on the bed to put on his cross-trainers.

Mosey pulled her trench out of the closet and, heading up the stairs, yelled back, "You got your keys?"

As he trailed up the steps behind her, he fumbled in his pocket. "Yep."

It was about five minutes later when they arrived at the station. Robert held the door, and Mosey rushed through. "Lauren, my goodness…"

She was stretched out on the bench by the door with a compress to her forehead. Olivera was standing beside her, his brow furrowed with concern or *utter stupor*, she couldn't tell. "What happened?" Mosey knelt next to the bench.

Lauren removed the cloth and sat up. "I fainted, but I think I'm okay. Lieutenant Olivera insisted—"

"Of course he insisted," Robert cut in, "and rightly so. You don't need to be driving."

"That's what *I* said." Olivera took a step toward Robert. "I offered to run her home, but she didn't want to alarm the neighbors."

"No need. We can take her home." Mosey helped Lauren to her feet. "Can you walk?"

"I think so. Could you carry this for me?" She handed Mosey her handbag.

"Of course."

Sergeant Springer came out of the coffee nook with a paper cup in one hand, a small paper bag in the other. "She said she hadn't had anything to eat. I'm guessing that's why she fainted. Said they haven't turned on the utilities. She hasn't even had her morning coffee." He handed the cup and bag to Mosey. "I put a couple of doughnuts in there. Get her to eat something if you can."

"Thanks, Sergeant." Mosey slipped the doughnuts and coffee into her tote.

Springer and Robert helped Lauren to the car, while Mosey hung back, wanting a word with Olivera. "What happened, Lieutenant?"

"One minute she was sitting over there at the table—" He gestured with his head toward the interview room. "—and the next, she got up and fell backwards onto the floor."

"Gosh." Mosey shook her head.

"I offered to call Dr. McGinnis, but she insisted she didn't need a doctor. If you could stay with her a little while? And, Ms. Frye, give me a call, please, when you get her settled." Not waiting for an answer, he walked away in the direction of his cubicle at the back.

Mosey headed out to Lauren's car. "Robert, toss me the keys, would you?"

Lauren rolled down the window. "They're in my handbag."

"Okay, got 'em."

Robert pulled out first, and Mosey followed along behind. "I've got to call Nadia," she mumbled, reaching in her pocket for her phone. She tapped on Favorites, then Nadia's number.

"Mosey?" Nadia answered.

"You at the store?"

"Yeah, just getting here. What's up?"

"Guess whose car I'm driving?"

"Huh?"

"Lauren Wilson's two-seat convertible. Snazzy, eh? You ought to see the interior—white leather upholstery."

"Why—?"

"Poor thing fainted at the police station."

"What the devil was she doing at the police station at this hour?"

"That's what *I'd* like to know." Mosey tilted the rear-view mirror slightly upward.

"So, where's Lauren?"

"Robert's got her in the hatchback. We're taking her to her place…Morris House. In fact, it's just ahead. I'd better hang up. I'll give you a call soon as we get her settled." She dropped the phone in her pocket and pulled to the curb. Robert drove past the drive and parked at the end of the street. She rolled down the window. "Robert," she called, "ask Lauren where she wants me to park."

He spoke to Lauren and yelled back, "In the driveway's fine."

Mosey nodded and turned into the gravel drive of the dilapidated Victorian. She got out and, setting her tote and Lauren's handbag on the hood of the car, waited as Robert and Lauren approached. "Be careful on the sidewalk," she cautioned.

"Huh?" Robert looked puzzled.

"The sidewalk," she repeated. "There're some uneven spots. And cracks, big cracks."

As Robert helped Lauren up the steps, Mosey let her eyes scan the front of the property. With its uneven pavement, peeling façade, and broken-down porch, it looked pretty much the way it did when she and Lauren first visited it some few weeks before.

"I bought the so-called half-house," she heard Lauren say to Robert.

"It may not be a half-house for long," Mosey chuckled, "if you finish out the missing rooms."

"Missing rooms?" Robert frowned at Mosey.

Lauren unlocked the door and pushed it back. "She means the dining room and first-floor bath."

"No bath on the first floor?" he asked.

"Nope, but it's not a big deal, with me living here by myself." Lauren pressed her wrist against her forehead.

"You okay?" he asked.

"I think I'd better lie down for a bit." She shed her coat, hung it in the foyer closet, then slipped her arm through Robert's. "Would you mind helping me up the stairs?"

"Be glad to." He hesitated before taking the first step up. "They seem to be in okay condition, well, considering the age of the house."

"Robert," Mosey said with reproach, "you think I'd sell Lauren a house with a faulty staircase?"

Paying no attention, Robert casually flicked the light switch.

"No power, sorry," Lauren said.

"Here…hold onto the banister." He changed sides with Lauren, and they slowly made their way up the stairs with Mosey coming along behind.

"The bed's pretty high," Lauren told Robert, as they reached the threshold to the bedroom, "and, if you don't mind…"

"Of course." He helped her to the bed. "I don't know why they used to make beds so high." He glanced around. "Amazing room."

"Yeah," she slowly nodded, "the furniture was all here. Belonged to the previous owner."

Mosey came through the door. "You ready to eat something? Think you can drink a little coffee?" She handed Lauren the cup.

"I might try one of those doughnuts, too."

Mosey peeked into the bag. "Which one you want— caramel-iced or jam-filled?"

"Doesn't matter." Lauren took a sip of coffee and set the cup on the nightstand.

"If you guys don't need me," Robert backed toward the door, "I've got an orientation meeting at nine."

"You'd better get out of here, then." Mosey nodded toward the door. "We'll be fine."

"Thanks, Robert." Lauren smiled. "I promise not to make a habit of this."

He chuckled. "You'd better not. I'm kind of a bear when I don't get my eight hours."

Lauren accepted the doughnut from Mosey and took a bite. "Not bad. You want the other, Robert?"

"Yeah," he took the sack, "I'll eat it on the way to school."

Mosey threw him a kiss. "Thanks, Robert."

Lauren scooted back against the pillow, and Mosey, sitting on the edge of the bed, asked the question she'd been patiently waiting to ask. "If you don't mind my asking, what took you to the station so early?" She picked up the cup and handed it to Lauren. But as Lauren accepted it, her hand jerked and coffee sloshed over the side.

"Oh, my, you *are* nervous." Mosey reached for the box of tissues on the nightstand.

Lauren set down the cup and lay back, while Mosey soaked up the spill. Then, slipping off her trench, she threw it over Lauren's legs. "It's cold in here. They haven't turned on the heat?"

"Not yet."

"Hold on a minute." Mosey reached for her phone and called the office.

"Shepherd Realty."

"Saffron, it's me. Do me a favor, will you?"

"What's that?"

"I'm at Lauren Wilson's, and they haven't turned on the utilities. Give them a buzz if you don't mind, please, ma'am."

"What's the address?"

"It's 313 McAllister."

"Got it. By the way, you coming in?"

"Soon as I finish here. Why?"

"I took a call for you yesterday afternoon. David Morell."

"Huh. What'd he have to say?"

"Left his number. Wants you to call him."

"Okay, I'll be in," she checked her watch, "by…well, I'll try to make it in by eleven." Mosey clicked off. "Saffron's going to get you some heat. They tend to fall behind at the beginning of the semester. People moving out, moving in."

"I'm starting to feel like a real whiner," Lauren said.

Mosey shook her head. "No, you're not. We

understand. You've got an awful lot on your plate right now. Moving to a new town, starting a new job. It's a lot." She walked to the window and, pushing back the heavy drapes, stirred up a cloud of dust. Turning away from the window, she sneezed into her elbow. "You'll never get this big place cleaned up—" She sneezed again. "—by the time school starts. You want me to see if I can get you some help?"

"Like who?" Lauren asked.

"Me, for one. And Nadia. Maybe Saffron. We could get a good start on the cleaning. Wouldn't take us more than a day or two."

"Gosh, Mosey, I don't know what to say. You sure you're up for all that?"

Mosey moved back toward the bed. "Things are really slow at the office. I could probably get away this afternoon…if that would work for you." She gathered up the damp tissues and threw them in the trash can.

"That would be a tremendous help."

Mosey sat back on the bed and gave Lauren a pat on the hand. "So, as I was saying before. That little business at the station this morning…"

"Well," she sighed, "I was working downstairs. I, uh, was in the front room." She reached for the cup, took a sip, and continued. "I, uh, spotted somebody outside the house."

"Who?" Mosey asked, a hint of concern in her voice.

"A man."

"Did you recognize him?"

She didn't respond right away.

"Anybody you know?" Mosey added.

"I don't know." She tightened her lips and gave her head a shake.

"What was he doing?"

"Walking away from the house." Lauren shrugged.

"He didn't knock?"

She shook her head. "I was cleaning the windows, in the front room, by candlelight. It must have been around six something. He had to have seen me. I was right at the window. But he didn't turn around. Just left."

"Did he get into a car?"

"I don't know. I don't remember seeing a car. I came down from the stepladder and checked the front door. It was locked. Then I checked the back door. It was locked, too."

"So you called the police?"

"Nope." She shook her head. "Not then. I was almost out of paper towels and needed to run to the store. But then, on my way back, I saw him again. That's when I called the station and spoke with Sergeant Springer."

"He didn't offer to come out?"

"To be honest, I was feeling so upset that I preferred to drive away rather than—" Lauren winced as tears rolled down her cheeks.

Mosey moved closer. "What are you afraid of, Lauren?"

"I thought when I left Philadelphia—"

"You mean this man has followed you from Philadelphia?" She looked at Lauren askance. "Surely not."

"I think he has."

"Did you tell Olivera?" That's what Mosey asked, but obviously Lauren hadn't. She hadn't told him squat, and that's why *he* had asked *her* to call him. Uh-huh. So, that's what that was about. He was thinking he'd use her—

"I couldn't bring myself to say it," Lauren interrupted Mosey's thoughts.

She handed Lauren the box of tissues. "Here you go, hon."

She had hidden her face in her hands but looked up and pulled a tissue from the box. "I thought I could tell him, but something made me hesitate. I'm gonna be working with Olivera, Mosey." She stopped and blew her nose. "I can't have him thinking—"

Mosey felt the cup, then picked it up. "Lauren, drink some of this. I don't want you to faint again."

She took a sip of coffee and, setting it down, lay back.

"Let me check your pulse." She picked up Lauren's wrist.

Lauren waited while Mosey counted off the seconds. "What was it?"

"Eighty. Is that high for you?"

"A little."

"Yeah, you're a runner, aren't you?"

Lauren nodded.

"I understand what you're doing, trying to get all this work done before the semester starts. But you need to eat, get some rest, and let us give you a hand."

A faint smile crossed Lauren's lips. "I know." She took one of the tissues she'd crumpled in her hand and dried her eyes.

"And," Mosey stood, "I think you'd feel better if you told us what's bothering you. If we're going to get to the bottom of this—and the sooner the better—you've got to tell us what you know. I mean—"

"Us?"

"Me...Olivera? Somebody."

"Not Olivera." She shook her head.
"Me, then." Mosey sat back on the bed.

Chapter Four

Half an hour later, Mosey left Morris House on foot. But not minding—she hadn't walked the length of McAllister Avenue in a good long while. The street stretched before her with its barren trees and lawns of straw-colored stubble. It wasn't going to be a humdrum day. "Nope." She smiled to herself. Between everything with Lauren and all the to-dos she needed to complete right away, she felt energized and ready to get started. She counted off her tasks on her fingertips. Speak to Olivera, Nadia, then David Morell… Before calling Morell, she definitely wanted to have a word with Nadia, preferably face to face. With that in mind, she picked up speed and high-tailed it to Abboud Antiques.

When she got there, the Closed sign was still hanging inside the door. So, she gave a loud knock and called out, "Nadia, it's me, Mosey."

"Hi, girl." Nadia opened the door wide and took a step back, making way for Mosey to come in. "I thought you were going to call."

"Things are getting complicated." Mosey walked past Nadia and, glancing around for a good spot to sit, decided on a wine-colored French settee close to the counter. "I wanted to talk to you in person." She shoved a collection of throw pillows aside.

"Must be important. You want some tea?"

"I'd love a cup." She pulled off her gloves and ran her hand over the soft chenille upholstery. "What do you call that—merlot? I can't keep up with the names of colors. You think Lauren would like something like this?"

"Nah, too frou-frou."

"I don't know why you'd say that." She glanced at Nadia. "I think it'd look pretty in the parlor. She needs something to brighten it up." To be honest, Mosey was feeling a little guilty. She had sold Lauren a monstrosity of a house, and now she was questioning the wisdom of it. "How much is it?" She got up to look for the price tag and, finding it, added, "Probably more than she would want to spend."

"Now, how do you know that? If she's driving a snazzy two-door convertible, well—"

"She's got that big ol' house to pull into shape," Mosey cut in, distress in her voice. "Something tells me it could be a money pit. Speaking of which—"

"Here it comes."

"Here *what* comes?"

Nadia, who was standing at the counter pouring tea from a pewter pot, didn't answer the question. She just kept pouring, then passed Mosey a cup.

"Nadia" —Mosey accepted the cup— "we need to help Lauren clean her house."

"Mosey!"

"I know, I know. You've got your hands full, and so do I, but she's in a terrible bind. I mean it."

"Mosey, you kill me."

"Oh, come on, it'll be fun—" She smiled. "—and

interesting."

"Interesting?" Nadia's face conveyed sheer disbelief.

"Of course, it will." Mosey's voice dripped with assuredness. Then, as she dove into the part that had truly sparked her curiosity, she opened her eyes wide and added, "But just wait till I tell you—"

"I think I'll pass," Nadia cut in.

"You don't want to hear about the man who's making Lauren's life a living hell?" She blinked a couple of times.

Nadia frowned and took a seat across from Mosey.

"That's why she was at the police station. But she fainted, didn't tell Olivera a blessed thing. But she told me just now after Robert and I took her home." Mosey sat up straight and set her cup on the drop leaf table between them.

"That's crazy. Why'd she call the police if—"

"She was scared to death," Mosey cut in. "Well, maybe not scared to death—"

"Mosey"—Nadia shook her head—"calm down, would you? And start at the beginning."

Mosey relaxed back. "Well, you see, she had some guy under her supervision—a grad student or another post-doc—and she suspected him of being a little deranged."

"Deranged? Deranged how?"

"Oh, I don't know exactly. Some sort of perversion. And she reported him to her supervisor, the chair of forensic psychology, but he didn't lift a hand. Typical..."

Nadia's eyes bulged. "Didn't suspend him—nothing?"

"They might have given him a warning, but Lauren

didn't feel safe around him. That's why she decided to give up the post-doc and look for a job. Or look for a job, then give up the post-doc. Whatever. That's how she ended up here. Ha! Their loss, our gain."

"This sounds serious." Nadia furrowed her brow.

"Oh, who knows. Lauren isn't sure that it even *was* the guy. Could have been somebody from the gas company, for all we know. She didn't get a good look at him. But I'm glad you're concerned. Maybe you'll be inclined to give us a hand with the cleaning. And, in passing, you could help her pick out some nice pieces for the house. Okay?" She gave the seat cushion another gentle rub. "This fabric is beautiful and so soft. I love it." Then, as if struck by a sudden impulse, she hopped up, saying, "I need to get out of here. Thanks, Nadia, for the tea."

"What's your hurry?"

"No hurry. I've just got a lot to do. Oh, for goodness sake." Mosey exhaled and flopped back down on the settee. "I forgot to ask you what I came for. David Morell…he called yesterday."

"What about David Morell?"

"You know him, right?"

"I wouldn't say I *know* him. I know who he is." She got up and returned to her spot behind the counter.

"Your father sold him the portrait of Fernanda de Lobos. Don't you remember?"

"Of course, I remember." Nadia cast her a sideways glance. "But that was ages ago, goodness, like fifteen, twenty years."

"I know. But it doesn't seem all that long."

Nadia dipped her chin in agreement.

"So, tell me, what do you know about him?" Mosey

knew that it was a lot, urging Nadia to dig deep into her memory and recollect the ins and outs of an encounter that occurred back when she was hardly more than a kid. But, hey, Mosey had faith in Nadia's remarkable memory, as she hardly ever forgot a thing.

"First, why this sudden interest?" Nadia shot her a probing look.

"Like I said, he called yesterday afternoon." Mosey shrugged. "Saffron took the call."

"And?"

"Nothing. It's just that before I call him back, I'd like to know who I'm talking to. So, you did see him when he came to the shop, didn't you?"

"Yes," she nodded. "He wasn't a bad looking guy. His horns were barely visible, though I did notice two little puckers on either side of his trilby."

"Very funny." Mosey rolled her eyes. "But, Nadia, I'm serious. I have a feeling about this."

"Mosey, what *don't* you have a feeling about? He's just a guy from New Orleans who happened to hear about the Bilyeu estate sale—through the grapevine, I'd imagine—and came in hoping to pick up something cheap. That's all. No mystery."

"But didn't you say your father had overpriced the painting, wanting to hold onto it for a while?"

"Yes, but what's that got to do with it? What's expensive around here could be cheap as dirt in New Orleans where there's more of a market for antique portraits."

"But that wasn't all he bought, right?" Mosey probed. "Seems like I remember your saying he bought everything left over from the estate sale."

"Yes, I guess he did, come to think of it."

"So, he didn't just come here out of the blue. He had a particular interest in the family."

"Possibly, but what if he did?"

"I think there's more to it. You just watch. His interest in the Bilyeus is more than coincidental. And…here he is back and calling *me*." She wandered in the direction of the mantel where, as Nadia had mentioned, the portrait of the infamous Fernanda—thief extraordinaire and accessory to murder—had once hung. "I don't like it." Mosey shook her head.

As she paced around the room, Nadia followed her with her eyes. "You mean you *do* like it. You're *so* disappointed to have finally sold a plain ol' house—no body, no bones, no ghosts—that you just gotta stir something up. And David Morell might as well be your man." With a look of exasperation, Nadia picked up a letter opener and slit open the top of a manilla envelope.

"That's outrageous," Mosey said in a huff. "I'm *thrilled* to have gotten out from underneath this curse, as Hugh calls it." She looked at Nadia, corners of her mouth turned down.

"What is it?" Nadia asked, apparently noticing Mosey's change of demeanor.

"The curse." Mosey walked back toward Nadia. "It may have gotten sidetracked, but I'm not so sure it's gone." A twinge of anxiety crept into her tone. "I'm thinking it's visited itself upon poor Lauren."

Nadia shook her head in disbelief. "Mosey, you take the cake. First, you're casting suspicion on Lauren, making us all wonder if *she* was involved in the death of Charles Ashby, and now you're acting like she's your bosom buddy."

"That's ridiculous. And back in November, we all

had questions about Lauren. Don't say you didn't."

"I absolutely did not," Nadia glared at Mosey, "until *you* started stirring things up."

"Oh, pooh, I didn't stir up a living thing."

"No, your specialty is corpses!"

Mosey broke into a smile before falling back on the sofa in an eruption of laughter.

Nadia shook her head, then burst into laughter, too.

"Oh, my. If I don't get out of here…" Mosey stood and buttoned her jacket. "But listen, seriously…"

Nadia sipped her tea to the bottom and set down the cup. "I'm listening."

"What if this guy turns out to be a stalker?" The thought of it was creepy indeed and yet a tad exciting.

"Mosey, really, how could Lauren possibly have a stalker? She just got here."

"Yeah, she did. Doesn't even have the lights turned on. Poor soul, she's making do with candles."

"Candles?"

"She was cleaning the front windows by candlelight—didn't I tell you? That's when it all started. She heard a screech, like an owl, then the cry of some poor little animal. I bet it was a baby rabbit. So, she looked out the window, and that's when she saw the guy walking away."

Nadia frowned. "And?"

"Well, first she checked the doors, then she went right on cleaning, but she ran out of paper towels and had to go to the Superette. When she got home and was just about to turn into the driveway, she saw the same guy again, coming from around the side of the house."

"So, she saw him twice, the same man?"

"Yep," Mosey nodded, "that's what she said.

So…she just kept driving. I guess she must have called the police station on her cellphone and said she wanted to go over there."

"So, what did Olivera say?"

"Not much. She fainted. Remember?"

"Oh, yeah, you did say that." Nadia lowered her brow. "But, Mosey, if you are smart, you'll let Olivera take care of this."

"Huh! Olivera—what does he know? Which reminds me, I promised I'd call him." She looked at her watch. "I got to get over to the office, or Saffron will have my hide." She stood and as she was heading toward the door, stopped and looked back at Nadia. "So…you don't know anything else about Morell?"

"Nothing."

"What about your daddy—you think he might know something?"

"I seriously doubt it."

"Give him a call, why don't you? He might. And this afternoon—" She softened her voice. "—can you get away for a little while?"

Nadia pitched the manilla envelope into the trash. "I'll try, but I'm not making any promises. You see that display window?" She pointed.

Mosey gave the window a quick glance. "What's wrong with it?"

"It's full of Christmas stuff—that's what."

"The sale's still going, isn't it?"

"Yes, but I need to set up for Valentine's Day, and I have the boxes from Sunny Banks to unpack."

"Sunny Banks!" Mosey said, mouth agape.

"Yes, Sunny Banks."

"When were you going to tell me?"

"I'm telling you now."

"Nadia, I cannot believe—"

"I tell you what," Nadia cut in, "you get yourself back over here and help me with the boxes, and I'll help you and Lauren with the cleaning. Bargain?"

"Bargain!" All smiles, Mosey was out the door and on her way.

Chapter Five

David Morell gazed in at the captivating exhibit of pigeon-blood ruby earrings. Strewn over a white velour mantle, they shimmered like fresh droplets of blood in the gentle morning sunlight. They were beautiful, yes, but were they enticing enough to lure in shoppers? Yes, he expected they might be.

He paused at the long front table to inspect the collections of rings, bracelets, and necklaces, some fashioned of delicately carved silver, others lavishly set with sparkling gems. He picked up a size-six ring tray and headed to the counter where his son Dave Junior was attending a customer. After the woman had left, he said to Dave, "If you've got a minute, check in the back for more of these, would you?"

Dave accepted the tray and walked toward the back.

Meanwhile, a handful of people had come into the store. Morell scrutinized the group, one of whom stood apart from the others. "Mr. Philpot." He waved. "I've been hoping you'd drop by."

Philpot waved back, and Morell politely escorted him into a softly lit room where the walls, painted a deep shade of crimson, were adorned with paintings from the eighteenth and nineteenth centuries. Toward the front of the gallery, a brass sconce cast a warm glow over the striking portrait of a woman. Philpot nodded approvingly as he exclaimed, "What an extraordinary painting, and I suppose the price reflects it?"

"Yes, I suppose it does," Morell responded, "but it *is* the absolute favorite."

Philpot stepped in closer to have a better look at the image that had so thoroughly captured his attention. Little more than an adolescent, the young woman in the painting wore a white silk organza gown with a vibrant blue cabochon pinned at the bottom of a plunging neckline. A black lace mantilla rested elegantly on her head, secured by a gold *peineta*. Her hands, fair and delicate, sat one above the other, adding the finishing touch to the stunning portrait. "Who is she?" he asked.

"Fernanda de Lobos, the wife of Hershel Bilyeu, one of the city's first pharmacists. Actually, his apothecary is still standing, around the corner, not far from here."

"I was told," he glanced at Morell, "that your collection was primarily of *casta* paintings, so I'm surprised to see this one."

"Yes, that's correct. But this *is*, in fact, a casta painting, one of my earliest acquisitions. The owner must have taken it with her when she left New Orleans around the time of the Civil War. I brought it back when one of her last descendants died some time ago."

Philpot took his time to admire the showpiece, then moved on to the next painting, which portrayed a heated argument between a couple—a man and a woman of diverse ethnic backgrounds. "This looks more like the casta paintings I'm familiar with."

"Yes." Morell nodded toward the painting. "This is more typical."

"But *that one*—" He glanced back at the portrait of Fernanda. "How is—"

"I'm often asked that," Morell replied. "Cardoso painted a good many portraits of men and women from various social strata, in addition to the paintings that portrayed ethnic interrelations. This one typifies *peninsulares*. You're familiar with the terminology?"

"She was born in Spain, you mean."

"That's right. She was brought here by her parents when she was still a child. It was here that she met her husband Hershel Bilyeu, who was French Bourbon…the pharmacist I mentioned."

Philpot, apparently satisfied with the explanation, moved on to the next painting, leaving Morell to assist a man who had been listening at a distance. The man, middle-aged and rather tall, dressed in a neat gray suit, approached and stooped to read the plaque next to the portrait. "I don't suppose" —he glanced up at Morell— "you are anxious to let go of it."

Morell chuckled. "For the right price, I suppose I could force myself."

"Is there something special…?" the man asked.

"Special?" Morell glanced at the painting and then at the man standing beside it. Something about him seemed oddly familiar. He had a strong feeling he'd come in before. "Well, it's part of the Mateo Cardoso collection, and I'm not anxious to break it up, now that the collection is almost complete."

"How does one ever know?" The man raised a questioning brow.

"That it's complete? In this case, the artist left a record of his invoices, which has proved extremely helpful. We knew the portrait existed, who commissioned it, and so on, but we had no idea where it was, until we, well, I, actually, learned of Larkspur Plantation, where—"

"A stroke of luck," he cut in.

"Luck?" Morell gave a slight frown. "I suppose you could think of it as luck."

He gave Morell a quick once-over followed by a wry smile. "I've been interested in casta paintings for a good long while, a couple of them in particular, but I haven't been able to track them down."

"Which ones, if you don't mind my asking?"

"I expect you're aware of them." He cast a side glance at Morell.

"Are the paintings you're referring to Cardosos?"

"I believe so."

"Which ones?"

"Well, one was commissioned before the Fernanda portrait, and the other one, some years later."

"I see. Might one be the painting of Hershel?"

The man nodded.

"I'm aware of it, but so far it has eluded me."

"Which isn't surprising."

"No, I suppose not." Morell's answer implied that he knew *why* it wasn't surprising when, in all honesty, he wasn't really sure. This man must know more than he, he thought, at least about the *whereabouts* of the painting if not the painting itself.

The man turned to Morell. "Do you suppose they took it with them to Arkansas?"

"Hershel and Fernanda? Well, that would be one explanation."

"Yet, from what I hear, no one in Hembree knows anything about it."

"Well, as far as I know," Morell stammered.

"I suppose if you *had* run across it, you would have purchased it and put it here with the others, unless, of course, someone persuaded you…" He trailed off, apparently waiting for Morell to respond.

"Persuaded me?" Morell thought for a second, pondering how to answer. The man's interest in the elusive Cardosos—and the Hershel portrait in particular—was clearly much the same as his own interest. Furthermore, it seemed likely he was privy to information regarding the whereabouts of the paintings, and yet his approach seemed rather oblique, evasive even. Morell shook his head and smiled faintly. "I'm not sure, Mr.—" He paused, silently hoping to elicit a name.

"Raines, Hollis Raines."

"As I was saying, Mr. Raines, I'm not sure I know what you're implying."

"I don't mean to offend—" He shook his head. "—but since you were able to find *this one*…" He eyed the Fernanda portrait, then looked back at Morell.

"Oh, if I had found the others, I would have bought them—if they had been for sale. And should I find the Hershel portrait, I would hang it here next to the portrait of his wife."

"But it isn't really a portrait, is it? It's a painting of Bilyeu and his Haitian *collaborator*, shall we say?"

Morell nodded uncomfortably. It wasn't just Raines's familiarity with the artwork but also his knowledge of the Bilyeu family history that caught Morell's attention. It made him wonder who exactly was this Hollis Raines. Had he come there not as a casual visitor but as someone with a particular purpose in mind? "So, I guess you're aware of the subject matter?"

"Yes, I am…*and* if I have the good fortune to locate the painting"—he nodded politely—"I won't put it in a gallery or museum, I don't think."

"No?" Morell probed. "I'm not sure you would determine the rightful owner if that's what you're suggesting."

"Could be problematic." He turned and looked at Dave Junior, who was walking quickly toward them.

"Father"—Dave touched Morell on the arm—"sorry to interrupt, but you have a call."

"Excuse me for a moment, will you please?"

Raines nodded and stepped back.

"Dave"—Morell turned to his son—"would you show Mr. Raines the rest of the collection? And check on Mr. Philpot for me when you can."

As Morell entered the front room, he gave a quick look back at the perplexing customer, now engaged in conversation with Dave Junior. Though he was fairly certain that he'd seen the man before—not often, but every now and again—it had never crossed his mind that his interest in the Cardoso collection might be anything but casual. In reaching the counter, he picked up the receiver. "This is David Morell."

"Mr. Morell, Mosey Frye here. I understand you called."

"Oh, Ms. Frye, thanks for getting back to me. I was speaking with Rafael de Lobos not long ago and your name came up."

"Rafael? Really?"

"He met you in Hembree, I believe."

"Yes, he was here just recently, in September."

"He told me you'd been helpful—"

"Helpful? Well, it's nice of him to say that, but—"

"If it hadn't been for you, Ms. Frye, I doubt he would have found what he was looking for. And now, you see, I am looking for something, and it occurred to me that you might be willing to help me out."

"But I'm in real estate, and he was looking for a house. It was Nadia, Nadia Abboud, well, her father, actually—"

"Then Nadia must have mentioned me to you."

"Yes, she did."

"She was very young at the time. I'm surprised she remembered."

"Of course, she remembered. They were quite fond of the portrait."

"Yes, her father said so at the time. I thought by now they might have visited the Cardoso collection."

"I wasn't aware there *was* a collection."

"Yes," he continued, "of casta paintings, but it doesn't matter. I'm sending my son, Dave, to Hembree to see if he can locate some additional Cardosos, one in particular."

"I'd be happy to help you with that, but I would need to consult with Nadia."

"If you want to bring her in, all the better. I would expect to pay a commission, of course."

"We can work out the details when your son arrives."

"Okay, thank you. He'll fly down on the company plane...tomorrow, if you're available."

"Tomorrow, yes, I think that'll work. Shall we say around midday?"

"Midday is good, and I'll let you know where he's staying—all right?"

"Yes, please do. I look forward to meeting him."

"And he'll bring proper documentation," Morell added. "You can't be too careful these days."

He placed the receiver on the hook and returned to the gallery. Not seeing Dave or Mr. Raines, he assumed they had moved into another room. He took a breath, unsure if he wanted to resume the conversation despite his curiosity. Had Raines come there on a fishing expedition, believing that, as a Cardoso specialist, he would know where the paintings were? If he *had* known, he wouldn't have let on in a million years. Determined to find the missing paintings himself, Morell had no intention of helping an inquisitive customer to discover them first. Once he had them, he might let the whole lot of them go, even the Fernanda portrait. He had realized some time back that it wasn't actually the paintings themselves that held his interest but, rather, the mystery that surrounded them. Why *had* they gone missing— those two in particular? And how had they managed to elude him for so many years?

## Chapter Six

Olivera, sitting comfortably at his desk, removed the remaining sheets from his daily desk calendar and inserted the 2010 refill through the rings. He flipped to January fourth and, at the top of the left page in the seven-thirty slot, printed, "Dr. Wilson, possible stalker." Though the year had started off peacefully—with Reagan and Ms. Hill still on holiday and only he and Springer there to keep things in check—a sense of unease had now settled in. Could a turn of events be just around the corner?

He sat back and allowed his eyes to drift over to the evidence board that hung on the partition beside his desk. It had been more than a month since the Sunny Banks case had been closed, and just for the purpose of keeping things tidy, he ought to have taken it down. But he hadn't. Glad as he was to see the case brought to a satisfactory end, he found himself still enjoying the snapshot Springer had taken of the gum brake. It was easily the most beautiful sight he'd encountered during his year and a half in Hembree.

Springer appeared in the doorway and, finishing off the cruller he was eating, followed it with a swig of coffee. "You reckon we ought to check on Dr. Wilson?"

"And why would we do that?" Olivera pulled a box of thumb tacks out of the desk drawer and got up from his chair.

"I don't know, Chief." Springer wiped his mouth with his handkerchief. "I have a funny feeling about this."

Olivera started clearing the evidence board of its contents, neatly organizing the different items into piles as he went along. "Funny feeling, eh?" He paused to look at Springer. "Grab an envelope and let's get this stuff put away." He picked up the gum brake photograph and held it to the light of his desk lamp. The banks and treetops were aglow with a radiance of fall color. "That's a beautiful picture, Springer. I'd blow it up if I were you…get it framed."

"We don't need it for the files?"

Olivera handed him the picture. "It wasn't part of the crime scene. The house and garage, yes, but not the gum brake. Take it if you want it."

Springer gestured toward the half-empty evidence board. "Before you know it, Chief, you're gonna be filling it up again."

Olivera gave him a quick look. "I will, will I? You're not going clairvoyant on me, are you, Springer?"

"Shucks, naw, Chief. Not me."

Olivera chuckled.

"I mean it," Springer emphasized. "I have a funny feeling."

Olivera waited to hear exactly what Springer was feeling funny about, but he didn't explain. He just leaned against the doorjamb, staring into space. "About what, Springer?"

Springer shook his head. "I don't know, Chief. Not

sure if it's her or that house of hers."

"You mean the Morris House?"

"I used to know a guy who worked there. Will Grayson was his name."

"And?"

"A ne'er-do-well, you could say, like Kit Morris, the owner. He used to be the owner 'fore he died."

Olivera swept the thumb tacks off the desk and into the box. "When was that?"

"A good while back."

Olivera relaxed in his chair. "Like when, Springer?" He licked a pre-printed label, stuck it in the corner of the envelope, and hammered it with his fist.

Springer scratched his head. "Must have been when I was in junior high. Yeah, 'bout then, early nineties."

"So, what about—what did you say his name was?"

"Grayson, Will Grayson. Oh, I guess he's all right, but I don't much care for him. He seems like a smart guy, and I've heard he's an artist. But I don't know of any art he's turned out lately. He mostly does odd jobs, works in people's yards, that sort of thing."

"Is he still around?"

"Far as I know."

"I guess we could head over to Morris House, take a look around. Might as well."

"Yeah, I think it's a good idea."

Olivera dropped the stacks of pictures, cards, and tabs into the envelope and handed it to Springer. "Could you add this to the file? We'll deal with the rest of the stuff later after we return." He reached for his sports jacket. "By the way, you got your gun, Springer?"

"Yep."

"Let's take the cruiser, and you drive." Olivera

crossed the outer office and entered the interview room to retrieve his hat. As he re-entered reception, he turned toward Ms. Hill's desk out of habit, only to remember that she was still on holiday. "You hear anything from Reagan?" He held the door open for Springer as they both headed into the garage.

"Nah, not likely to hear anything till he gets on the road again."

"Why is that?"

"Are you kiddin' me? Reagan and his brother-in-law might as well be dead. They're on the freaking lake fishing from early morning till the sun goes down. They step into the house to eat. That's about it."

Olivera chuckled to himself. *Might as well be dead.*

They pulled out of the drive and took off down Lee to McAllister, which was no more than a couple of blocks away.

"You ever seen this place?" Springer asked.

"Can't say I have."

"It's rough looking. I can't imagine why a classy lady like Dr. Wilson would pick a house like that. If you ask me, she'd a' done a sight better to wait on Sunny Banks. You release the property yet, Chief?"

"It's not up to me. It's up to Judge Hendricks, but he'll get around to it. If it hadn't been for the holidays, he'd have released it already, I imagine."

"And what about ol' Martin's Tyche XL500?"

"I drove it over to the garage a couple of days ago."

"That's a fine automobile, Chief. I wouldn't mind buying it myself if I had the dough."

"Not I, thank you very much."

"Why not?" Springer shot him a quizzical look.

"The body, Springer. Gotta have a strong stomach."

Springer laughed. "Never figured you for a hot-house tomato, Chief."

"Hot-house tomato?" Olivera muttered, exaggeratedly rolling his eyes. "Springer, you kill me." He chuckled.

As he glanced from Springer to the road ahead, he noticed that they had reached the historic district. Springer veered onto McAllister, gradually reducing his speed as they passed by the beautiful Queen Anne belonging to the Raines family.

"You hear any more about those folks, Chief—the Raineses?" Springer nodded toward the house as they passed.

"You mean Matthew and Charlotte? Now, why would I hear anything about them?"

"Just making conversation."

Springer went on making conversation till they reached the end of McAllister, where he slammed on the brakes just shy of the drive that led onto the property.

"Whoa!" Olivera raised up slightly out of his seat.

"What's the matter?"

"Your driving, Springer." He released the Jesus strap. He opened the door, stepped out, and scanned the front of the property. "That is a rough looking place. I don't envy Dr. Wilson the cleanup." As he approached the front of the house, his eyes wandered toward the wooded area off to the right. The trees had dropped their leaves and seemed to be stretching their lifeless arms upward from the tangles of undergrowth. Apart from a handful of stubby evergreens, that whole section of the property had blanched to a dusty gray.

He and Springer walked cautiously along the broken sidewalk to the entrance. With midday approaching, the sun shone through the branches of the cottonwood that stood opposite the wraparound porch. On their way to the door, they passed under an elaborate arch. Olivera glanced up. "A person well-versed in Victorian houses would have a name for that, I expect."

"One mess of a house, I'd call it." Springer dodged a cobweb that stretched from post to post along the edge of the porch.

"Lower your voice."

"Huh?"

"Shh…she'll hear you." Olivera opened the screen door and tapped lightly on the etched pane.

"Coming," Wilson called from within. She opened the door a crack. "Lieutenant?" She opened it wider. "What brings you to my humble abode?"

"It was Springer here if you want an honest answer. He thought we might stop by, make sure things are okay around the place." He took a step in, and Springer followed. "Looks like we caught you cleaning. We won't keep you long."

"No problem. Glad you're here." She pulled the scarf from her head and brushed the hair back from her face. "I'd offer you a cup of tea, but the stove isn't working. No gas. No electricity, either."

He glanced around the foyer, dimly lit by the flickering flame of a chunky candle set atop a wooden crate.

"Come in if you'd like. I'll show you the place."

Olivera followed her from the foyer into the parlor. "We'll see it another time. I thought we'd look around the grounds if that's okay. See if we can pick up any sign of an intruder. You haven't noticed anyone in the yard since this morning, have you?"

"Not a soul. Mosey left a short while ago. She stayed till I was feeling steadier."

He eyed a stepladder in front of a window. "I wouldn't recommend getting back on a ladder today, Dr. Wilson."

"I'm afraid I don't have the luxury of waiting, Lieutenant. I've got to finish the cleaning so I can move on to the next task. You know, classes start next week."

Springer, who hadn't spoken since entering the house, stood tapping his hat against his leg and gazing up the staircase into the darkness. "Dr. Wilson—" He came into the room. "—you haven't heard anything from the utility people, I suppose?"

"No, I haven't," she said with disappointment. "Not a word, but I'm hoping they show up today. Saffron Smiley offered to give them a call."

Springer eyed the window. "So this is where you were when you saw the guy?"

"No, actually I was in there." She gestured toward room opposite the parlor. "The first time, anyway. But when I came back from the Superette, I saw him walking across the lawn. He was coming from back there." She motioned toward a corner window that offered a view of the yard.

Springer approached the window and looked out. "Ma'am, I'd get that woodsy area trimmed back soon as I could."

"I haven't been able to find anybody to do it. Looks like a lot of people are still on vacation. I guess I picked a bad time to move in, but it couldn't be helped."

"Talk to Mosey, ma'am. She can help you with that."

"We won't keep you, Dr. Wilson," Olivera said.

"We'll look around outside, check for footprints, that sort of thing." He stepped back into the foyer. "We'll let you know if we find anything suspicious."

"Thanks, Lieutenant." She followed him and Springer through the foyer and onto the porch. "I appreciate your concern."

After she'd gone back inside and closed the door, he and Springer stood on the porch for a moment. "You check that side"—he pointed to the left—"and I'll check over here." He took the steps down to the sidewalk, passing under the arch, and entered the clearing that ran the length of the side yard to a rickety fence at the back. He walked along the bottom of the porch, shining his flashlight through the latticework that stretched from the porch floor down to the ground. Nothing caught his eye except for a few small heaps of mulch and garden debris here and there. Coming to a spot where the latticework was damaged, he hunched over to get a better look. The porch itself was high off the ground. A person a little shorter than himself might have easily walked under it, standing up. As best he could tell, the house had a crawl space or maybe a basement. Unlikely, the latter. He'd learned that few houses in the Delta had basements. He continued on till he came to another break in the latticework where someone had evidently used the space underneath for storage. "Gardening tools, huh…" he mumbled. "A shovel, a rake, and a hoe." He deposited his flashlight in his pocket. Why would anybody leave his tools under the porch and not in the tool shed? He looked toward the back of the lot and, spotting a small shack near the fence, headed in that direction. As he reached the back corner of the house, Springer emerged from the other side. "You see anything?" Olivera asked.

"Nothing suspicious, no footprints, nothing outa place. There wasn't much to see…a few shrubs and an old garden patch, a couple of old trellises."

"Yeah, same here. Somebody left some gardening tools under the porch. Not the best place to store tools. Let's check out the shed."

They followed the pavestone path to the back of the lot and, reaching the shed, found the door ajar. There was a latch but no padlock, and when Olivera nudged the door, it swung back, giving way to a small room with a concrete floor. The sun, streaming in through a tiny window at the rear, illuminated the upper part of the room where there were rows of shelves along the side walls. An old lawn mower was tucked away under the shelves, and a jumble of old cans—paint cans, oil cans, and the like—were stacked on the floor. "That's not good." Olivera slowly shook his head. "Looks like a fire waiting to happen."

"Sure does. If you ask me, Dr. Wilson oughta clear all this outa here."

Olivera sniffed. "What's that smell?"

"Smells kinda fusty in here, don't it?" Springer reached down and picked up a paint can, and as he did, the pile shifted and cans rolled hither and yon.

"Good God!" Olivera gasped.

Springer looked up startled. "What is it, Chief?"

"Look closer, Springer."

Chapter Seven

*Monday, 11:15 a.m.*
*Morris House*

As Olivera waited for the coroner, his eyes idled over the front of Morris House. Despite the new owner's arrival, the saggy Victorian showed no sign of human warmth or seasonal cheer—no wreath on the door, no twinkling lights tacked to the wide overhangs. Wilson evidently had prioritized spotless windows over holiday trimmings. To him, her cleaning seemed obsessive, skeptical as he was of too much tidiness.

The coroner's van pulled up. Olivera, with a bit of swagger—as if to conceal his eagerness—approached the driver's door and tipped his hat. "Dr. McGinnis, can I help you with anything?"

A faint grin played at the corners of her mouth. "This is a switch, Lieutenant, you getting here before me."

He cleared his throat. "Yes, I suppose it is."

"Who lives here, by the way?" She glanced toward the house.

"You met her, didn't you? Dr. Lauren Wilson? She was with Mosey Frye at Sunny Banks."

"That's right." She nodded. "I remember. She's the new forensic psychologist at the college."

"Kinda weird, isn't it?"

"What?"

"She keeps showing up at crime scenes. This makes two in a row."

McGinnis shrugged. "Is she at home?"

He turned toward the house, where a faint glimmer of light came from the downstairs windows.

"Yes, but I haven't mentioned anything yet. Now you're here"—he looked down at the ground—"I'll let her know about this."

Over the phone, he'd given McGinnis a general description of what he and Springer had discovered in the tool shed—a man, middle-aged, apparently indigent, and most certainly dead. But not wanting to disturb the body hidden behind a stack of paint cans, Olivera hadn't been able to determine just how the man died.

McGinnis retrieved her instrument case and photographic equipment from the back of the van, and as she was closing the doors, Olivera reached down for the camera case.

"I got it," she said.

"You sure?"

She nodded.

He led the way to the back of the lot. Skirting the area he and Springer had taped off, they crossed over to the shed, where Springer had stationed himself in front of the door.

"Sergeant Springer," she acknowledged.

"Dr. McGinnis." He stepped aside. "It's kind of dark in there, Doc, but I've got my flashlight."

"Yes, that would help."

Olivera followed her in, while Springer, hovering nearby, shot a beam of light into the shed. After taking a couple of photographs, she stretched on latex gloves and removed the paint cans that had tumbled onto the body. Then stepping carefully from side to side, she scrutinized the corpse before pulling out her recorder. After noting her time of arrival, she proceeded to document her findings. "Middle-aged man, approximately sixty, recently deceased." She opened the dead man's jaw, then bent his left arm at the elbow. "Some rigidity in the limbs."

"Any idea of cause of death?" Olivera asked.

She clicked off the recorder. "Not right off. I don't see any obvious signs—no bleeding, no visible wounds. Until I can get him to the lab…"

"Time of death?"

"Three to eight hours." She picked up the victim's hand. "I'd say closer to three than eight."

Olivera checked his watch. It was eleven thirty. "That would put the time of death around seven thirty."

"Or an hour or two before."

"You notice that smell?" Olivera swatted away an annoying fly that had landed on his nose.

"How could I not?"

"What *is* that?"

"Acetone?" She shrugged.

"Huh. From paint?"

"Possibly, or from metabolic changes," she conjectured. "Fluids, breath, skin. It's part of the chemical breakdown. Does seem strong, though." She took her camera out of her bag and snapped several pictures of the body. "I'm not sure I can accomplish much more here." She turned to Springer. "Let's get the stretcher, Sergeant."

Springer followed at a few steps as they headed toward the van. "This is a tough one, ain't it, Doc?"

"We'll see when I get him to the lab."

Olivera watched from near the side of the house as Springer helped McGinnis unload the stretcher and body bag. But before they cleared the edge of the porch, Lauren Wilson stuck her head out of the front door and yelled to Springer. "What's going on, Sergeant?"

Springer looked at Dr. McGinnis, and McGinnis, apparently registering the awkwardness of the situation, said something to Springer, then walked toward the porch. "I'm Eads McGinnis, the county coroner. We met briefly at the Eldridges' a few weeks back."

"Yes, I remember. What's going on?"

"I'm afraid the back of your property has become a crime scene, well, not necessarily, but could be. From the looks of it, someone has died in your tool shed. I can't say for sure, but on the surface—"

"My God, you found a body?" Wilson stepped out on the porch, wrapping her jacket tightly around her.

"Not I. Lieutenant Olivera." McGinnis glanced toward Olivera. "I'm sure he'll want to speak to you as soon as we've completed the preliminaries."

"Of course. Who was it—do you know?"

"A middle-aged man, but we haven't identified him yet. Sorry, but that's all I can tell you."

"I understand." Wilson, backing toward the door, glanced down at her overalls. "I'll get dressed."

"Springer, let's get on with it." McGinnis took hold of her end of the stretcher, and Springer, his, and they proceeded toward the shed.

"Can't imagine what she's thinking of Hembree, Arkansas."

"Given her profession," McGinnis said, "she may be thinking she's come to the right town and just in time."

"In time for what, pray tell?"

"To help us solve this murder, if it was a murder."

They placed the stretcher near the door to the shed and, going in, cleared away the paint and oil cans to create a path for the removal of the corpse. McGinnis opened the top flap of the body bag, and with Olivera holding up the flap, she and Springer lifted the body into the bag. Once she'd zipped it up, the three together carried it outside and placed it on the stretcher.

"Did you find anything suspicious in the yard?" McGinnis asked Olivera. "Any footprints?"

"Nothing in the yard. Just some gardening tools underneath the porch." He followed along as she and Springer pushed the stretcher toward the van. As they passed the side porch, he gestured toward the area where he'd seen the tools. "See that break in the latticework? I stooped down to check under the porch, and spotting the tools, well, that's what prompted me to check the shed."

"And you came here why?"

"I spoke to Lauren Wilson this morning at the station. She'd seen an intruder. Well, not exactly. She'd seen a stranger in the yard."

They reached the van, and McGinnis opened the doors. "So, you and Springer came over?"

"Not right away. It's complicated. I'll tell you about it later at the morgue. Got any idea where this is going?"

"To be honest, not the foggiest. By the way, looks like you're short-handed. Where's Reagan?"

"On vacation. And, yes, I am feeling a bit short-handed." He turned to Springer. "I need to fill Dr. Wilson in on a couple of things. When you finish here, get into your slip-ons and give this area a thorough going over." With a sweep of his arm, he indicated the patch that ran from the sidewalk at the front to the fence at the back.

"Sure will, Chief."

"We'll take a closer look at the inside of the shed later," Olivera added. With that, he tipped his hat to McGinnis, climbed the porch steps to the front door, and tapped on the pane. Wilson came to the door, now dressed in jeans and a checkered shirt, and led him into the parlor. With no place to sit, he positioned himself in front of the fireplace—absent a fire, unfortunately. Wilson, meanwhile, propped herself against the stepladder by the window and rested her arm on the top step.

"Would you prefer to go to the station?" he inquired. "We might be more comfortable there."

She looked up, her expression full of confusion. "What was that?"

"I thought you might be more comfortable at the station."

"No," she shook her head, "I'm all right here. Please, what did you want to ask me?"

"Our conversation was interrupted this morning."

"Yes, sorry."

"You've got a lot going on." He glanced around the room that was destined to be the parlor, still bare except for cleaning supplies and paper toweling crumpled and strewn about the floor.

"Do you have any idea who that man is?" she asked.

"No, but do *you*?" he responded.

Her eyes opened wide. "I don't think so." She shook her head. "He wasn't the man I saw this morning, I mean, judging from his age. Didn't you say he was middle-aged?"

"The man you saw was younger?" he asked.

"I thought so, but it's hard to say. The first time I saw him, his back was turned. Then later, he was moving fast, and I only saw him at a distance. I didn't see his face either time…not really. And it was sort of dark. I couldn't even be sure about his clothing."

"But you're fairly certain he was younger?"

"Judging from his movements, yes, but I can't be sure."

"So, let's say the man you saw *wasn't* the victim. But he could have been—"

"—the assailant?"

"Yes," he nodded, "I guess that's what I was thinking. But let's not get ahead of ourselves. Our John Doe could have died of natural causes, though the circumstances do suggest foul play. I suppose what I'm getting at is this. Do you have any reason to believe that the person you saw—or even if not *that* person, some other person—?"

"Yes," she cut in, "I do have reason to believe…"

"So, what's going on?" He moved closer.

"I had a situation"—she looked away—"back in Philadelphia."

"Go on."

"There was a guy, a colleague, well, another post-doc like myself. I suspected he had a problem. I wasn't really sure, but I decided I had to report it to my supervisor. Nothing was done about it, and I, well, didn't feel comfortable. I thought it best to look for another job."

"You say he had a problem. Can you be more specific?"

"Technically, probably not. But if you give me your word that you will keep this in confidence."

"Of course."

"I suspected he suffered from a form of paraphilia." A slight blush rose to her cheeks. "How could I *not* report it? He was furious, of course, and, since nothing was being done, well, I didn't feel I could continue in the department. That's why I decided to leave. Fortunately, I was offered the position here. So I stayed on one more semester, hoping to make a smooth transition, but it was difficult. And this morning, when I saw someone in the yard—" She leaned into the ladder. "—I suppose I lost it." She let out a sigh and gave her head a shake. "I don't know…maybe I overreacted."

"Well, we should be able to find out if the man in Philadelphia has an alibi."

She had been avoiding eye contact, but now she looked his way. "And how do we do that, Lieutenant, without tipping him off?"

"Don't worry about that, but I would need at least his name and address."

She reached for her handbag on the floor next to the ladder and pulled out her phone. Moving toward him, she pointed to a name in her contacts. "This is the man."

Olivera looked at the screen. "Paul Krueger. That's the guy?"

She nodded.

"And that's his picture?"

"Yes."

"Mind if I share the contact to my phone?"

"Go ahead."

"This information is current?"

"I assume so, but you could check the Rutherford directory."

"That's where you were?"

"Yes, Rutherford College, for a year and a half."

"What I'd like to do is offer you some protection, and I will, but as you may have noticed, we're understaffed right now. In the meantime, would you consider—"

"—getting a room somewhere? No, out of the question. I must get my life in some sort of order before classes start." She approached the fireplace and, opening a small box on the mantel, showed Olivera the contents. "I have a gun, and I know how to use it."

His brow lifted. "It's registered to you, I assume."

"Yes, of course."

"Are you sure you don't want to move into the Tavernette? It'd be just a couple of days, till we can figure out what's going on."

"And who's going to cover my expenses?"

"Well, actually—"

"That's what I thought. Look...I'll be very careful, and Mosey and Nadia should be here later to help with the cleaning."

He shook his head and sighed. "I don't like it, but if you won't be convinced..." For a moment he stood glancing around the room, then passed into the foyer and picked up his hat, which he'd hung over the end of the banister.

She followed him to the door. "You'll let me know...whatever you find out?"

"Yes, I'm going to the morgue now. I'll be in touch."

## Chapter Eight

*Monday, 1:30 p.m.*
*Morgue at Delta Infirmary, Hembree*

On the way to the morgue, Olivera grabbed a burger at the Dairy Bar at the intersection of McAllister and Lee, thinking he'd give McGinnis time to start the autopsy. It was about one thirty when he arrived at Delta Infirmary and, pulling up at the back of the three-story stucco building, he parked in his designated spot—having at last convinced the ladies' guild he deserved such a privilege. Once inside, he followed the darkish corridor to the grand mahogany door at the end. The architecture and furnishings reminded him of his home in Santa Clara, where remnants of the Spanish Colonial style were common in the older parts of town. The hospital administrators were clearly in no rush to modernize the place. The cracked plaster walls, the old light sconces at intervals along the hall, the terrazzo tile flooring, the ornately-carved table below the painting of the infirmary's founder... To Olivera it seemed comfortable and nostalgic, and he savored it all.

As he pushed through the door to the morgue, a pungent odor irritated his nostrils. It was the same stench they'd smelled in the shed but not as strong. "Dr. McGinnis."

"Lieutenant."

He joined her at the gurney.

Without so much as lifting her head, she'd offered him a small tin of eucalyptus balm. "You want some of this?"

"Thanks." He rubbed a dab under his nose, then looked down at the open thorax. She'd already removed the stomach. "What do you have so far?"

"An explanation for the strong smell of acetone," she said, going on with what she was doing. "Oftentimes you get that," she added, "especially if there's a problem with the digestive tract. She brushed the back of her hand across her forehead. "Our friend here was close to death, aside from whatever occurred at Morris House." She pointed toward the scale where an organ lay. "It looks like advanced stomach cancer."

"Hmm. So, if not for—"

"—exactly what," she cut in, "I don't know yet, but I do know he was a very sick man."

"What else have you got?"

She put down the scalpel and removed her gloves. "No defensive wounds, no significant signs of a struggle. I am seeing some slight bruising that might have resulted from a fall."

"You think he just fell?"

"Or was pushed."

Olivera took a step back. "And the impact—" He butted his fist against his palm. "—would have been enough to cause death?"

"Maybe. It wouldn't have taken much, given his condition. Of course, he could have had a stroke. I haven't checked the brain cavity."

"What was this seriously ill man doing on the grounds of Morris House?" He paced away from the gurney. "And on a dreary morning at that?"

"Can't tell you that, but I could take a guess."

He lifted his brow. "Let's hear it."

"Now that I've gotten a better look at the face, I believe I know him. Will Grayson is his name. He did gardening, odd jobs around town. He might have worked for the Morrises at one time, but I doubt he had lately."

He looked down at the corpse's frail arms. "He's almost, well, emaciated. Surely, he was under a doctor's care. Think you could ask around?"

"I'll check the hospital records. There weren't any scars from an incision, no radiation burns. If his cancer was diagnosed, I doubt he received treatment. He probably didn't have any insurance." She approached the head of the deceased and, using both thumbs, opened his eyes. "See that?"

"Green eyes."

"My grandfather called him Mr. Green Eyes."

"To his face?"

She laughed. "I doubt that."

"Your grandfather knew this man?"

"Somewhat. He knew the man he worked for, Kit Morris."

"The owner of Morris House?"

"The same."

"Is your grandfather still around?"

"No, he passed away some years ago, but Daddy might know something."

"Would you want to ask him, informally, I mean?"

"I could, or *you* could." She tore off a sticky note from a pad on the counter and scribbled a number. "Give him a call. You know him, don't you?"

"Yes, of course. We worked together on a couple of

cases before he retired." He inserted the note into his tablet. "This puts a new spin on the case. Grayson here might have had cause to be there, though it's unlikely he was known to the current owner. Maybe he'd left something in the tool shed and dropped by to pick it up."

"That's possible, but Grayson was a sick man. I'm not sure he would have been out and about without good reason."

"Yes, I expect you're right about that. But if there *was* a compelling reason to go, and he felt pressured… Well, since Dr. Wilson had already moved in, maybe…"

She nodded. "That could be it. He felt he needed to get over there, do whatever it was he needed to do, and get away unseen."

"He didn't exactly knock on the door, did he?"

"No, I expect not." She turned to face him. "You mentioned Lauren Wilson saw someone?"

"Yeah, she did, but didn't think it was *this* guy." He nodded toward the corpse. "She thought it was a younger man. She saw him twice. Once early this morning, before seven, then a little later she saw the same man coming from the back of the house, but she seemed somewhat unsure about the description."

"If the man she saw *wasn't* Grayson, maybe that man *saw* Grayson."

"He could be the man who put Grayson in the shed."

"Well, the body doesn't show any signs of being dragged." She lifted the sheet, uncovering first the feet and then the upper torso. "No bruising in the usual places. He might have picked him up and carried him."

"How much did he weigh?"

"A hundred and twenty-seven pounds."

"Light for a man. Wouldn't have been difficult—"

"Yes, and he wouldn't have been able to offer much resistance, well, if he had needed to. In the late stages of gastric cancer, he would have experienced exhaustion, weight loss, muscle thinning…"

"So"—he rubbed his knuckle against his chin— "we have two men on the property, possibly three, at approximately the same time. By the way, do you have a more exact time of death?"

"Before I said three to eight hours, closer to three, and I'll stick with that. I would say somewhere between six and seven this morning."

"So, it's likely they *were* there at the same time." He wheeled around. "We've got to go back to the crime scene."

"If a crime occurred," she reminded him.

"Not that again." He rolled his eyes toward the ceiling.

"Sorry, but *that again*. And this time, there's no sign of an altercation, as in the Ashby case, much less a conk over the head."

"But what about the circumstances?" He threw out his hands. "Grayson didn't pass out in the tool shed, then pile cans around himself to block the view."

"Of course, not." She rolled her eyes. She covered the body and walked toward her desk at the back of the lab.

Olivera followed. "So, what are you thinking?"

She reached for a folder and opened it, revealing a stack of photographs. "From the crime scene." She handed the stack to Olivera.

He shuffled through the photographs, giving each one a quick look. "Someone else must have arranged those cans over and around the body." He set them back on her desk. "And Dr. Wilson believed the man she saw was a younger man. Probably most young men, especially if they really needed to, could pick up a man Grayson's size, carry him into the shed, and so on."

"Or he could have died in the shed. We don't really know where he died."

"True."

"For the moment, *how* he died seems more important."

"Maybe, just maybe we're looking for a suspect who didn't *kill* Grayson but wanted to get him out of the way. Didn't want to raise suspicion or call attention."

She leaned against the desk. "Sounds like a reasonable assessment of the situation."

"By the way, mind if I take one of these?" He gestured toward the photographs. "I could use one for the evidence board."

"Sure, I have copies. Take all you want."

"You know it's funny," he continued. "Springer mentioned Grayson this morning. He didn't care for him, called him the town drunk."

"Yes." She nodded. "He had that reputation."

"Seems like Springer also said something about him working for the Morrises and some other people on McAllister. I need to ask him about that." He picked up his hat, which he'd set on McGinnis's desk. "By the way, I got a lead on the *other* uninvited visitor—at Morris House, I mean."

"Who?" Her tone implied surprise.

"Dr. Wilson suspects she has a stalker."

"She's only been here a couple of weeks, hasn't she?"

"That's right, but this guy's not from around here.

He's from Philadelphia, a former colleague, a post-doc who was under her supervision. She reported him to her supervisor, who did nothing. Typical." He set his hat back on the desk and, taking out his notepad, opened it to the interview with Wilson. "Rutherford College in Philadelphia. She was there a year and a half and moved here mid-year, as soon as the semester ended."

"Wow. That puts a new spin on it, doesn't it? This stalker, assuming it's the same man, might have run into Grayson, then—"

"Yes, then what?" he asked.

"I'd better see what else Grayson can tell us." She glanced at the corpse.

"You do that, please, Dr. McGinnis." He picked up his hat and put it on. "And call me as soon as you know something." He pulled the note she had given him from between the pages of his notebook. "Meanwhile, I'm going to give the other Dr. McGinnis a call." He crossed the morgue and, on his way out, pulled a handkerchief from his pocket and wiped the salve from beneath his nose. Turning and tipping his hat to the younger and more appealing Dr. McGinnis, he smiled. "I'll be in touch."

Chapter Nine

*Monday, 2:30 p.m.*
*Morris House*

Mosey, Nadia, and Saffron were on one of those
missions common to Delta women, who go rushing off
at the drop of a hat to help a friend in need. The object or
rather, subject of their mission was Lauren Wilson, a
newcomer from the City of Brotherly Love. She'd been
in Hembree only a fortnight and was about to get her first
taste of real Delta hospitality.

With their obligations for the afternoon set aside, the
trio climbed into Nadia's SUV and drove toward Morris
House, one of many historic homes on McAllister. Nadia
had been in each of them before, and Mosey had visited
most. But Saffron, it being her first time and all, seemed
edgy, as if she weren't sure *what* to expect.

"So, that's the Raineses' big Queen Anne?" Saffron
asked, as Nadia turned off Lee onto McAllister.

"That's it." Nadia slowed to a crawl.

During most of the year, it was hard to make out the
architectural details of the house because of the big tall
trees that circled the property. But now that the leaves
had fallen, the expansive wraparound porch came into
view, with its ample spindles and brackets and a neat row
of Ionic columns high on stone piers. As they drove by,
Mosey caught sight of the upstairs window beyond

which stretched the plush boudoir of Charlotte Raines, née Bujeau. The lights were on, which suggested Charlotte was likely there. The lights were off in the cavernous first-floor living room where, almost a year before, Matthew Raines had treated Mosey to a beer. She had thought of going back to smooth the ruffled waters if indeed there were any in need of smoothing. She somehow doubted, however, that the May-to-December couple held *her* responsible for the outcome of the Crump case. Admittedly, her snooping had essentially prompted its reopening, even though Olivera had chalked up the final solution to himself. She sat back in her seat and crossed her arms. "Doesn't seem so pompous as it once did, does it?"

Nadia glanced at the house. "I had never set foot in the place till a while back when Matthew phoned, wanting me to look at his collection of casta paintings."

"Casta paintings!" Mosey gasped. When she went there before, she caught a glimpse of the artwork that lined the corridor from the study to the living room. But back then, she was hot on the pursuit of Delaney Crump's killer and hardly paid any attention at all to the subject matter of the paintings.

"Yes, casta paintings," Nadia repeated.

"Oh, my." Mosey clutched the back of Nadia's seat. "That's exactly the excuse I need to get back in the house."

Saffron twisted around. "What are you talking about, girl?"

"David Morell...casta paintings. Weren't you paying the least bit of attention to what I was telling you earlier? He called about some casta paintings he thinks are in Hembree. Wants me to track them down." She sat back in her seat.

"And how you gonna do that?" Saffron asked, her voice growing sharper.

"Well, I don't know, but if Matthew Raines is a collector, I might as well start with him."

Saffron turned back around and glanced over at Nadia. "And what, please ma'am, is a casta painting?"

"Late eighteenth century into nineteenth," Nadia explained. "They were common among the painters of the Spanish Colonial period."

"So, what are they?" Saffron asked with impatience.

"*Casta* means 'caste.' The paintings depicted the various classes and ethnicities of the Spanish colonies. Turns out our friend David Morell specializes in the genre."

"Your *friend*?"

"Not a *real* friend," Nadia clarified. "I hardly know him, and Mosey doesn't know him at all."

Mosey tapped Saffron on the shoulder. "You talked to Morell. Didn't he tell you what he wanted?"

"No, he did not. And why'd he call *you*?"

"Well, if you must know, Rafael told him I'd been very obliging."

"Rafael. Morell knows Rafael?"

"Evidently."

"All these rich folks seem to know one another," Saffron observed. "But tell me this." She turned back to Mosey. "Do you actually know anything about casta paintings?"

"No, but I can learn, can't I?"

Prattling away, the threesome arrived at the end of the street where Saffron, mouth agape and eyes agog, delivered a last cutting commentary. "So, *this* is Morris

House?"

"Yep." Mosey's gaze drifted to the spider-web arch on the porch. She shot a glance at Saffron, whose eyes had come to rest on the same spot. "Not much to look at, is it?"

"I suppose I've seen worse."

"We've all seen worse," Nadia said, "but it's a crying shame what's happened to the place. The old Morrises built themselves an elegant house, then let it go to pot. You gotta wonder—"

"Never even finished it," Saffron cut in.

"Yeah." Mosey chuckled. "That's why I used to call it the half-house."

Nadia shook her head. "Well, houses, like people, have their good moments and their bad."

"True, and this one's hit rock bottom." Saffron opened the car door and got out.

"So, where was the body found?" Nadia asked.

"In the tool shed," Mosey replied. "Did you know Will Grayson?"

"Not really." Nadia closed the door and opened the rickety gate. "I've heard of him but can't say I ever met him."

"What about you, Saffron? Did you know Grayson?"

"Me? Never had the pleasure." She started down the sidewalk behind Nadia.

"*Pleasure*," Mosey repeated. "Not sure ol' Will was well thought of around town." She closed the gate behind her. "You ladies be careful. If the sidewalk doesn't get you, the cobwebs will."

Saffron, passing under the arch, glared up. "They could have saved themselves the trouble on that bit of embellishment. I've never seen such a thing."

"Shh." Mosey frowned and pointed to Nadia, who'd already tapped on the door pane.

"Come in, come in." Lauren opened the door. "Thanks for coming." She stepped back and invited them in. "I could use some company."

"—and some help, we were thinking." Mosey stepped in behind Saffron. "Have you got enough cleaning supplies? I could have brought some, but we came straight from work."

"I've got plenty, but I could use the extra hands. Sure you guys don't mind?"

"Guys?" Saffron repeated.

"Yankees say that," Mosey explained. "We'll have her saying *y'all* in no time."

"Sorry," Lauren said, "we do tend to say that where I come from. Can I take your jackets?"

"It's chilly in here," Mosey noted. "Think I'll keep mine on."

"I know. The utilities people still haven't come."

"First thing in the morning, the man told me," Saffron said.

Lauren took Saffron's and Nadia's jackets and hung them in the foyer closet. "Come in, won't you?"

She led the way into the parlor. "I've just about finished in here. I thought we'd get started on the upstairs bedrooms."

"Sure," Nadia said, "whatever you need us to do."

"Why don't you head up, and I'll grab the supplies. I've got rubber gloves if you want them."

"Sure, I'll take a pair." Saffron followed Mosey up the stairs.

"Be careful, ladies. I've set out candles, but it's a

little dim up there."

Even though Lauren had pushed back all the curtains, it was dark on the north side of the house. But Mosey didn't mind. Yes, the chilliness bothered her but not the darkness. It reminded her of when she and Nadia were kids, and just for fun, would turn off the lights and light a candle. As soon as Lauren was out of sight, Mosey whispered to Nadia, "Kind of creepy, isn't it?"

"Yes, and you're loving every minute of it."

At the top of the stairs, Mosey opened the door to the room on the left. "This is Lauren's bedroom. Check out the beautiful old furniture."

"You reckon she wants us in here?" Saffron glanced around the room.

"She said upstairs rooms." Mosey walked over to the armoire and opened it. "Looks like she hasn't unpacked her clothes."

"Mosey, for Pete's sake," Nadia scolded.

"I'm not snooping." Mosey calmly closed the door. "I just wanted to see if it was empty."

"And it is." Lauren came in. "As you can see. I'm living out of a suitcase till I get the whole place cleaned up." She set the cleaning supplies on the dresser.

"I don't blame you," Saffron said. "You don't want to put your clean clothes in dusty drawers. You wouldn't happen to have any drawer liner, would you?"

"As a matter of fact, I do. Rolls of it. I think I left it in the other bedroom. I'll get you a pair of scissors if you don't mind bothering with it."

"Course not."

"I'll be right back."

Mosey followed Lauren out with her eyes, then quickly turned to Nadia. "How does the furniture strike you?"

"It's pretty," Nadia casually remarked. "In good condition, but it's not that unusual. I've seen a lot of pieces like this. It's Eastlake. Simple, clean designs. Often hand made." She opened the top drawer of a three-drawer dresser. "Sometimes there's a stamp in the drawer. See this?"

Mosey looked. "So, all this is Eastlake? Looks like a matched set."

"I would say so. I'm a little surprised Lauren would go for this, but somehow, I didn't expect her to go for the house, either."

"What do you mean?" Saffron asked.

"Well, I don't know. I thought she might want something more modern."

"Modern," Mosey repeated. "She doesn't care for modern, from what she's told me." She opened the bottom drawer of the dresser. "Look at this. There's stuff in here." She picked up a handful of old photographs in cardboard frames. All this must have belonged to the Morrises." She opened one of the folders and held it up for Nadia and Saffron to see. "Momma Morris, Daddy Morris, Kit, Eleanor, and Peggy."

"Wait a second. You knew them?" Lauren, her arms stacked with rolls of drawer liner, had come in and, laying the rolls on the bed, looked at Mosey.

"Not the parents. They died long time ago, but I knew Mr. Kit and his two sisters. The sisters are still alive. They're out at the Magnolia Nursing Home."

Lauren picked up a photograph. "So the sisters must have left these here. You'd think they would have wanted them."

"Yes, you would," Mosey agreed.

"Look at this one." Lauren passed the picture to Mosey. "Looks like a poker game."

"My goodness." Mosey pointed at one of the men in the group. "That's my granddaddy. He's so young. I'd love to have this one if the sisters don't want it."

Lauren picked up a handful of loose snapshots, then held up two. "Check out these. Must have been taken during the war."

Saffron, who'd made herself comfortable on a chaise in the corner, got up, sauntered over to the group, and began browsing coolly through the pictures.

"You aren't fond of old snapshots, huh, Saffron?" Lauren fished out a picture of the Morris kids as children and held it up for her to see.

"Sure, they're okay." She dropped the bunch she'd gone through on the bed. "But ladies, I don't mean to rush y'all, but shouldn't we get on with what we came to do?"

"We really should." Nadia checked her watch and turned to Lauren. "Where should we start?"

"Well, there're three rooms up here, and I've already cleaned the bathroom. "Saffron, what if you take this one." She glanced around. "There's not much to do. Just give the furniture a good cleaning. Too bad we can't run the vacuum. If you have time to line the drawers, great, but not to worry if you don't. I'll take the other bedroom, and there's a small room I'm going to use for a study." She motioned in the direction of the room. "It's got built-in shelves." She looked at Mosey. "Maybe you and Nadia could run over the shelves and desk with a dust cloth and, if there's time, unpack the books—just the ones staying here. I'm taking most of them to my office at the college."

"Sounds like a plan to me." Saffron said.

Lauren handed Saffron a pair of gloves, then gestured toward the scissors and drawer liner. "It's all right there, should you feel like dealing with it." She gave her a faint smile and then walked Mosey and Nadia across the hall to the room she'd chosen for her study.

It was a little cubbyhole of a room, furnished only with an antique walnut desk and an old-fashioned task chair, hand-crafted and upholstered in hand-tooled leather.

"Look at that!" Nadia beamed. "What a beautiful piece." She sat in the chair and, reaching underneath for the lever, lowered the seat, then raised it. "If you've got some lubricant, I could fix that squeak for you."

"Not sure I do," Lauren replied. "I'll pick up some at the Superette."

"I've got a can at the store. I'll drop it by."

"I don't know what to say. You guys are amazing."

"Not really," Nadia said with a wave of her hand.

"It's true what people say about small towns." Lauren smiled.

"What?" Mosey asked.

"That people are friendlier, more helpful."

"I wouldn't know. I've never lived anywhere but Hembree."

"And I've never lived anywhere but Philadelphia."

"If you decide you'd rather have something more modern—" Nadia got up from the chair. "—I'd be glad to take this desk off your hands." She opened the desk drawer. "Hey, there's stuff in here, too."

Lauren, who was on her way out, stopped. "What stuff?"

"An old letter opener." Nadia held it up. "Pretty."

"Looks like rose gold." Mosey approached.

"It *is* rose gold." Nadia passed the piece to Lauren.

Lauren turned it over in her hand. "Nice, twenty-four carats. Must have belonged to one of the Morrises. It's got an *M* on the handle."

"This house is a treasure trove," Nadia said.

"Yeah, it is." Mosey furrowed her brow, eyeing the letter opener. "Wonder why the Morris sisters didn't hold on to it or sell it at the estate sale."

"*Was* there an estate sale?" Lauren looked at Mosey.

"If there was," Nadia said, "I didn't hear about it."

Fat chance of that, Mosey thought. "For the time being, why don't we put whatever we run across into a box?"

"Good idea." Lauren picked up an empty cardboard box and set it on the desk.

"Shall I speak to the sisters for you?" Mosey asked. "Leaving it all here like this, you have to wonder if they cared about it." Of all the things a person might leave behind—family pictures and an item like a letter opener that probably was a gift. Didn't seem right to her.

"Maybe they got overwhelmed," Nadia suggested. "Dispensed with what they could and the rest, well…"

"Yeah, I guess."

"If you wouldn't mind checking with them, I'd feel better about it," Lauren said.

"I may want to buy a few things." Nadia glanced at Lauren.

"It's not really mine, but maybe the sisters would be interested."

"Don't worry about it, Lauren. We'll figure it out."

Lauren shrugged and headed out the door.

"Hey, Lauren," Mosey called. "You want us to

unpack the books, right?"

Lauren paused and looked back. "Yes, just the three boxes next to the shelf, please, and you don't have to concern yourself with putting them in any kind of order. I'll get around to that as soon as I can."

Once she'd gone, Mosey opened the other desk drawers. "Look at this," she whispered to Nadia.

"What?"

"More pictures." Mosey laid a couple of black-and-white snapshots on the desk. "More military pictures." She turned one over. "This one has a date, December 1945." She held the back of the picture to the light that poured through the only window. " 'Amos Frye, Timothy McGinnis, Colton Raines,' " she read, then turned it back over. "Look how happy they look." She picked up another picture. "There's Granddaddy Amos again. I would *love* to have this one."

"Doesn't seem like anyone's particularly interested in this stuff. If you want it, ask Lauren."

Mosey shook her head. "Not without asking Eleanor and Peggy first."

"So ask them. And by the way, how come you're not sneezing?"

"I took a pill." Mosey set the picture aside and moved on to the next. "You know, I think I'll run by to see them after we leave here." She went on sorting. "Military, military, military. The same group, over and over."

"Must have been a close bunch."

"They were. My grandfather knew Mr. Morris well. Timothy McGinnis, too. But Colton Raines? Not sure about him. He must have moved away."

"Come to think of it, the other day Matthew

mentioned he had a brother, and I think he called him Colton. Hand me one of those. I'll ask Daddy. He'll know who they are."

"Here's a good one." Mosey handed her the picture.

"Nice." Nadia smiled. "So handsome, the whole bunch, and sort of sexy. Look at the hairstyles and the poses." She held up the photograph and, Mosey accepting it, began to laugh. "What?" Nadia said.

"I never thought of Granddaddy as a sexy man, but you're right. Look at the hair, all poofy on top. That's hilarious."

"Servicemen were *supposed* to be sexy—didn't you know?"

"I never thought about it, but come to think of it, they always look like that in pictures, don't they? Sexy, sort of sophisticated, happy."

"Any women in that stack?"

Mosey shuffled through till she came to a picture of two girls. "Eleanor and Peggy. Says here, 'December 1945.' What in heaven's name happened in December 1945?" She continued thumbing through the stack. "Another 'December 1945' and another."

"That's when the war ended, silly. That's when the troops came home. Germany surrendered in May, then Japan followed in September."

"Are you sure?"

"Look it up if you don't believe me."

Mosey pulled out her cellphone and keyed in *end of World War II*. "I know you're right. You always are," she muttered. "Good lord, 'One million men were discharged from the military in December 1945.' This bunch must have come back about the same time. No wonder they were happy. They didn't die."

"Right." Nadia rolled her eyes.

Mosey shuffled some more. "But you know something, there aren't any pictures of Kit. You'd think there would be. Likely the pictures belonged to him."

"Maybe he was taking them," Nadia suggested.

"Possibly, but you'd think he'd be in some of these."

"Maybe the sisters kept the ones of Kit. Take the whole stack to the Magnolia. Ask them."

"I think I will."

"But in the meantime"—Nadia gave Mosey a determined look—"would you pick up a rag and get to dusting, please, ma'am? I'd like to get out of here before dark."

Mosey looked at her watch. "We've got plenty of time."

"*You've* got plenty of time. I've got to get back to the store."

## Chapter Ten

*Monday, 3:30 p.m.*
*Police Station*

On the way to his cubicle, Olivera spotted the box of doughnuts. He was ravenous. Hadn't touched a bite since the night before when he and Eads had ordered a pizza and watched the Razorback game at her place. He pulled out a pumpkin spice and closed the box. Finding the coffee carafe empty, he rinsed it out, prepped a new filter, and placed the basket in the machine. He pressed the On button and, resting his back against the counter, bit into the doughnut.

He needed to call the personnel office at Rutherford College, he thought as he chewed, but he wasn't sure how to get information on Krueger without arousing suspicion. A call from Hembree, Arkansas, was likely to raise eyebrows.

But all that aside, what Wilson had passed along concerning her supervisor had hit a nerve. Shouldn't have surprised him, hearing about yet another dismissive administrator. He'd learned firsthand that indifference was the hallmark of the breed. A year had passed—more than that now—since his run in with his old super, but it hadn't taken much to set that broken record to spinning. He was getting over it…a little. At least Santa Clara was no longer at the forefront of his concerns.

The light went off on the coffee machine, and he poured himself a cup, then headed to his cubicle. Once settled into his high-back executive, he reached for the pyx he'd been using for a pencil holder, a going-away present from his old partner, Nick. Indeed, a strange souvenir. Maybe not for the average Joe—but for him? Nick was well aware he wasn't the church-going type. But there it was—a receptacle for transporting the holy eucharist, filled with pencils, ballpoints, a couple of felt pins, and a letter opener.

A moment later, as he was finishing his doughnut, a voice called out from the front office.

"Anybody here?"

He rose from his chair. "Reagan, is that you?"

Reagan's tall, lean frame soon appeared at the door. "Course it's me, Lieutenant. Who'd you think it was?"

"I didn't expect you back today." He shook Reagan's hand. "Have a seat. How was the trip?"

"Fine, just fine." Reagan sat in the folding chair to the side of the desk and crossed his spindly legs at the knees.

"Glad you're back. We were starting to feel a little short-handed."

"How's that?"

Olivera paused, tapping on the desk. "It's possible we've got a murder." He looked at Reagan. "Will Grayson—you know him?"

Reagan's head jerked back. "Will Grayson? *Yeah,* I know him."

"He was found dead this morning in the tool shed at Morris House. You know the place?"

"On McAllister?"

He nodded. "House at the dead end of the street."

"You said in the tool shed?"

"Yeah, Dr. McGinnis thought he'd been dead several hours. She's got him over at the morgue."

Reagan leaned back, stroking his chin with his thumb.

"Looks like he was in the advanced stages of stomach cancer."

"You think that's what it was?"

"I don't know." Olivera shrugged. "The body was behind a bunch of old cans. He couldn't have set it up that way, I don't believe. Well, I don't know, maybe he could have." He reached in his briefcase for the picture Eads had given him and handed it to Reagan. "Somebody put him there, I suspect. Then stacked the cans around him."

Reagan studied the photograph. "Who found him?"

"We did, actually."

"You and Springer?"

Olivera nodded.

"Huh." Reagan laid the picture on the desk, then thought a minute. "How'd y'all happen to be back there?"

Just as Olivera was about to answer, Springer popped his head in. "Reagan!" Springer exclaimed, stepping in. "When did you get back?"

Reagan stood and shook Springer's hand. "Just drove in."

"We didn't expect you till tomorrow."

"Yeah, we came back a day early. Jenny got bored, was ready to get back."

"And none too soon." Olivera turned to Springer. "If you'd fill Reagan in on what's been going on—" He checked his watch. "—I've got to make a couple of phone calls. By the way—" He looked back at Springer. "—what I said earlier about you going clairvoyant—"

"Yeah, Chief?" His eyes grew big.

"Will Grayson is the dead man."

"You don't mean it." His eyes bulged. "Good grief." He shook his head. "I can't believe it. Ol' Will?"

"You didn't recognize him?" Reagan asked Springer.

"Naw, I didn't."

"He was in bad shape," Olivera said. "Skin and bones."

"Yeah, he didn't look like himself." Springer frowned.

"Poor ol' Grayson," Reagan shook his head. "He's been a fixture around here forever."

"Sure has," Springer agreed. "Did Dr. McGinnis say what happened to him?"

"Stomach cancer—stage four."

"That's not a big surprise."

"Yeah, the man had a drinking problem," Reagan added.

"The town drunk, you might say."

"He looked pretty bad, didn't he?" Olivera said.

"He might have just been looking for a place to die" —Reagan shrugged— "like some homeless mutt."

"I guess I could believe that" —Olivera nodded— "if not for the effort to hide the body."

"Yeah," Springer agreed. "He was *put* there, I'd imagine."

"You sound like you picked up some evidence." Olivera looked at Springer.

"A thing or two, but I think we oughta go back over there. Finish going over the property. I was hoping Dr.

McGinnis would give us cause of death."

"Uh-huh. Would save us some crime work, wouldn't it?" He sat up straight in his chair. "Let me make these calls, men" —he pulled the telephone toward him—"and then we'll take another look. But in the meantime, Springer—"

"Yeah, Chief?"

"I was just about to tell Reagan how we happened to be there—at Morris House."

"Sure thing, Chief, I'll bring him up to date."

"Yeah, and start at the beginning." Olivera stifled a yawn.

"You need a refill on that?" Springer pointed to Olivera's empty cup.

Olivera handed him the cup. "I just made a fresh pot if you guys want some."

Springer and Reagan left, and Olivera checked his watch again. It was almost closing time in the Eastern Time Zone, and if he didn't call Rutherford soon, he'd probably have to wait till the following day. Who should he say he was—a friend, family member? It was risky, but he had to give a name…other than Lieutenant Gustavo Olivera of the Hembree Police Department. He wasn't one for subterfuge, but he owed it to Wilson to keep her name out of it if he could.

"Chief, here's your coffee."

"Tell me something, Springer. I know colleges don't like to give out information about students, but who do you suppose they might open up to?"

"I don't know. Another college?"

"Brilliant. I'll try that."

Olivera punched in the number, and when the receptionist answered, he cleared his throat. "Tell me, who might I speak to about a man named Paul Krueger? He's a postdoc in your department, I believe."

"Paul Krueger," she repeated. "I'm afraid he's not here anymore."

"I see. Do you have a forwarding address?"

"May I ask who's calling?"

"Professor Olivera, University of Arkansas."

"He told us he'd be in touch as soon as he got settled."

"I suppose you wouldn't know if he has accepted a position elsewhere."

"I'm afraid I couldn't tell you that, Professor, but if you want to speak to—"

"No, I'll see if I can locate him some other way, but thanks."

"Hmm." He hadn't expected to hear that. So…Dr. Paul Krueger had flown the coop…or been kicked out of the coop. He twisted around in his chair and, reaching for his cup, took a few sips of coffee, then twisted back around. He picked up the receiver again, thinking he'd take a chance, call back, and ask to speak to the chair. He set his cup down. No, he wasn't going to do that. He would look up the number and call him directly. He keyed the name of the college into the computer and, pulling up the forensic psychology department webpage, located the name of the chair. "Raymond Davis, Ph. D.," he mumbled. "Okay, Professor Davis, let's see what I can get out of you." He punched in the number. Drat! Voice mail answered. He waited for the beep, then said, "Professor Davis, I would like to speak to you about a person of interest in a case I'm investigating. Please give me a call as soon as you can." He left his number and hung up.

"Chief," Springer stuck his head in again, "you ready?"

"No, Springer, one more call."

He left, muttering to Reagan, "He's got to make another call."

Olivera punched in Sam McGinnis's number. "Sam, how are you? Gus Olivera here."

"Good, and yourself?"

"Can't complain. Listen, I'm investigating a death, Will Grayson. Maybe you've heard."

"No, I haven't."

"Yes, he passed away. Well, we found the body this morning."

"I'm sorry to hear that."

"Seems like he was known around town, but I didn't know him. Eads thought you might be able to provide us with some background information."

"Well, I know Will, but I haven't spoken with him in a long time."

"His body was found at the Morrises' old house."

"He died at the Morrises'?"

"Looks like."

"Not too surprising, I guess. He worked for Eleanor and Peggy. He was a longtime friend of their brother."

"Yes, I think someone mentioned that."

"He and Kit were of the same persuasion, you might say. Artists of sort. Neither one of them had much success. Kit kinda looked out for Will. I don't think he had any family."

"But it occurred to me that, with Morris gone and the sisters out at the Magnolia, Grayson wouldn't have a reason to be there, at the house, I mean, unless you might know of something."

"He's not working for the new owner?"

"No, I don't think she knows him."

"Then, I'm afraid I wouldn't know."

"Okay, Sam, I appreciate your help. If you think of anything, please give me a call."

"Sure will, but tell me something. You don't suspect foul play, do you?"

"Too soon to say. Eads is working on it."

"Okay. I'll be in touch if I think of anything relevant."

Olivera got out of his seat and grabbed his hat and sports coat off the rack. "Springer, let's go."

About ten minutes later, he, Springer, and Reagan rolled into the gravel drive at Morris House just as Mosey, Nadia, and Saffron were driving away. Olivera waved and gave a half smile. "Don't those women ever work?"

Springer sniggered. "If there's snooping to be done, Mosey's on it. You know that, Chief."

Olivera sighed, shook his head, and stepped out of the SUV. "I'll speak to Dr. Wilson, let her know we're here, and you two go ahead. By the way, Springer, what was it you found before?"

"A cigarette butt, over there." Springer pointed toward the wooded area.

"Check it again...closely." Olivera climbed the steps to the porch and tapped on the door pane. As he waited, his eyes wandered to the thicket. If somebody was watching the house, that'd be an ideal place to hide.

Wilson opened the door. "Didn't expect you back today, Lieutenant."

"I won't keep you. I just wanted to let you know we're here to finish going over the yard."

"I thought you finished this morning."

"No, I had to get to the morgue. I don't really expect to find much more. Just following procedure."

"Sure, I understand. By the way, do you know what happened to the man?"

"We're still working on it, but we were able to identify him. Will Grayson. He used to do yard work for the Morrises. I don't suppose you met him, spoke to him?"

"No, I didn't."

"By the way, I contacted Rutherford, spoke to the receptionist in forensic psychology. Seems Dr. Krueger is no longer with the department."

"Oh, dear." Her brow creased with apprehension. "Maybe they *did* do something about him."

"Possibly. I couldn't get into it deeply. I didn't want to raise suspicion, and I doubt I would've gotten very far. So, I placed a call to the chair, Raymond Davis, and got his voicemail."

"You didn't mention me, did you?"

"I haven't spoken to him yet, but, no, I won't." He glanced away, then back. "I'll manage it the best I can, but we need to know what's going on—the circumstances of his dismissal, if he *was* dismissed, and his whereabouts."

"Yes." She looked thoughtful. "I'd like to forget the matter entirely, but if it has followed me here, I need to know. Must know."

"I hate to even mention this but, being realistic, if Krueger was dismissed and blames you for his dismissal, you need to be aware of that and take precautions."

She sighed and leaned against the doorframe.

"I'd at least keep a paper trail of any contact with

the alleged stalker." He paused. "Of course we don't know yet that you *are* being stalked. But if Krueger calls, sends you anything through the mail… And if you see him, don't confront him, just call us. If necessary, you can get a restraining order." He stopped, threw out a hand. "But surely you must know all this."

She shook her head. "No, I'm in psychology, not criminal justice."

"Let's hope nothing comes of it, but better to be safe—"

"—than sorry. I know."

"I still wish you would consider staying somewhere for a few days."

"Unless something more tangible comes up, I'd prefer to go on with my work. Mosey, Nadia, and Saffron were here earlier, helping me clean and unpack. It helped, having them here."

"Yeah, I just saw them drive away."

"I think this small-town thing might grow on me."

"Yes." He smiled and nodded. "I hope it does." He stepped away. "So, I'm going to see what Springer and Reagan are up to. I'll speak to you before we leave."

"Thanks, I appreciate your concern." She smiled faintly and stepped back in.

Olivera descended the steps and rounded the house to the spot where he'd noticed the gardening tools earlier that day. "Springer," he called, "can you help me with this?"

"Sure, Chief." Springer approached. "What you need?"

"You know it was those tools" —he gestured toward the tools—"that led us to the shed in the first place."

"That's right."

"So, why don't we get under there and take a look?"

"Good idea." Springer turned toward the thicket. "Reagan!"

"What's up?" Reagan called back, emerging from amidst the trees.

"Come over here a sec." Springer motioned. "We need to get under the porch. See what we can see."

Reagan came to the porch and stood looking at the broken lattice. "If you can hold that back, I imagine I can squeeze through."

As Olivera and Springer tugged at the break in the lattice, Reagan hunched over and stepped through. "It's dark under here." He switched on his flashlight.

"Watch out for footprints," Olivera said.

"Don't see any. Nothin' but tools."

"Slip on your gloves and hand them out here. Maybe we can pick up some prints."

"You know what?" Reagan handed out a shovel. "There's a door under here."

"A door? What kind of door?" Springer asked.

"It's flat on the ground. Sure looks like a door. The tools are lying on top of it."

"Hold this, Springer. I need to get under there." Letting go of the lattice, Olivera propped the shovel against the porch and squeezed through the space.

"Don't it look like a door to you?" Reagan stepped aside.

"Most definitely a door." Olivera stooped down. "But where to? I guess it could be a basement door—if the house has a basement. Or maybe some sort of underground storage area. The lock's open. That's strange—or maybe it isn't. Maybe there's nothing down there worth stealing."

"You gonna open it, Lieutenant?"

"Technically, I need a warrant or permission from the owner. Hey, Springer."

Springer stuck his head through the opening. "Yeah, Chief."

"Knock on the door and ask Dr. Wilson to step out here a minute."

"Okay. I'll be right back."

Reagan squatted next to Olivera. "I'd be surprised if this place has a basement. Crawl space is usually what you find in these old houses."

"Yeah, I imagine you know more about that than I do, but this door must lead somewhere."

"I'd have to agree with you on that." Reagan looked over at the stone structure that ran the length of the porch, then, moving closer, flashed his beam over the surface. "That wall's in good shape, considering."

"It is, isn't it? Don't see any sign of cracking or crumbling."

"Nope, looks pretty solid to me."

"What's your guess at the age of this place, Reagan?"

"Hun'erd years or more." He shrugged.

Olivera, hearing Springer's and Wilson's chatter, made his way out from under the porch. Brushing a cobweb off the sleeve of his jacket, he squinted at Wilson. "Sorry to bother you again, but are you aware there's a door under there?"

She stooped and peered underneath. "A door? A door to what?"

"I thought you might know. I didn't see it this morning. There were some gardening tools on top," he explained, "but with your permission, I would like to take a look."

"Certainly. I'm curious myself."

"Okay, so I'll get on with it." With a nod to Wilson, he squeezed back through the opening. He squatted next to the latch, removed the padlock, and handed it to Reagan. "Bag this for me."

"Sure, Lieutenant."

Tugging at the latch, he lifted the door. "If you could hold the door back…" Olivera switched on his flashlight and shot a beam into the darkness below. His light caught a wooden staircase leading down. "Not really the kind of stairs you would expect in a basement," he said to Reagan. Then, after taking half a dozen steps down, he glanced back at the faint rectangle of light above. "Hey, Reagan," he called up, his voice resounding within the space, "you got any slip-ons handy?"

Reagan tossed down a pair, and Olivera, after pulling them over his shoes, cautiously proceeded down the steps.

"Can you see anything, Lieutenant?"

"Can I *see* anything? You bet."

Chapter Eleven

*Monday, 5:15 p.m.*
*Magnolia Nursing Home*

By the time Mosey pulled up at the Magnolia, it was close to the residents' dinnertime. She wouldn't have much time to talk to Miss Eleanor and Miss Peggy, but she wasn't too concerned about that. Her purpose was to get her foot in the door and establish a friendly relationship with the sisters. Luckily, she had a splendid prop for the undertaking—the family photographs, dozens of them tucked away in dresser and desk drawers at their former abode.

She took a seat in the reception area and waited for the two women to appear. They soon came in and, after looking around, smiled and waved in her direction. They were wearing the same double-knit pantsuits and chunky lace-up shoes as when she had last seen them. Miss Peggy's pale lavender hair was coifed into a French twist and heavily sprayed. Evidently to her, grooming still mattered despite her advancing age. Her sister, of a different mindset entirely, wore her dull gray locks cut short, with severe bangs that implied a no-nonsense perspective.

"Miss Eleanor." Mosey stood and approached. "Miss Peggy."

Miss Peggy offered her hand, and Mosey obliged

with a friendly clasp. "Would you like to sit in the sun parlor?"

"Yes, indeed," said Peggy, the slightly younger and sprightlier of the two. "I don't like this cold weather we've been having, do you?" She gave her chubby arms a good rubbing.

"Not a bit. What about you, Miss Eleanor?"

"Cold doesn't bother me, but yes, let's do catch a little sun while it's up."

The sisters took the settee, and Mosey, the wicker chair across from them. "I brought some photographs we found at Morris House." She reached up and switched on the floor lamp. Then, scooting forward, she took the black-and-white snapshots out of her tote and piled them on the glass-covered table between them. "We were helping the new owner, Lauren Wilson, with the cleaning and ran across these old photographs. We just wanted to make sure you didn't leave them behind…accidentally." She smiled and looked from one sister to the other.

For a second, they stared blankly at the stack, as if they didn't recognize the photographs. Then each sister, with some hesitation, picked up a handful and began going through them one by one.

"I think I see my grandfather in some of these. Amos Frye—did you ladies know him?"

Peggy glanced up. "Oh, yes, we knew Amos." She pulled out a picture of the poker players and, holding it up for Mosey to see, added, "We knew all of them. They were friends of ours…well, mostly. That's Amos right there—" She pointed. "—and Colton Raines." She passed the snapshot to Eleanor. "You remember Colton?" She glanced back at Mosey, half covering her mouth as she whispered, "I always thought Colton was sweet on Eleanor."

"That's not Colton," Eleanor snapped. "That's Timothy McGinnis."

Peggy took the picture and looked again. "I think you're right." She chuckled. "Eleanor was fond of Timothy."

"No, I was not." Eleanor frowned, deepening the furrows that ran from the corners of her mouth down her chin.

Mosey, not expecting to stir up emotions so quickly, cleared her throat and pointed at the picture. "Those other men around the table, do you recognize them?"

Ignoring the question, Peggy turned to her sister. "If that's not Colton, which one is *he*?"

"*That's* Colton." Eleanor gestured toward the only man who was standing, then paused and looked across the table at Mosey. "I didn't care for Colton Raines, and I don't care if the world knows it." She raised and lowered her brow.

Mosey looked again. "I don't recognize him."

"You wouldn't have known him," Peggy said. "He moved away, probably before you were born."

"Is he related to Matthew Raines?"

"His *older* brother," Eleanor added.

"Matthew's older brother," Mosey repeated. "May I see that again?"

"Certainly." Peggy handed her the picture.

"Yes, now I see the resemblance." Actually, the man in the picture looked a good bit like Matthew, tall, fair, attractive…

"Colton was a handsome man like Matthew," Peggy opined in a reflective tone.

As Mosey studied the faces in the photograph,

Peggy continued flipping through her stack, as if searching for a particular picture.

"The whole group got together once a week for a game," Peggy explained, "and afterwards, Kit and Arnold would stay up half the night—" She leaned in Mosey's direction and cupped her hand around her mouth. "—*drinking*."

"Surely not." Mosey feigned disbelief.

"Yes, they *did*."

Peggy pulled out a snapshot and handed it to her sister. "Remember him?" She pointed to a boy sitting at the table with the men. "That picture was taken some years later, after some of the men married and had children."

"Hmm," Eleanor droned. "Yes, that was little—"

"—Hollis. Remember Hollis, Colton's little boy?"

Mosey picked up the photograph Eleanor had laid on the table. "He's just a kid."

"Indeed." Peggy nodded. "He *was* just a kid, about five when he started coming with his daddy to the games. Hollis and Matthew were about the same age. You see, Matthew was a good bit younger than Colton, and after Colton left town, Matthew stayed on in the house. You must know the Raines house, just down the street from our old house."

"Yes, I've been there a time or two."

Peggy looked at her sister. "We never saw much of Hollis after he grew up, did we?"

Eleanor shook her head. "Not after he left Hembree."

"And Colton?" Mosey asked. "Whatever happened to him?"

"I have no idea," Peggy answered. "He might have

passed on by now. He'd be about Eleanor's age. We didn't keep up with either of them—him or his son—did we, Eleanor?"

Eleanor shrugged. "Why are you asking me?"

Ignoring her sister's reply, Peggy stared down at the picture of the poker players. "That one on the left is Kit." She looked up at Mosey. "Did you know our brother?"

"Not well, I'm sorry to say, but he and my grandfather were friends."

"Yes." Peggy gave a gentle nod. "Kit thought a lot of Amos."

Mosey looked on the back of the picture she'd picked up. "December 1945. That same date is on quite a few of these. Looks like a good many were taken at the end of the war."

"That's true," Eleanor agreed. "A lot were taken around then."

"Those were exciting times when the men came back." Peggy stopped to examine a picture she'd pulled out of the stack. As she studied the image, her sunny expression clouded up, and when at last she spoke, her tone had saddened. "I'd have to say, though, that it was sort of hard for Kit. Yes." Her head slowly bobbed. "Very hard for him."

Hard for Kit? Interesting. She looked at Peggy for a moment. Dare she ask why? She wanted to know. Getting more information about Kit could be crucial to—

*Mosey!* Her dad's ubiquitous voice cut in. *That is entirely too personal a question to ask. You don't really know these women, and even if you did—*

"Shush, Daddy," she whispered.

Peggy glanced up. "You say something, dear?"

She shook her head.

Peggy continued. "Kit didn't get called up for service."

"He didn't?"

"He was let off because of his occupation." Eleanor's brow slightly raised.

"Occupation?"

"Yes, Mosey," Peggy added, "he was a farmer. You didn't know that?"

"Huh!" Eleanor interposed. "Kit wasn't a farmer, not a *real* farmer. That's why it was hard for him and Arnold—Arnold Bilyeu. They didn't do their duty like the others, and the town wasn't about to let 'em forget it." She waggled her head.

Something in Eleanor's voice sounded harsh, as if some incident from the past had never been resolved or forgiven. So… she mused, Kit and Arnold had managed to dodge the draft. Quite a revelation. She couldn't imagine how that would have sat with her granddaddy, who was as patriotic as they come. "Well." She opened her eyes wide. "I guess that explains it."

"Explains what?" Eleanor barked.

"What I was saying before, about Kit not being in many of the pictures. Arnold, either. They weren't in uniform like the others."

"Yes." Eleanor's brow rose and fell. "I guess that was it." She sat up straight and scooted closer to Mosey as if suddenly they were confidantes. "And that was just the surface of it. Before the war, all these men were a close bunch." She glanced down at the photographs, now sorted into smaller stacks. "But afterwards, it was never quite the same." She shook her index finger. "Kit and Arnold were sort of left on the sidelines, when at one time they were the leaders of the group."

"That's right, they were," Peggy said.

"But not *after* the war," Eleanor corrected.

"Well, they—I mean the others—kept coming to the house, didn't they?" Peggy huffed.

Eleanor inhaled deeply and closed her eyes. "As if it matters now…"

For a second, Mosey became pensive, unsure she could agree with what Eleanor had said. In her experience, what mattered *once* could, indeed, matter again…and more than anyone would expect.

"Well, I'm glad Kit didn't go to war." Peggy looked at her sister. "How would we have managed without him?"

"What do you mean?" Eleanor said in a gruff voice. "Our parents took good care of us."

*Mosey, you see what you've stirred up, girl. Lordy mercy!*

Mosey glanced sideways but didn't respond.

"That's true, they did," Peggy agreed. "But later, after they passed away—"

Mosey interrupted the tiff. "I didn't see many photographs of your parents."

Eleanor tensed and turned toward Mosey. "Long ago, there *weren't* many cameras around, not like today."

Mosey might have been annoyed by Eleanor's patronizing tone but instead took a calming breath. "Yes, I sometimes forget that, but it's true. I have lots of pictures of Daddy but hardly any of Granddaddy."

Peggy held a picture out to Mosey. "Would you like to keep this one, dear?"

Mosey accepted the picture, a really nice one of her grandfather and ol' Doc McGinnis, Eads's grandfather. "Thank you, Miss Peggy." She looked at Eleanor. "Is that all right with you, Miss Eleanor?"

"Let me see." She took the picture. "Those two were close back then, the smartest of the bunch. Very studious, both of them." She handed the picture back to Mosey.

"Thanks, Miss Eleanor."

Eleanor set the stack she'd been going through on the table. "It's true. We left some things behind. We couldn't bring it all with us. We kept saying we'd go through these, put some of them in albums, but we never got around to it."

"I'd be happy to pick up an album for you. Why don't I do that? And I can help you with the pictures if you'd like."

"That would be much appreciated" —Peggy smiled at Mosey— "if you're sure you wouldn't mind."

"Shall I hold on to these for the time being?"

"Yes, might as well."

Footsteps sounded nearby, and Mosey glanced toward reception. Some of the residents had emerged from the corridor. Some shuffled along, while others came in wheelchairs. She sensed it was time to go and gathered up the photographs.

Eleanor looked around, then down at her watch. "Must be time for supper." She stood, as did Mosey and then Peggy.

"Just let us know," Eleanor said, apparently ready to join the train of residents. "We'll be here."

Mosey dropped the photographs in her tote and followed along with the sisters. As they entered the dining hall, she glanced at the residents already seated at the table. "I thought I might catch sight of my friend Saffron Smiley's uncle, Mr. T. Patrick Brown. Do you know him?"

"Isn't that Mr. Brown?" Peggy gestured toward the end of a long table crowded with patrons chatting cordially as servers filled the table with steaming platters of food.

Mosey offered a friendly wave to Uncle T., who was helping himself to a piece of cornbread. "My goodness," she observed, "the Magnolia serves up quite a spread, doesn't it?"

"It surely does," Eleanor nodded, "and if Peggy doesn't watch what she eats—"

"Oh, fiddlesticks!" Peggy cut her off. "Since when have you ever watched what *you* eat?"

Eleanor merely shrugged, then added an eye roll in Mosey's direction.

"Well, I'll speak to Mr. Brown and get along home." Mosey turned and waved back. "Enjoy your supper, ladies, and I'll be in touch very soon. So nice to see you both." She nodded to one, then the other, and headed off to speak to Uncle T.

Chapter Twelve

"Must be a cellar," Olivera said to himself. Though, oddly, the way down looked surprisingly well designed. As he descended, he flashed a beam over the steps. Stopping about halfway down, he called up to Reagan. "Looks like some sort of cellar to me, but not exactly what you would anticipate."

"What was that, Lieutenant?"

"A cellar," he repeated, raising his voice, "but rather posh. Looks like nobody has been down here in quite a while."

He brushed away the cobwebs and made his way into semidarkness with only the light from his flashlight to guide the way. What kind of place *was* this? He scanned the walls of the staircase. The top half was papered in a light striped pattern, and the bottom half was paneled in dark wood. He wiped dust off the paneling. "Mahogany, must be." Apparently, what at one time must have been a handsome space had suffered serious neglect. Splotches of dampness blackened the walls, and in spots, it looked as if someone had taken a hammer to the wallboard—or a fist, maybe. As he reached the last step, he passed under a decorative overhead division, some sort of arch made of plaster, looked like. "You won't believe this place," he called up to Reagan.

"What'd you say, Lieutenant?"

He repeated, louder this time, "I said you won't believe this place. *Elegant*, I guess you could call it." Elegant, yes, but in deplorable condition. A real mess, and talk about stuffy… Not an ounce of air was moving. Apart from that, it was eerily silent, like the silence of a grave.

He ventured forth through the arch into a room about twenty by twenty. Bookshelves lined all but one of the walls. The books were still on them, but not upright, as books are usually arranged. Some tilted in one direction, others in another, and the volumes at the top lay flat in disorderly piles.

He aimed the beam toward the side of the room where an armchair sat, a battered old thing with stuffing poking out through a hole in the seat cushion—the handywork of pesky mice, no doubt. The bookcase behind the chair was crammed top to bottom with books, and the volumes that hadn't found a home on the shelves had ended up on the floor—mounds of them, mostly hardbound and oversized. Amidst the landslide of books, a stretch of rug came into view. It was dusty and soiled, but he could make out the pattern. "Red-and-black checkerboard," he muttered. "Interesting choice for a library."

He turned around, and against the only empty wall—the wall adjacent to the staircase—his eyes came to rest on a small desk. On top of it, there was an old manual typewriter, a real antique. He approached, feeling an urge to peck at the keys to see if they still worked, but held back. He wasn't there for his entertainment but, rather, to pick up clues in a possible murder investigation. Hunching over, he examined the cloth ribbon where imprints of letters had left their mark. Before moving on, he paused to look at the analog desk clock that stood beside the typewriter. The clock—like the typewriter—had outlived its usefulness, but there it stood, aimlessly recording the hour when whatever had gone on there had ceased. "Yeah," he mumbled, pondering aloud, "I wonder what *did* go on here—and when?"

He glanced around at the furniture—the tattered armchair, the old desk, and toward the middle of the room, a round table with five straight-back chairs. The table drawer hung open, and with gloved hands, he pulled it gently toward him, exposing a deck of cards and dozens of poker chips. He picked one up. It wasn't plastic. Judging from the color and texture, he'd say it was either bone or ivory. Each chip was edged in a color—teal, amber, purple, royal blue—and a horse's head was etched in the middle of each. He hesitated, then dropped a chip into his jacket pocket. Yep. The checkerboard pattern of the rug was beginning to make sense. This wasn't just a library. It was a *game room*, a poker room.

He stood musing for a moment, flashing his light over the floor, ceiling, shelves, and furnishings of the disheveled room. Then, thinking he'd seen enough for his initial once-over, he pushed the table drawer shut and, following his tracks up the stairs, stepped out onto the ground.

"What'd you see, Lieutenant?" Reagan asked.

"Well, it's not clear. Either a library, some sort of game room, or both, I suppose." He pulled off his slip-ons and gloves. "Strange place for either, if you ask me.

Nobody's been down there in God knows how long. The whole place is covered in dust and cobwebs." He stepped through the break in the latticework and, taking the chip from his pocket, handed it to Springer. "Ever seen one of these?"

Springer turned it over in his hand. "Can't say that I have." He passed it to Wilson.

"What is it?" She looked at both sides.

"There's a whole bunch of them down there in a drawer, along with a deck of cards."

"Must be a poker chip, then," Springer suggested.

Olivera nodded. "I'd say so."

Wilson handed him the chip. "Can I go down?"

"I wouldn't, at least until we get this thing figured out. Those gardening tools"—he gestured toward the foundation where the tools were now propped—"might have been put there for a reason. Maybe to cover the door or—who knows?—maybe to mark the spot." He raised his brow. "Not sure what to think. By the way"—he turned to Reagan, who was stepping out from under the porch—"you didn't lock the cellar door, did you? We don't have the key."

"No, it's open. We bagged the padlock, remember?"

"Yes, that's right." He turned back to Springer and Wilson. "There must be some sort of connection but exactly what I couldn't say. You know, spotting the tools is what pointed us to the shed in the first place—and the body. Again, it was the tools that led us to the underground room." He looked at Wilson. "When Ms. Frye showed you the house, did she mention anything about a cellar?"

"Not a word."

He believed her. From the expression on her face,

she seemed as mystified as he. "You didn't see a blueprint, I suppose."

"No, but I do remember Mosey's mentioning the floor plan. She thought the people who built the house must have had a cross structure in mind but, for whatever reason, didn't finish out the cross. When she was a kid, she called it the half-house."

"I guess I should speak to Ms. Frye." He glanced at his watch. "I think we'd better leave the rest of it till tomorrow. We'll be back over, Dr. Wilson, if you don't mind."

"No problem. I'm sure I'll be here."

He started to walk away but then turned back. "Are the locks on the doors and windows secure?"

"Seem to be, but I'll check again."

"Springer, please help Dr. Wilson with that, and Reagan, let's package the tools and get them in the van before we go." He looked again at Wilson. "You want a receipt for the tools?"

"No, Lieutenant, I trust you." She grinned.

After a brief stop by the station to deliver the evidence, Olivera drove to the Tavernette for a bite of supper before heading home. He circled the square a time or two until a parking space opened up near the entrance. Tucking his car keys into his coat pocket, he felt the poker chip. He took it out and toyed with it, not really thinking about it, while he mulled over what he'd seen in the underground room. In going down into that dank closed-off space, he felt like he'd intruded upon a secret world where very few people had ever trod—maybe only a handful of poker enthusiasts whose host did an awful lot of reading, apparently, and writing, too, and on the occasional evening, engaged in a game of poker with his buddies. He looked down at the chip, rubbed it, turned it over, and rubbed it again. If only that chip, like some magical charm or talisman, could somehow help him connect with that distant past. At one time or another, all the players must have handled it, set it forward in a stack, won it back, or lost it.

He had to confess he didn't know much about the time period encapsulated in the room. The hefty volumes, the checkerboard rug, the ancient typewriter— it all suggested to him a different era. Since his family, still in Mexico back then, had yet to relocate to California, he lacked the collective memories that might have helped him connect with that chapter in Hembree history.

Still, maybe there *was* something that could help him to understand more deeply what he had seen. A strange idea, right? But wasn't that the way it worked? If you wanted to get to what drove a generation— understand not only *what* they did but *why* they did it— you had to get inside their heads, figure out their values and aspirations.

He got out of his car, walked into the Tavernette, and took a seat at the bar. Happy hour was winding down, and the counter had filled up with empty glasses and crumpled napkins. Clinton, the bartender, his sleeves rolled to the elbows and a towel over his shoulder, grabbed two clean glasses, scooped ice from a bag in the sink, and raced off toward the end of the bar, where two guys were blithely chucking darts at a dart board. As he returned, Olivera called out to him, "Hey, Clint, a lager when you can." Clinton promptly poured him the usual. "And could you get me a ham sandwich from the kitchen?"

"Sure can, Lieutenant."

"And pass me that bowl of nuts, please, Clint."

The bartender obliged, and Olivera fished out a couple of salted cashews and popped them in his mouth. He sat sipping his beer and waiting for his sandwich until he heard a feminine voice speak his name. He glanced around. It was Mosey Frye, all bundled up and ready to brave the cold. He gave a chin nod to Robert and Hugh, who stood a few paces away, evidently on their way out of the bar.

"How's the case going, Lieutenant?" Mosey asked.

He put on a pleasant face. "Making progress. As a matter of fact" He twisted around. "something *has* come up." He faced the bar again, pondering what to say next. He'd managed to catch himself before saying too much, or maybe he hadn't. Maybe he'd *already* revealed more than he ought to. As always, she'd caught him off guard.

"What was that, Lieutenant?"

"Oh"—he drummed his fingers against the counter—"the Morris house. I thought I might mention—"

"What in particular?" She lifted a booted foot onto the brass footrail.

He eyed her foot briefly, then the exit, where Hugh and Robert were chatting. "Don't want to hold you up."

Mosey gestured toward Robert and Hugh. "Doesn't matter. They're on their way to a meeting at the college."

"Well, if you wouldn't mind joining me here at the bar, it wouldn't take long."

Mosey walked over to where Robert and Hugh were standing, spoke briefly with Robert, and came back to the bar. She took off her gloves, more like woven mittens, then her dark blue beret, a shade darker than her eyes, and laid them on the counter.

"Would you care for something to drink?" he asked.

"No thanks. Well, maybe a coffee." She slid onto the stool.

He caught the bartender's attention. "Clint, a coffee for Ms. Frye." He turned back to Mosey. "Something unexpected came to light this afternoon as we were checking the grounds." He picked up his glass.

"Unexpected?"

He hesitated. "We discovered a room, an underground room. I suppose you'd call it a basement or cellar—not sure I'd know the difference but you would, I imagine."

"Morris House has a cellar?" Her expression suggested curiosity.

"Funny, that's the same reaction Dr. Wilson had when I brought it to her attention." He took a sip and set down the glass. "I'll tell you how we found it. When we were checking for footprints, we came across a door under the porch."

"Which porch?"

"If you're facing the house—" He held up his hands and wiggled the little finger of his right hand. "—it'd be the porch on the right."

"You found a regular door *under* the porch?"

"Yep, flat against the ground. We didn't see it when we first searched the grounds. Couldn't see it. Somebody'd left some gardening tools on top of it, but once we removed the tools…"

"Well, I checked the property." She rubbed under her bottom lip.

"So, you weren't aware of it, either? Interesting."

She stared blankly. "How'd I miss that?"

"It'd be easy to miss. We missed it, too. The latticework blocks your view."

Clinton arrived with her coffee, and Mosey, pushing it to one side, picked up the paper napkin he'd set beside the cup. She dug in her tote. "Here, Lieutenant." She handed him a pen and the napkin. "If you don't mind…"

He made a quick sketch of the side of the house with the porch and latticework and handed the napkin back to Mosey. He pointed with the pen. "There's a break about there. When I was checking along the porch, I noticed it and decided to take a closer look. That's when I spotted the tools. Later, I checked it again with Springer and Reagan, and when we moved the tools, we discovered the door. We lifted it up and saw stairs leading down. You know anything about that?"

"No, I don't." She shrugged.

"The blueprint didn't indicate—?"

"If there *was* a blueprint," she cut in, "it must be lost. That's a very old house, Lieutenant. I guess the former owners might have held on to the house plans, but I doubt it."

"The former owners?"

"The Morris sisters, Eleanor and Peggy."

"How might I get in touch with them?"

"They're at the Magnolia, moved in a few months ago. Well, I don't know exactly when. They're elderly, moved out, then put the house up for sale. We got the listing some time back."

He reached into his breast pocket and brought out his pad. "Let me get those names again."

"Eleanor and Peggy Morris, Magnolia Nursing Home."

He made a note.

"By the way, the man you found, Will Grayson…"

"What about him?" He slipped the pad into his breast pocket and handed Mosey her pen.

"You don't think anybody might have—"

"—killed him? No, I don't. He died of natural causes." That's what he told her, which was what McGinnis had suggested so far, though he wasn't convinced of it, not yet. Even so, he wasn't inclined in any way, shape, or form to say anything to pique Mosey's curiosity.

"I can't imagine what he was doing there," she pondered, "and at that hour of the morning. Doesn't make sense."

"Reagan tells me he did odd jobs. Maybe he did some gardening in that part of town." He blinked and stared ahead.

"He was friends with Kit Morris," she added, prolonging her assessment of the situation, "but Mr. Kit died ages ago. Mr. Kit was friends with my grandfather. They played poker together."

"Hmm." He felt in his pocket for the poker chip he'd found in the drawer, thinking he would show it to her, then changed his mind.

"In fact—" She dug a small photograph out of her tote. "—there they are, the whole group. Mr. Kit"—she pointed—"Mr. Arnold, Grandaddy Amos, Doc McGinnis…" She hesitated, tapping the only one of the group who was standing. "That's Colton Raines."

He took a look. The one she had singled out, much like the others, seemed cheery and young, as if he didn't have a care in the world. "Must have been taken a long while back."

She turned the picture over. "Yeah, it says here

*December 1945*, see?"

"Huh." He paused to do the math. "That's sixty-five years ago." He picked up his drink and took a swig. Then, sticking his hand in his pocket, felt the poker chip. Like Springer, he was beginning to feel a little clairvoyant himself. Was the poker chip "working"? Or did he have it all wrong? Was Mosey herself— *diablos!*—the lucky charm?

"Great picture, isn't it? They must have just gotten back from the war, World War II, except Mr. Kit didn't go. Mr. Arnold, either. But the rest went." She fished in her tote again and brought out another photograph. "Here they are in uniform, see? My granddaddy was in the Navy."

He cleared his throat. "Uh, how do you happen to have these, if you don't mind my asking?"

"We found them in a drawer at Morris House, just today when we went over to help Lauren. We passed you as we were leaving. Remember?"

"Oh, right." He nodded. "And the pictures were left there?"

"Yes, Eleanor and Peggy must have gotten overwhelmed. You know how it is. Old people having to move out of their home after so many years. It's sad. Poor women…they hardly have any room where they are now. So, I offered to take the pictures to the Magnolia…not just these, a whole bunch"—she glanced down at her tote—"to see if the sisters wanted them."

"And did they?"

"Oh, yes." She pushed the photographs back in her tote, which bulged with old snapshots. "I told them I'd pick up an album."

"That's kind of you." And it really was. Mosey was

a good soul, but she had this annoying little habit of prying, getting into his business.

"You know, if you wanted to, you could ask them about the cellar," she said. "Or I could ask."

He thought for a second. He wasn't sure he wanted her involved any more than necessary. More to the point, how might he take advantage of this magical force of hers without tying himself to her apron strings. He shivered at the thought. But the matter of the cellar—the sisters either knew or they didn't—seemed rather simple, harmless. "I don't suppose it would hurt to raise the question. And I'd appreciate it if you'd let me know what they say."

"Sure, I'll be going over there tomorrow, likely." She finished her coffee, thanked him, and after gathering up her hat, gloves, and tote, left the bar.

"Clint," he called to the bartender, "could you check on that sandwich for me?"

"Of course." Clint rushed off toward the kitchen.

So ultimately, he thought, Mosey was the *real* good luck charm, which, in this case, made a ton of sense, given that she was the one who usually offered up the dirt on Hembree's less than glorious past. With a quiet groan, he confessed it to himself—if to no one else. Had to. For, clearly, this nemesis, this agent of divine punishment—ha!—had totally kick-started the investigation. In a minute, she'd told him more about the poker players than he might have learned on his own in a month of Sundays. With a shake of his head, he grabbed his glass and downed the last gulp of beer. "Clint," he called out to the bartender, who, back at the end of the bar, was serving something to the dart players, "another lager when you can."

Chapter Thirteen

*Tuesday, 11:00 a.m.*
*Shepherd Realty*

When Mosey reached Shepherd Realty the next morning, she couldn't wait to talk to Saffron about the mysterious cellar Olivera had mentioned the night before. But to her disappointment, Saffron confessed that she had absolutely no idea. They diligently searched through the paperwork but found no reference to a cellar. So Mosey, in an attempt to take her mind off the problematic issue, plopped down in her swivel chair and reached for the letter opener. She sat mindlessly flipping through a stack of advertisements and announcements until Dave Morell called. They had a brief chat, and then Mosey, clicking off, walked toward reception. "Saffron, that was Dave Morell, David Senior's son. He's on his way from the airport. We got anything to offer him when he gets here?" She glanced toward the coffee niche. The cookie plate was empty, though the room still smelled divinely of Saffron's fresh gingerbread.

Saffron checked her watch. "It's almost lunch time. Why don't you take him to the Tavernette?"

"I'm bored with the Tavernette," she moaned, leaning against Saffron's desk. "We were there last night."

"Then take him to Al's."

"At this time of day?"

"Mosey, this is *not* New York City." She rather noisily closed a file drawer.

"I know, but this guy's from New Orleans."

"Then take him to the Yacht Club, for heaven's sake. They're open for lunch."

"Too cold for the Yacht Club."

"They got heat."

"Oh, all right." Mosey slumped off. "When he gets here, give a yell." She returned to her office, phoning Nadia as she went.

"Abboud Antiques."

"It's me."

"Hi, what's up?"

"Morell just called. You wanna meet us at the Yacht Club?"

"No, I *don't* wanna meet you at the Yacht Club. What's wrong with the Tavernette?"

"It's too bloomin' crowded."

"I don't have *time* to go to the Yacht Club. Let's go to the Tavernette."

"Fine," Mosey grumped. "I'll text you when he gets here."

When Mosey spoke to Nadia, she had been eager to tell her about Olivera's revelation. However, Nadia seemed preoccupied, and with Dave's impending arrival, she decided to wait for a more suitable moment to share the information.

She busied herself with one thing and another until Saffron shouted from the outer office. "He's coming up the walk."

"Okay, thanks." She slipped on her corduroy jacket and walked toward the front. As the door swung open, a nice-looking man, not drop-dead handsome but distinctive, strode confidently into the room. "David Morell?" She greeted him with a smile.

"Dave." He smiled back at Mosey as he tugged at the tips of his gloved fingers.

"Nice to meet you. I'm Mosey Frye. Did you have a good flight?"

"A little bumpy." He removed his hat, a handsome dark fedora, and smoothed back his light brown hair.

"Not the best weather for flying, I suppose." Mosey nodded toward Saffron. "This is Saffron Smiley. You might have spoken to her on the phone."

Saffron rose out of her seat. "Hi, Dave, nice to meet you."

"Yes," he smiled, "I believe we did speak, didn't we?"

"This morning, in fact." She offered him her hand.

Mosey turned to Dave. "I was thinking you might like to have lunch?"

"Sure."

"Nadia Abboud's going to meet us at the Tavernette. It's just around the corner."

"Good. I look forward to meeting her."

Mosey and Dave took his rental car to the square and found a parking spot near the Tavernette.

"This is a charming town." He opened the car door for Mosey. "Father mentioned that it was."

"You think so?"

"Yes, I do, and it's nice to get out of New Orleans." He pronounced New AHL-lee-ins just like the natives did.

"I like the way you say that."

"You wouldn't be teasing me about my accent,

would you?"

"No," Mosey grinned, "I wouldn't do that."

They entered the restaurant, stopping at the hostess stand.

"Ruby, could we get a table for three? Nadia's joining us." She checked her cell. A text had come from Nadia. "She's on her way."

Ruby picked up three menus. "I can put you in the back."

Mosey glanced around the bar. All the tables and booths were taken. "Okay, we'll take it."

They followed Ruby through the bar and slid into a corner booth.

"Can I get you something to drink?" Ruby placed menus on the table.

Mosey looked at Dave. "Would you care for a cocktail?"

"Sure, what about a Bloody Mary?" He glanced up at Ruby.

"Make that two," Mosey said. "Not sure what Nadia will want."

"I'll catch her on her way in."

"Dave, if you'll excuse me just a minute." Mosey got up and slipped off her jacket. "I think I'll hang this up. Shall I take your hat for you?"

"Yes, thanks."

As she walked back toward the bar, she crossed paths with Nadia coming in. "Hi, did you give Ruby your drink order?"

Nadia nodded, then looked past Mosey. "So that's David Morell." A playful grin played around the corners of her mouth. "He's cute…and, wow, young."

"This is the son, not the daddy."

"I know that."

After Mosey had hung up the jacket and hat, they returned to the booth, and Dave rose and nodded to Nadia.

"Hi, Dave." Nadia offered her hand. "Nadia Abboud."

"I'm glad to finally meet you." He waited for them to sit. "Father has talked about Hembree for a long time."

"Well, that's a surprise." Nadia laughed.

"Not really." He shook his head. "We come across some of our best finds in out-of-the-way—"

Mosey interrupted with a laugh. "You've come to the right place, then."

"Of course." Nadia gave him a knowing look. "Small wonder Hembree would have what you're looking for."

Dave's brow lifted. "Which brings us to the subject that brought me here."

"It was my father, Toni Abboud, who sold your father the painting. I was just a kid, but I remember them wrangling over the price."

"Sounds like Father." He chuckled. "He's a good businessman. I imagine your father is, too."

"True," she nodded, "but in that case, I think it was sentimentality more than money. Daddy was *very* attached to the Fernanda portrait."

"As is my father."

Ruby set a tray with three Bloody Marys on the table. "Would you like to order now?" she asked as she distributed the drinks.

"I don't think we've given Mr. Morell a chance to look at the menu," Mosey said.

"Would you like to hear the specials?"

"Actually, I think I'll just take a burger and fries." Dave passed Ruby his menu.

She jotted down the order and turned to Nadia and Mosey. "What would you ladies like?"

"A burger sounds good." Nadia handed Ruby the menu.

"I'll take a green salad," Mosey said. "Blue cheese dressing on the side."

After Ruby had gone, it was Dave who picked up where they'd left off. "You know my father still has the Fernanda portrait."

"I didn't know that," Nadia said, "but I can see why. Daddy held on to it from the time he bought it at the Bilyeu estate sale till when your father showed up, looking for—"

"—anything Bilyeu?" Dave smiled.

"Uh-huh," Nadia sipped her drink. "Anything left over from the sale."

"So, why the interest?" Mosey gave Dave a pensive look.

"The Bilyeus are an old New Orleans family." He glanced at Nadia. "You know them, I take it."

"Yes, of course, I've heard plenty about the Bilyeus." Nadia knitted her brow. "I guess you know what happened to Arnold's only heir."

"Yes, what a pity." He raised his brow. "I read about it in the paper."

"The last of the Hembree Bilyeus." Mosey let out a sigh. "Some of her New Orleans cousins were here for the funeral. It was my understanding that one of the heirlooms, the apothecary, in fact, would go to the Apothecary Museum in the French Quarter. I don't suppose you've seen it." She picked up her drink.

"Yes, I have." He picked up his and clinked Mosey's glass, then Nadia's. "Here's to you, ladies."

"And to you, Dave." Mosey smiled, then took a sip of her drink.

"I believe the other heirlooms," Nadia said, "were returned to the De Lobos family, the Spanish De Lobos, were they not?"

"That's right. You met Rafael, I believe."

Mosey glanced at Nadia. "When did we meet Rafael—this past September?"

"Yes, in fact, the day Ninon was killed."

Mosey rubbed her brow. "Yes, I suppose it was."

"He contacted us in October," Dave said, "not long after he left Hembree. Asked us to keep an eye out, should additional heirlooms surface. He suspected Fernanda's parents might have brought over even more than the items we know about."

"Right," Mosey nodded. "Makes sense."

"And did they?" Nadia asked.

He shrugged. "Not as far as we know, but it was Rafael's call that got Father to thinking about the Bilyeus again in connection with the casta paintings. According to the invoice—"

"Wait," Nadia interrupted, "there was an invoice?"

"Yes, the artist's invoice."

"I didn't know there *was* an invoice."

"The artist—his name was Mateo Cardoso—was a good recordkeeper, and according to his inventory, the Bilyeus contracted for a few paintings, all completed, all paid in full. But the Fernanda portrait was commissioned by her father, not her husband. In fact, when Father learned about the existence of the Fernanda portrait, it took him a while to make the connection between the De

Lobos family and Larkspur. When he finally did, it occurred to him that the painting might be among the family heirlooms. He knew the New Orleans Bilyeus didn't have it. Well, he was delighted, of course, when he found it here." He took a sip of his drink. "He's kept it in the gallery on Royal ever since."

"I understand your father has a sizeable collection," Nadia said.

"Yes, he's been interested in casta paintings since his early days as a collector. There aren't that many in existence…maybe a hundred. Many have been destroyed."

"Destroyed?" Mosey asked.

"Yes. Have you ever seen one?"

"Can't say that I have, unless you count the portrait of Fernanda."

"That one's a special case, but most of them are rather distasteful." He frowned.

"Oh, I didn't know."

"But Father thought they ought to be saved…for the historical interest, and he hoped to find a few more in Hembree, including one of Hershel Bilyeu. When he didn't, I guess you'd say he was left with a sense of dissatisfaction."

"I'm surprised he hasn't paid us another visit," Nadia said.

"I suppose he thought he had exhausted his leads."

Mosey spotted Ruby with plates of burgers and fries. "That must be our lunch."

"Here you go." Ruby set plates in front of Nadia and Dave. "Mosey, I'll be right back with your salad."

"Wow, I haven't had one of these in a while." Dave lifted the top of the bun and salted the patty.

"No?" Nadia reached for a bottle of hot sauce. "You want some of this?"

"Go ahead. I think I'll take ketchup."

Mosey passed him the bottle. "Would you care for something else to drink?"

"Yes, I would. A glass of tea, thanks."

Ruby arrived with Mosey's salad, and Mosey ordered a pitcher of iced tea for the table.

"So, this painting"—Nadia placed a fry on Mosey's napkin—"what can you tell us?"

"According to the description in one of the paintings, the background is Bilyeu's pharmacy…or 'apothecary,' as they called it back then." Dave paused to taste a fry. "His was one of the earliest in New Orleans, the whole country, for that matter. He's pictured in the painting with a woman, most likely the Haitian priestess with whom he collaborated. The two of them are posed before a table stocked with tools of the trade— mortar and pestle, scales, and so on. There's another painting, but we're less certain of the content. As far as we know, it's a composite with sixteen vignettes, which is a fairly standard configuration." He bit into his burger and chewed.

Nadia nodded. "I can see why he would want those for his collection, especially the first you mentioned."

"Not sure *I* do," Mosey interjected.

Dave paused to wipe his mouth. "The subject is dark, given what we've come to know, but from a historical perspective, the apothecary painting, should it come to light, would bring more at auction than the Fernanda portrait."

"I suppose," Mosey said. "But I'm confused about something. If your father lost hope of finding the paintings…"

"When the museum received that small apothecary, Father was encouraged, would have come here himself, but he doesn't travel much."

"You feel sure, then, the paintings are *not* in New Orleans?" Nadia asked.

"Hard to be sure, but Father thinks it's every bit as likely they are here."

"If they *are* here, I haven't seen them."

"We thought, well, *hoped* you'd be interested in helping us track them down."

"If the Bilyeus brought them here," Mosey chimed in, "it seems funny they didn't show up at the estate sale."

"But if you think about it," Nadia glanced at Mosey, "the Bilyeus weren't exactly *forthright* about their heirlooms."

"Indeed." Mosey lifted her drink. "It's pretty obvious why they kept some things hidden."

Nadia nodded. "Because they were stolen."

"But the paintings wouldn't have been stolen," Mosey said.

"That's right," Dave agreed. "Commissioned and purchased from the painter himself."

"So why—?" Mosey turned to Nadia.

"Don't ask me. We did business. At least my daddy did business with the Bilyeus for years, and as far as I know, there was never a mention of a painting other than the Fernanda portrait."

"I suppose we could check with Carlotta," Mosey said.

"Carlotta?" Dave tilted his head.

"My step-aunt, Carlotta Humphrey. She took over

the family practice when my father died. Arnold Bilyeu was one of Daddy's clients. Mr. Arnold died before Carlotta moved to Hembree, but she has access to the Bilyeu records."

"We might as well start there, then," Nadia said. "Where else?"

"So, you've got a nice little mystery to solve." He took a sip of tea.

Nadia looked thoughtful. "Paintings don't just disappear without a reason."

"I don't suppose they do."

"You wouldn't happen to know," Mosey ventured, looking at Dave, "if there might *be* a reason."

"I've heard theories but nothing concrete."

"If there is something you know…" Nadia paused.

"It would help if we had some sort of lead," Mosey added.

"I don't think this would help, but it could be that Hershel was not at all anxious to display the paintings *publicly*."

"Because?" Nadia asked.

"The subject, well, might have raised suspicion."

"Suspicion?"

"Yes. The Haitian woman he was pictured with was hanged."

"Oh, my." Nadia's eyes widened. "I see what you mean."

Chapter Fourteen

*Tuesday, 2:00 p.m.*
*Magnolia Nursing Home*

No sooner had she left the Tavernette than Mosey buzzed by the office supply store and picked up a photograph album. She had intended to drop back by the office. She wasn't about to delay another much-anticipated conversation with the Morris sisters. After the bomb Olivera had dropped the night before—"That old place has a cellar, *a secret cellar!*"—how could she do otherwise? She dug in her tote for her cellphone and called Nadia.

"Abboud Antiques."

"Hey, is Dave still there?"

"He had another appointment—why?"

"I heard the weirdest thing last night. I wanted to tell you today at lunch but didn't get a chance. Well, I didn't want to bring it up in front of Dave."

"What?"

"Morris House has a cellar, *a secret cellar.*"

"Huh?"

"And you won't believe how I came by that information. Olivera told me!"

"Mosey, that's bizarre. Start at the beginning, would you?"

"There's nothing much to tell. We were at the

Tavernette last night—Robert, Hugh, and I—and as we were leaving, I saw Olivera at the bar and stopped to say hello. He mentioned they'd found a cellar under the side porch and wanted to know if I knew anything about it."

"Very strange."

"They were checking around the foundation of the house—looking for footprints, I imagine—and came across a break in the latticework. They checked it out and found some gardening tools under the porch. They spotted the door when they removed the tools."

"A door in the foundation?"

"No, no, not in the foundation, *under* the porch, flat on the ground."

"Did they open it?"

"Of course, and there it was, plain as day."

"How did you *not* know this, Mosey?"

"That's what I'd like to know, and I'm gonna find out one way or the other."

"Mosey," Nadia warned.

"Don't go trying to stop me. I need to do this, for professional reasons. I've sold a house with a cellar I didn't know existed, for heaven's sake. I'm going out to the Magnolia. I'm on my way out there now. I picked up an album for Eleanor and Peggy. Turns out they *do* want the photographs."

"I suppose you know what you're doing," she sighed, "but don't say I didn't warn you. And call me later. Let me know what you find out."

"I will. By the way, I don't suppose you've had a chance to talk to your father."

"About the photograph?"

"Yeah...and you know this thing seems to be heating up. Photographs, poker players, and now, a *secret cellar*."

"I don't know why you're calling it *secret*?"

"Nobody knew about it, obviously."

"You and Olivera didn't know, but so what? I'm sure the people who *lived* in the house knew. What's down there?"

In hindsight, Olivera's silence regarding the contents of the cellar seemed a bit strange. And silly her, she hadn't even thought to inquire. "I have no clue," Mosey admitted to Nadia. "Olivera never mentioned it, but now that I think about it…" Lost in thought, Mosey left her sentence dangling in mid-air.

"Mosey, are you there?"

"Yeah, I'm here."

"So, how are you going to approach this?"

"Approach?" Mosey asked. "I'm just gonna ask them plain and simple. I think I'll say, 'Eleanor, I had no idea your house had a cellar. There wasn't a word about it in the specs.' Oh, Nadia," Mosey exclaimed, "I can't wait to see the expression on her face."

"You be nice to those ladies. They've been through a lot."

"They have?" In the same instant Mosey realized that, when she'd been at the Magnolia the day before, Eleanor had had a sort of world-weary look about her eyes. Not Peggy, though. She seemed cheerful…bordering on giddy.

"Well, I'd imagine," Nadia said.

"We don't know much about them, do we?" And it was true. The Morrises were staples in Hembree. They'd lived in the big house at the dead end of McAllister forever. Even so, she had no idea *who* they were. She knew they were farmers, *had been* farmers, but she didn't know anything about what Mr. Kit had done with himself as a young man. She'd only known him as an old gent and Eleanor and Peggy as old ladies.

"Nope," Nadia said. "But before the day's over, I imagine we will."

"Okay, I've got to go. I'm getting close. Don't want to miss the turn." She clicked off and laid the phone on the seat.

*Mosey, what are you doing, girl?*

"Daddy—"

*Don't daddy me. You're up to no good. What are you snooping into now?*

"If you were here, I bet you'd know all about the Morrises, but you aren't here, so I have to go digging all by my lonesome."

*And stop trying to soften me up.*

"Daddy, it's starting all over again, a new case. I knew something was bound to come up. I just sold another house—to Lauren Wilson, the new forensic psychologist—and no sooner had I handed her the keys, a stalker showed up. Well, *maybe* a stalker. But when the police went to check out the house, they found Will Grayson, dead in the tool shed at the back of the property.

*Will Grayson, that old coot?*

"The same."

*What happened to him?*

"They don't know yet."

*And what was he doing back there?*

"Dying, I reckon."

*This sounds like quite the mare's nest—a stalker, maybe…an old drunk dead in the tool shed. How come you going out to the Magnolia?*

"I need to ask Eleanor and Peggy about the secret

cellar—"

*Secret cellar?*

"—and to take them an album for some old photographs. By the way, Granddaddy's in some of them…when he was young, right after the war. December 1945. What about that?"

*How should I know? I was barely born.*

"You never heard anything from Granddaddy about a poker game? Him and a bunch of other guys?" She'd almost said, "young and sexy." Oops. She was talking to her daddy, who would have balked at such a comment from a woman.

*Poker game…*

"You think about it, Daddy. I got to go. I'm here already at the Magnolia."

She pulled off Little Smith onto the lane that led to the Magnolia Nursing Home. She downshifted and drove along, glancing from side to side at the dark spindly branches fanned out like broomstraw against a gray-blue sky. The twigs at the tips seemed eager for the invigorating sunlight of spring—as was she—while the knobby limbs of the old gnarled trees seemed to be waiting around for whatever came their way, maybe a roaring windstorm or an *ice storm*—perish the thought!—either one of which might topple them to the ground. On behalf of these veterans of nature's ravages, she silently pleaded for nothing more taxing than a cloudburst.

At the end of the lane, she pulled up in front of what at one time had been the Magnolia Hunting Club, now converted into a home for the elderly. The ladies she was returning to see were in pretty good shape. Neither Eleanor nor Peggy appeared to require much help. They could still do for themselves, though keeping up a big place like Morris House may have exacted more energy than their aging bodies could muster.

She parked near the entrance and reached for the paper sack that contained the album. She'd picked the nicest one Miss Evelyn had in the store—leather-bound, hand-sewn, with rough-cut pages and a leather tie. Miss Evelyn had said that if the sisters wanted, Mosey could bring it back and get the family name engraved in gold letters. She stepped down from the cab, slid her tote and the sack off the seat, and headed across the gravel lot.

Inside, she spoke to the receptionist. "I'm Mosey Frye, here to see the Morris sisters."

"Let me give them a buzz."

The receptionist phoned the room, then said, "They'll be right down."

She took a seat in the sun parlor. In a minute or two, Eleanor appeared in the passageway between the corridor and the reception area, with Peggy following along close behind.

"Is this okay?" Mosey stood and gestured to the cozily arranged spot she had chosen, where two comfy armchairs faced a sofa. A nearby floor lamp cast a warm glow over that corner of the room.

"Of course," Peggy said. "This is the most pleasant spot in the whole place, if you ask me. I love to sit in here, and nobody much seems to use it."

Eleanor and Peggy took the armchairs, and Mosey sat back down on the middle cushion of the sofa. She took the album out of the sack and placed it on the small wicker table between them.

Peggy reached for the album right away. "Oh, Mosey, this is a nice one." She ran her fingers along the hand-stitched binding. "Very nice." She handed the album to Eleanor.

"Let me pay you for this," Eleanor said.

"I wouldn't think of it." Mosey quickly crumpled the receipt that had fallen onto the floor. "Shall I help you with the photographs?" She pulled a handful out of her tote and laid them on the table.

"Well, if you wouldn't mind." Eleanor handed the album back to Peggy, who opened it, flipped through the blank pages, and closed it again.

"I'll tell you what." Mosey picked up the photographs. "I'll place them for you, but if you want to change them around, you can. You see, each picture goes into one of these little slots." She showed them how the slots worked, then slipped the album back in the sack. "And if you'd like, I'd be glad to take the album back to Miss Evelyn. She'll engrave it for you if you want."

"Oh, I don't know," Eleanor said, "but for the time being—"

"We're anxious to see the pictures placed," Peggy interrupted. "We've been saying we were going to do this for years, but if you don't mind doing it for us…"

"Okay, but should you change your mind about the engraving, just let me know." When she'd finished putting the photographs back in her tote, she placed two pictures she'd held back on the table. "By the way, if you don't want these snapshots of my grandfather…"

"There's quite a few similar to those. I think we can let you keep them." Peggy looked at Eleanor, who agreed with a dip of her chin.

"I appreciate that." Mosey smiled and dropped the snapshots back in her tote. "I also wanted to update you on the investigation."

"Investigation?" Eleanor frowned.

"Maybe not an investigation," Mosey hurriedly added, "but Lieutenant Olivera had to follow up on Mr. Grayson's death, make sure—"

"Of course," Eleanor interrupted, "I see what you mean."

"So, in checking around the outside of the house," Mosey continued, "he came across a door to a cellar."

Eleanor raised her brows and pursed her lips, while Peggy, still holding the album, seemed to grip it a little tighter.

"I had no idea the house had a cellar," Mosey said.

"Yes, it does, but we never used it," Peggy explained.

"Did Mr. Kit use it?"

"It was *his* study," Eleanor said. "That's what he called it. Funny place for a study if you ask me. He kept his books and typewriter down there, though his writing never amounted to much."

"Your brother was a writer?" Mosey asked.

"Huh!" Eleanor frowned again. "He'd have done a sight better if he'd farmed, as Daddy wanted him to."

"Are his things still there—in the cellar, I mean?" Mosey asked.

"I suppose they are," Peggy said, "but who knows? The cellar was terribly inconvenient for us to get to, or we might have gone down there and given it a good cleaning—at least that. Though when dear Kit was alive, he did the cleaning himself." She looked away and, with eyes filling with sadness, stared out a nearby window.

"I'm not sure if the lieutenant has checked it out," Mosey said, "but he asked me if I knew about it, and I was surprised, that's all. When I did the market analysis,

I really should have known about the cellar."

"I'm sorry," Eleanor said. "I guess we didn't think to mention it."

"Well, I doubt Lauren will have any objection. I can't imagine that she would. But I suppose sooner or later something will need to be done about whatever is down there. What would you want done with the books?"

"Well, obviously"—Eleanor threw up her hands—"we can't have them here. I suppose they might be donated to the library."

"Excellent idea," Peggy agreed, coming back into the conversation. "And I bet Mosey"—she looked from Eleanor to Mosey—"wouldn't mind seeing to that, would you, Mosey?"

"I'd be glad to. And I'm sure the Hembree Library would appreciate the contribution." She checked her watch. "Ladies, I need to be running. But I'll stay in touch."

"Yes, please do." Peggy patted Mosey on the hand. "And thanks so much for helping us with the album and all."

The sisters accompanied Mosey to the entrance, and she waved back as she crossed the gravel parking lot to her truck. "So, then," she mumbled to herself as she climbed in, "they *knew* about the cellar, all right, but they didn't go down there, not even to clean. It was Kit's cellar, his study. Hmm."

Chapter Fifteen

*Tuesday, 1:30 p.m.*
*The Tavernette*

Olivera took one last bite of his burger and wiped his lips with his napkin. He raised his index finger to catch the bartender's attention. "The bill when you can, Clint." As he reached down for his briefcase, which he'd deposited on the floor, he caught sight of a portly figure that instantly registered in his mind. A. B. Bilyeu, he thought. What was *he* doing back in Hembree? He blinked and looked again. Yep, for sure it was he, with that slick nephew of his, Cecil DeGroat. He gave the elder of the two gentlemen a polite nod. "Well, well, Mr. Bilyeu."

"Olivera, isn't it?" Bilyeu drawled as he padded slowly toward him. "Fancy meeting you here."

Fancy meeting *him*? Harrumph. Olivera was practically a fixture at the Tavernette, but Bilyeu? He figured that after their last visit, A. B. and DeGroat had journeyed back to where they'd come from…New Orleans…Memphis. "That's right, Gus Olivera." He extended Bilyeu a hand. "Come to pay us a visit, have you?"

"You remember my nephew, Cecil DeGroat?"

Olivera glanced at the man at Bilyeu's side. Lanky, dressed to the nines, dark hair pulled back and tied at the neck. "Of course." He shook DeGroat's hand. "Good to see you, Mr. DeGroat."

"Join us for a drink if you will." Bilyeu scanned the bar for an available table.

"Thanks, but I've got to get back to work."

"Another time, then." Bilyeu smiled coolly.

"Just one thing. I suppose everything worked out at the Apothecary Museum." Olivera smiled, too, but not coolly, his intention being to inject a bit of mockery into his comment.

"Yes, it did." Bilyeu lifted his chin and looked down his nose at Olivera. "But the less said about that the better." With those parting words, he followed his nephew to a table a short distance away.

Olivera was not one to *rub it in*, but on that occasion, he'd been tempted. Clearly, the Larkspur incident was still fresh in the old gent's mind. The leather-bound apothecary—which if not a book of poisons, a collection of dubious remedies—had ended up at the Apothecary Museum near Bilyeu's residence in the Quarter, serving henceforth as a reminder of an episode in Bilyeu family history that the proud man evidently preferred to forget. In direct violation of Louisiana's Code Noir, Bilyeu's distant ancestor Hershel had tested some herbal remedies on his house servants with devastating results. But by the time the authorities caught wind of it, Hershel had fled the city for more remote climes—the Arkansas Delta, in fact. His dodge had been effective, and, in fact, his part in the offense hadn't been entirely known for a hundred years or more—yes, more—and then not in the Crescent City but in Hembree.

Back in September, at the time of the Larkspur incident, Olivera had wished for a clearer picture of the murderous legacy of the Bilyeus, especially as it pertained to the Hembree branch of the family. But after Ninon's tragic end, it seemed like Hembree had seen the last of the Bilyeu clan. He was confident in his own mind that A. B.'s distant cousin Arnold had killed Eugene Brown and that Melvin Moody was no more than an accomplice—albeit an accessory to homicide. But now, with Arnold and his accomplice dead, it was doubtful he'd be able to dig up more skeletons than he already had. Yeah, he might as well let sleeping dogs lie. And, as far as current company was concerned, though he really wasn't one to rub it in, it was tempting. Yes, indeed.

Clinton came with the check, and Olivera paid it, lifted his briefcase, and, before leaving, nodded again to A. B. and DeGroat. "By the way—" He stepped closer to their table. "—I suppose the work at Larkspur is going well."

Bilyeu cast him an apprehensive look that segued into a smile. "Yes, as a matter of fact it is. You oughta come out and let us show you around the place. You wouldn't recognize it."

"Thanks, I'll take you up on that." That is what Olivera replied, even if he had no intention of following through. He adjusted his hat and, nodding again, sauntered toward the door.

Once outside the Tavernette, he paused to gather his thoughts regarding the case at hand. He could drop by the morgue, see if Eads had come to a more solid conclusion regarding cause of death. "Or," he mumbled aloud, pausing to ponder his options, he could pay Lauren Wilson a visit, see how she was getting along. He felt uneasy about her decision to stay at Morris House, especially with the whereabouts of the suspected stalker unknown. But now that the matter of the cellar had cropped up, he had justifiable reason to go back over there to take a closer look. He pulled his phone out of his pocket and called Springer. "Springer, you finished lunch?"

"Sure have, Chief."

"I'm just leaving the Tavernette, and, uh, I was thinking about that cellar at the Morris place."

"Me and Reagan just been talking 'bout that."

"Let's get back over there and see what we can turn up."

"I guess we still don't know cause of death, do we?"

"Let's give Dr. McGinnis a little more time. But between you and me, she's no more convinced than we are that Will Grayson went to his grave *unassisted,* shall we say."

"Maybe, maybe not, but seems like something's developing on that front."

"I can't disagree with you there, Springer. So listen. Get the van ready. I'll be there in five."

Minutes later, he pulled up behind the station, parked, and headed in through the back door. Springer, stretched out in a chair next to Reagan's desk, got up and slipped on his jacket. "What equipment we gonna need, Chief?"

Olivera scratched his head. "Hard to say. I seriously doubt we can pick up any prints. Didn't look like to me that anybody had been down there. The whole place was covered in dust."

"Reckon we'll need boxes?" Reagan asked.

"Yeah, maybe," Olivera said.

"Ammo?"

"I doubt it. What we're looking at is an old library. I'm guessing the owner used it for a study or a game parlor. I ran into Mosey Frye last night, and she agreed to check with the Morris sisters, see if they knew it was down there."

"How would they *not*?" Springer asked. "If you got a cellar, you got a cellar."

"Well, *Mosey* didn't know it was there and wondered if *they* knew. They had never mentioned it."

"Weird, if you ask me." Springer patted his upper lip.

"Yeah," Olivera nodded, "to say nothing of the fact that tools were covering the door. I bet those tools were put there for a reason."

"Why else?" Reagan asked.

"You assumed that from the beginning, did you, Reagan?" Olivera said. "I didn't. Sloppy upkeep. That's what I was thinking. Like maybe the yard man hadn't bothered to put his tools away. Just left 'em lying there."

"So, Chief, you think Grayson was involved?"

"Involved in what?" Reagan asked.

"Hard to say," Olivera said, "but seems to me—"

"—somebody was hiding something," Springer cut in. "And if the cellar was the scene of whatever, the culprit must have been Grayson." He stared into space.

"How you figure?" Reagan asked.

Springer looked at Reagan. "He covered up the door with the gardening tools, didn't he?"

"I'm not sure he did." Olivera crossed the office to the front door. "Did he?"

Springer shrugged and followed Olivera into the garage. "Where'd Reagan go?"

"He's coming."

With Springer on the driver's side, Olivera on the passenger's side, and Reagan—who'd run back for boxes—in the back, they headed down Lee toward McAllister, talking as they went about who might have done what, when, and why. As they drew nearer to Morris House, Reagan, ever the considerate one, scooted up and asked, "Oughtn't we to let her know we're coming?"

"No need," Olivera replied. "We'll let her know when we get there. We're not going in the house, just the cellar."

"But the cellar's in the house."

"You'd think, but in this case—"

"This is it," Springer cut in, slowing down. "Shall I park on the street?"

"Yeah, let's not block the driveway in case Dr. Wilson needs to get out. That's her sporty ragtop." He pointed toward the car. "Looks kind of out of place, doesn't it?"

"Sure does, Chief. That's one cool ride, but the house—?" he added, apparently still perplexed about Wilson's decision to buy the Morris place.

While Springer and Reagan waited in the yard, Olivera spoke with Wilson, and once he'd gotten her okay, recommended the scrutiny of the cellar. Reagan lifted the cellar door and laid it back against the ground. Then the three of them descended the stairs, flashlights in hand. Springer, the first one to reach the landing, flashed a beam around the walls. "I've never seen such a place. There're more books here than in the Hembree Library."

"I doubt that," Olivera said.

"You ever been there, Chief?"

"No, can't say that I have."

"Reckon what Dr. Wilson will want done with all this," Reagan mused.

"I doubt that's up to her." Olivera shot a beam toward the desk where the typewriter sat.

"Who's it up to, then?" Reagan asked.

"The Morris sisters—who else?" Springer said.

Olivera approached the desk and, with his right hand paused above the keyboard, pressed the space bar with his thumb. "It still works."

"Would you look at that." Springer joined him at the desk. "Reckon they make ribbons for these things anymore?"

"I doubt it." He pushed the return lever and the carriage slid to the right.

"I don't know. People like these old machines." Springer opened the desk drawer and peered in. "Look, there's a key in here."

"Wonder what it's to." Olivera fished it out and handed it to Springer. "Bag that, would you?"

"Looks like a house key." Springer took a plastic bag from his pocket, labeled it, and dropped in the key.

Olivera left the desk and moved toward the table. "Remember the poker chip I showed you guys?"

"Yeah." Springer moved in Olivera's direction.

"Here's where I discovered it." Olivera first illuminated the top of the desk, and after double-checking for prints and finding none, he grasped the drawer pull and, removing the drawer from its slot, set it on the table.

"Wow." Reagan approached. "Chips…cards, ever'thing you'd need for a game of blackjack, five-card stud…"

"I wonder why they played down here," Olivera said. "Darn inconvenient to the kitchen and bathroom."

"That's easy, Chief."

"So enlighten me, would you?"

"Gambling," Springer said, excitement in his voice. "Unlikely they played just for the fun of it. Gambling's illegal in Dent County—you know that, Chief."

Olivera thought back to the picture Mosey had shown him the evening before. "Of course!" he exclaimed. "And Hembree's upper crust wouldn't have wanted it known—"

"Wouldn't do at all," Springer cut in. "Rich folks getting caught in an illegal poker game? Nope, wouldn't do at all, not 'round here, it wouldn't."

"Who you talkin' about?" Reagan asked.

Olivera fished out another chip and handed it to Springer. "Might as well bag this, too." He turned to Reagan. "Mosey Frye showed me a picture of a bunch of guys taken after the war. Said it was her grandfather's poker buddies. Kit Morris, Amos Frye, Arnold Bilyeu. There was a McGinnis, too. Must have been Dr. McGinnis's grandfather. And one other guy. Not sure who she said it was."

"Yep," Springer confirmed, "that's Hembree's upper crust, all right. They must have been young, *real* young if it was soon after the war."

"Unlawful gambling." Olivera focused his flashlight on the drawer. "That would be reason enough to keep this place secret…back then, anyway. But now? They're all dead. Well, Kit's dead for sure. And Amos. Arnold Bilyeu's dead."

"Is old Dr. McGinnis still alive?" Springer asked.

"Nope, but his son is. I just talked to him. Guess I'll

have to call him back."

"You figure Will Grayson was keeping the place up?"

"Ha. Fine job he did." Olivera slid the drawer back into place and walked over to the armchair, nestled against a towering bookcase. He lifted the cushion and felt down into the crevices of the seat. "Nothing here." He ran a beam up the corner of the room, then along the floor in front of the chair and on either side. He pulled the chair away from the bookcase, and shining the light around the back, he spotted a mark on the floor. He motioned to Springer and Reagan. "Come look at this."

"What you got, Chief?" Springer walked over with Reagan at his heels.

"What's it look like to you?" He illuminated the area behind the chair.

"Huh," Reagan said. "Looks like a scuff mark."

"But what made it?" Olivera ran the light over the shelves behind the chair. "There's no door here, just bookshelves."

Together, the trio took down the books and piled them on the chair. Just as Reagan removed the last book from the middle shelf, a keyhole appeared. "Look at that!"

"Give me the key you bagged, Springer." Olivera held out his hand, and Springer emptied the key into his palm. When he inserted it into the hole, it fit, and when he turned it, the shelf creaked and jogged forward. "Let's get the rest of these books off the shelves."

They scooted the armchair out of the way and hurriedly removed the books. After they'd given the case a couple of tugs, it swung open, revealing an alcove about the size of a wardrobe.

"What's in there?" Springer asked.

"I haven't a clue." Olivera stepped inside the space and ran his flashlight around the sides. Shelves lined both sides, top to bottom, and a large container rested against the back wall. He lifted the top and looked in. "Hmm, paintings…" He handed his flashlight to Springer and, reaching in with both hands, lifted out an ornately framed canvas. "Take this, will you? It's heavy." After handing the first painting to Springer, he pulled out the other one and passed it to Reagan. "Looks like that's it." He double-checked the inside of the container, then, stepping out, rubbed the dust off his gloves.

"Wow, check this out," Springer said, a hint of disbelief in his voice. "This looks like a masterpiece, don't it?"

"Yeah, it does," Reagan agreed, sharing the same awe. "This 'un, too. Pretty incredible."

Though inclined to concur with his sergeants, Olivera preferred to remain silent on the subject. "Let's get these pieces back to the station, guys."

"You gonna leave that open, Lieutenant?" Reagan motioned toward the alcove.

His inclination was to leave it, but Reagan was right. "Probably better not."

Reagan propped the painting he was holding against the armchair. "Give me a hand here, Springer."

Together, they pushed the case into position and smoothly aligned it with the wall. Afterward, they quickly gathered handfuls of books and set them back on the shelves.

Olivera picked up a stack of books that had toppled off the chair, and before reshelving them, checked the titles. "I wonder if any of these are worth anything."

"I wouldn't know," Springer said.

"I suppose I could ask Nadia Abboud. If anybody around here would know…" Not that he was anxious to get Nadia involved, but if he had ever needed the advice of an antiquarian, indeed, it was now. "Let's go, guys."

Chapter Sixteen

*Abboud Antiques*
*Tuesday, 2:30 p.m.*

Once Nadia and Mosey had gone through most of the treasures Nadia picked up at the Sunny Banks estate sale, they took a break to enjoy a leisurely cup of tea. Mosey nestled into a navy velour wingchair, while Nadia settled down on a stunning creamy-yellow tufted sofa across from the chair. After savoring her last drop of tea, Nadia lay back and let her mind wander, imagining herself sinking into a sumptuous bed of hay. But, alas, her blissful moment was abruptly interrupted by the intrusive ring of the phone. She raised up, pulled the phone off the counter, and lazily spoke into the receiver. "Abboud Antiques, Nadia Abboud speaking."

"This is Gus Olivera."

"Lieutenant, what's up?" She sat up straight, casting a quick glance at Mosey.

"I'm just leaving Morris House."

"Yes?" She glanced again at Mosey as a spark of curiosity flitted across her friend's face.

"We stumbled upon, uh, some items of interest, and I'd like your opinion, if you wouldn't mind swinging by the station."

"Well, I'd be glad to help you out, but I can't leave the store right now."

He hesitated. "I suppose I could, uh, drop by."

"Fine with me."

"Okay, in a few minutes… Let's say around three or a little before."

"I'll see you then." She placed the receiver on the hook. "I wonder what *that's* about."

"What'd he say?" Mosey's initial curiosity morphed into a grin.

"What are you grinning about?"

"I'll wager you this," Mosey declared with confidence, "that whatever it is, there's definitely a connection to that cellar."

"I guess that's a possibility. He's come across some stuff at Morris House and wants an opinion."

"Wow." Mosey's face lit up. "I wonder what he found."

"We'll know soon enough." She nodded toward the clock above the counter. "He should be here any minute."

"He won't like finding *me* here."

"Must be desperate or he wouldn't have called *me*." Nadia sat back on the sofa and, picking up a plush taffeta throw pillow, fluffed it into shape.

"We aren't his favorite people, are we? But I really don't get it. We've walked him through an awful lot of cases. By now, you'd think he'd wanna put us on the payroll."

Nadia laughed. "I never thought of it that way, but it's true. We've done a ton of free work for the Hembree Police Department."

"Not that I mind," Mosey added. "Without a crime or two to solve, I'd be bored to tears."

Nadia shook her head. "Mosey, you're crazy."

"Ha! No crazier than you."

As they waited for Olivera to arrive, they tidied up the clutter from the unpacked boxes and carried it to the rear of the store. They had just returned to the front when the rumble of a car engine caught Nadia's attention, causing her to pause and peer out the window. "That's him."

Mosey, who had resumed her position in the wingchair, pulled a magazine out of a stack on the enamel tray table in front of her and, leaning back, crossed her legs.

Nadia raised an eyebrow at Mosey. "What are you doing?"

"Looking nonchalant."

"Just keep quiet. We don't wanna annoy the lieutenant."

As Nadia held the door open, Olivera lugged in a very large parcel wrapped in brown paper.

"Looks like a painting," Nadia said.

"It *is* a painting." As he tore into the wrapping, it dropped to the floor, exposing the painting inside.

"You found *that* at Morris House?" Nadia exclaimed.

"I did…in the cellar…well, more or less in the cellar."

"What do you mean, 'more or less'?"

"Sort of secreted away off the…well, I guess you could call it a study," he explained. "Whoever put it there didn't want it disturbed. I've heard of closets hidden behind bookcases, but I never expected to actually see one."

"It's a dusty old thing." Nadia reached for her dust cloth. "Mind if I tidy it up a little?"

"I don't see the harm in it."

When Nadia had removed most of the dust, Mosey, an elbow covering her nose, got up and cautiously joined the group. She eyed Olivera. "How'd you ever think to look behind a bookcase?"

He nodded politely to Mosey. "There were scuff marks on the floor, actually, like a door makes when it drags, but oddly enough, there was no door." He looked back at Nadia. "Just a bookcase behind an old armchair. We took some of the books down and, presto, a keyhole. But before that, we'd seen a key in a desk drawer. It fit perfectly in the hole, so I opened the case and found *this*—" He gestured toward the painting with a wave of his hand. "—this one and another one in a large container. The other one's in the van." Looking quite pleased with himself, he glanced from Nadia to Mosey.

"Wow, in a secret compartment," Mosey exclaimed.

He nodded. "Where shall I put it?"

"Well, for the time being, set it over there." Nadia motioned toward the counter.

After he'd propped the painting against the counter, Nadia briefly examined it. "My word. Mosey, come look at this. It's a casta painting."

"Wait, what?" Mosey moved closer.

"Yep." Nadia smiled at Olivera. "Lieutenant, you may have saved us a heap of trouble."

"Really?" His voice was laced with puzzlement. "How's that?"

"I guess it won't hurt to tell you this." Mosey took a step toward Olivera. "One of Nadia's father's old customers—David Morell's his name—has commissioned *us*, Nadia and me, to look for a couple of casta paintings."

"Well, that's—" Olivera began.

"You know," Nadia cut in, "Morell's been on the lookout for paintings he *thought* were in Hembree, and now I'm beginning to think he may have been absolutely right. Wouldn't it be just the craziest thing if Kit Morris had them squirreled away in his cellar all along?"

"This opens up a can of worms, doesn't it?" Mosey glanced at Nadia.

"Certainly does."

"Mr. Kit must have had a good reason, hiding a painting, two paintings…"

"Especially if you consider that there was a market for them," Nadia added.

"I wonder what he was thinking."

Nadia turned to Olivera. "Could we possibly see the other painting?"

"Sure, I'll bring it in."

Nadia and Mosey watched through the display window as Olivera walked quickly toward the van and, opening the back doors, pulled out a parcel. "I bet it's another casta painting."

"I surely hope so." Mosey's face beamed with excitement. "What kind of unbelievable luck is this? Dave shows up, and the same day…!"

"Yeah, but how do we get our hands on them?"

Mosey's expression gloomed. "Hadn't thought of that."

Olivera came back in and propped the second painting beside the first. He removed the wrapping and stepped aside. "So, what about this one?"

Nadia picked up her dust cloth and knelt in front of the painting. "Clearly, it's another casta, but this one is different," she noted as she lightly ran her cloth over the canvas and frame. "I've seen this vignette pattern before. Four images across…four images down. Sixteen vignettes in all. Each segment of the grid represents a phase in a sort of progression."

"Not following you."

"Well, evidently, the artist had a kind of hierarchy in mind that began with the *peninsular*," she tapped the top lefthand corner of the painting, "and ended with the *meco*." She directed his attention to the last vignette, in which an indigenous woman was comforting an irritable child. Her eyes then drifted to the artist's signature in the lower right corner. "My, my, Lieutenant, you've brought us *exactly* what we were looking for," she said excitedly before turning to Mosey, who was standing at her back. "This *is* a Cardoso, Mosey. Kinda unreal, isn't it?"

"Let me see." Mosey stepped closer.

"Cardoso?" Olivera asked. "I don't think I've ever heard of him."

"*Mateo* Cardoso," Nadia elaborated. "He painted the Fernanda portrait, the one my father sold to David Morell. His son Dave, by the way, is here now."

"Here now?"

"Yes."

"Wait…you mean here in Hembree?" he asked, his confusion growing.

"Yes, but it's got nothing to do with this—your find, I mean. Not directly at least."

"That's right." Mosey glanced up at Olivera. "I spoke with Dave's father just yesterday. We didn't know anything about this—the missing paintings, I mean—until recently."

Though Olivera looked quite baffled, he didn't question the unlikely coincidence. He just paced a bit before saying to Nadia, "So, can you tell me something about this man…Mateo Cardoso?"

"I don't really know much about him, other than the basics. I believe he lived in New Orleans and was primarily known for casta paintings. But wait a second." She rounded the counter to the file cabinet. "I'm pretty sure I've got some notes." She opened the top drawer and flipped through the folders till she came to the one she was looking for and, laying it on the counter, opened it and lifted the top sheet. "Okay, this is the bill of sale for the Cardoso that Dad sold Morell. Dad picked it up at the Bilyeu estate sale after Mr. Arnold died. It was a portrait of Mr. Arnold's great-grandmother, Fernanda de Lobos."

"Indeed," Olivera said, obviously taken aback.

"I'm guessing you remember—"

"How could I not?"

About to take a seat, Nadia realized her *guest* was still standing. "Forgive my manners, Lieutenant. Wouldn't you like to sit down?" She motioned toward the tufted sofa.

He nodded, then perched awkwardly on the edge of the seat cushion, as if he wasn't entirely sure he wanted to join the hen party.

"Can I offer you something, a cup of tea?" she asked.

He looked up. "Sure, if it's no bother."

She reached for the teapot and swished it. "Plenty left. Would you care for sugar? Lemon?" She gestured toward a silver tray of condiments on the counter.

"Lemon, please."

She skewered a lemon slice, then dropped it in a cup before pouring the tea. "Mosey, can I warm yours up?"

she asked as she passed Olivera his tea.

"Yes, please." Mosey took a seat again in the navy wingchair.

Nadia refilled Mosey's cup and her own, then settled into the other wingchair across from Olivera. Having brought the folder with her, she took a quick peek, then passed it to him.

He folded back the top sheet. "So, this is the infamous Fernanda de Lobos."

"You haven't seen her before?" Nadia remarked.

"No, but I've heard plenty about her." He raised a brow. "Just for the sake of clarification—" He cleared his throat. "—let me ask you ladies something." He placed the folder on the tray table and continued. "How much do you know about this, uh, Bilyeu matriarch?" He glanced from Nadia to Mosey.

"She was Hershel Bilyeu's wife," Mosey volunteered, "and the two of them founded Larkspur Plantation."

"Well, yes...but what else?"

"Her portrait hung on the wall over there, right above the mantel, from the time we were kids—junior high, high school? What's the date on that?"

He opened the folder and referred to the top sheet. "Says here 1989."

"We were in high school, right?" Nadia looked at Mosey.

"Must have been."

"That's when we first learned about Fernanda"— Nadia turned to Olivera—"some years after Mr. Arnold's death. There was an estate sale, not that there was much left. I remember Daddy's speaking of that."

"Not much left?" His tone implied confusion. "I

assumed there would have been quite a bit left. Weren't the Bilyeus well-off, *very* well-off?"

"Yes, at one time, but Arnold fell on hard times. He had to sell off what he could to keep the farm running."

"I see." Nodding, he thought for a second. "But even so, he held on to the portrait of this…woman."

Noticing contempt in his voice, Nadia remarked, "I'm guessing you're familiar with the De Lobos family history."

"Yes…as told to me by Rafael, who seemed to know it like the back of his hand. I suppose there's no point in keeping this under wraps," he added with a sigh. "Now that the apothecary is in the museum in the Quarter, I imagine the whole story, I mean of Hershel and Fernanda's departure, their reason for leaving New Orleans and coming here…"

She and Mosey exchanged glances. "Fill us in, Lieutenant," Nadia said, then added, "if you can." *She* knew the story, as did Mosey, but she couldn't resist the urge to see what *he* knew.

"Rafael," he said, referencing his source again, "was loath to speak of it, but Hershel and Fernanda came here, uh, running from the law."

"Running from the law, eh?" Nadia feigned puzzlement.

"I suppose that's not putting it too strongly. Yes," he went on, "running from the law, after committing a *serious* crime. Turns out Hershel Bilyeu was a pharmacist and, in collaboration with a Haitian priestess—well, according to Rafael, and, as I mentioned before, he was none too keen to tell me this—Hershel and the priestess concocted some herbal remedies and tested them on the Bilyeu house servants, who soon became ill and died, every one of them." He lowered his eyes, then, looking up, continued. "Hershel left the priestess to face the music, and he and his wife took off. They ended up here in the Delta, which was rather unpopulated at the time."

"Horrific." Nadia shook her head.

"Gotta wonder how they got away with *that*," Mosey ruminated.

"Well, I don't know all the details," Olivera added, "just the essentials as Rafael told them to me. He seemed quite disturbed by it all."

"Of course, he would be. Rafael seemed like a good person." Nadia glanced at Mosey, who nodded in agreement.

"Yeah," Mosey said, "I don't believe he thought much of the Hembree branch of the family."

"I can certainly see why not," Nadia agreed.

"But," Olivera continued, "he was anxious to follow through on the task the Conde de Lobos entrusted to his descendants. Rafael's father had failed to carry out the conde's wishes, so Rafael, in anticipation of inheriting the title himself, was determined to locate the heirlooms that Fernanda stole from her father. Above all, he hoped to find the dagger and dueling pistols, uh, with which you are familiar."

"So *that's* what he was looking for," Mosey broke in, playing along with Nadia's ruse. "Not the house…but, rather, something *in* the house." She looked at Nadia. "I wonder why he didn't tell *us* that."

Nadia shrugged.

"I'm surprised he didn't." He turned to Mosey. "I suggested he speak to you before he left, given that he'd pulled you into it." He took a sip of tea. "So, he didn't tell you."

Mosey, evidently as unwilling as Nadia to tell Olivera an outright lie, simply shrugged.

"He seemed ashamed of what Hershel and Fernanda had done," Olivera went on, "and anxious to put that part of the family history behind him. He potentially had a claim on Larkspur, given his relation to the founders, but wanted nothing to do with the place."

"Come to think of it," Mosey said, "it was Rafael who passed my name to David Senior. I suppose he credited me with helping him locate the heirlooms."

"Must have," Nadia said, "which would explain his recommendation."

"I guess so. I wondered about that."

Nadia, feeling uneasy about the charade that she had kicked off and Mosey had willingly played along with, suddenly changed subjects. "But back to the matter at hand." She gestured toward the paintings. "How did these paintings end up in Kit Morris's cellar? I can't imagine why he wouldn't have sold them. They must be valuable. Or if he wanted them for himself, why didn't he go ahead and hang them for people to see?"

"Good questions," Olivera said.

Nadia got up and moved back to the paintings. "This one—" She knelt before the composite. "—is fairly typical. The enlightened despots of the Spanish Colonial period carefully *monitored*, shall we say, the opinions of their subjects, especially concerning the so-called castas." With a bit of uncertainty, she added, "Lieutenant, you must be familiar with that sort of thing, right?"

"*Mestizo*, c*riollo*, that sort of thing?"

She nodded. "In the casta system, they even

155

distinguished between Spaniards born in Spain and Spaniards born in the Americas. *Peninsulares* and *criollos,* they called them."

Mosey drew near and studied the composition closely, looking from one vignette to the next. "How…unfortunate," she uttered, after apparently struggling for the right word.

"I know." Nadia wrinkled her nose.

"But that other one…" Olivera got up from his seat. "You said it's a casta painting as well?"

Nadia nodded. "It is, but in that one, Cardoso abandoned the grid format and, instead, focused on just one couple, not a married couple, however. Note there is a man and a woman but no offspring." She motioned toward the man in the painting, who was young, fair-complexioned, and dressed in foppish eighteenth-century attire. "His clothing suggests he's upper class and probably European—either Spanish or French. The objects around the room indicate the same." She cast a quick glance at Olivera, who was gazing intently at the painting. "You see, casta painters often added household items to the backdrop…to denote status. Earthenware and rough-hewn furnishings suggested humble origins, while more precious items, like clocks, fine porcelain, crystal, gemstones, and books, implied wealth. Notice the items in the case." She pointed to a small wooden case off to one side, which, spatially, served to balance out the central figures of the middle portion.

"Yes, I see." He rubbed his chin. "Looks like the artist has put a *peninsular* or maybe a *criollo* alongside a woman of African or Caribbean descent."

She looked back at the painting. "Yes, but the woman doesn't look like a house servant, does she?"

"No, she doesn't, and judging from her dress, I'd say she was better off than a servant, wouldn't you?"

"Absolutely. Look at her hair style" —she motioned toward the woman— "her earrings, the detail on her dress…"

"Yes, and all the things on the table." He became pensive. "I wouldn't be surprised if that's not Hershel Bilyeu himself."

"Could be, I suppose, and just imagine…" Nadia gestured toward the man in the painting, who was standing behind a worktable scattered with implements. "If that's Hershel Bilyeu, the vial he's holding could have contained the brew that poisoned his house servants."

Olivera nodded. "Yes, I suppose it could."

"Heaven knows what sort of excruciating demise it could have caused."

"I'd rather not think about that if you don't mind," Mosey said, turning away.

Passing over Mosey's remark, Nadia went on with her re-enactment, envisioning the dreadful ordeal the pharmacist's victims must have endured after ingesting the toxic beverage. As she proceeded with her fabulation, the facial expressions of those who were listening gradually changed from unease to disgust. Once she had finished, she said, "The Bilyeus have a lot to live down, don't they?"

"What Bilyeus?" Mosey moved back to her wing chair. "There aren't any left, not of the Hershel-Fernanda line."

"True." Nadia sat down in the other wing chair. "I guess Ninon was the last one, as far as we know."

Olivera returned to the sofa. "A. B. and DeGroat,

then, are only distant cousins of the Hembree Bilyeus?"

"That's right. And Rafael wasn't related to Hershel at all except by marriage."

"I don't know how you keep it all straight." Olivera sighed.

"I'll show you how." Mosey scooted to the edge of the seat cushion. "On a sultry Sunday evening, when my parents had nothing better to do than sort out who was who, it kinda went like this. *So-and-so married so-and-so*. That was my momma. Now my daddy. *Naw, he didn't, Marie. That was his uncle, Old Man so-and-so.* Now Momma. *Whatchu talkin' 'bout, Ellis? That old man never married. It was his nephew who married so-and-so, not he.*"

Olivera let out a chuckle. Apparently, he was ready for a little comic relief, which Mosey was more than happy to provide.

## Chapter Seventeen

*Abboud Antiques*
*Tuesday, 3:30 p.m.*

Despite bidding farewell to Olivera and finishing their tea, Nadia and Mosey remained glued to their wing chairs. It was that time of the afternoon when inertia creeps in. A stack of cardboard boxes stood near the display case, ready to be filled with merchandise left from the after-Christmas sale. Yet Nadia and Mosey, in no mood to get moving, sat cogitating over a matter they considered of greater importance.

"You know," Nadia began, "I can't believe I convinced him to leave the paintings here."

Mosey looked askance. "Neither can I."

Nadia studied Mosey's face, not sure what to make of the look she'd given her. "You aren't jealous, are you?"

"No, fool!" Mosey rolled her eyes at Nadia. "On second thought, maybe I *should* be. He's nicer to you."

"Not true. Remember last year after the hassle over the Haviland vases?" She threw a thumb in the direction of the elegant pair of Havilands that sat on a rustic buffet cabinet on the other side of the room. "I thought he'd never speak to me again."

"You're exaggerating."

"No, I'm not."

"So, how'd you get past that?" Mosey asked.

"The dagger." A faint smile surfaced. "I helped him out with the dagger."

"Huh?"

"Yeah." Nadia's face brightened. *That was it.* He came into the shop, asking about the dagger, wanting to know what it looked like and how much it was worth."

"And?"

"I had the information on file. Daddy assessed it for Mr. Arnold—it and the dueling pistols—for insurance purposes, I assumed. But maybe that wasn't it at all. Maybe Mr. Arnold was thinking of selling them."

"Yeah." Mosey sat up in her chair.

"Of course. This whole thing—"

"What whole thing?"

"The Bilyeu estate. These paintings must have belonged to the Bilyeus." She glanced at the paintings, still propped against the counter.

Mosey looked doubtful. "So, what were they doing in Kit Morris's cellar?"

"I don't know, but I have a good idea who would." She walked to the counter and, placing a call to her father, got the desired result. "He's coming over." She placed the receiver on the hook. "He'll be right here."

By four o'clock, Toni Abboud had arrived and, giving a hug first to his daughter, then to Mosey, seated himself on the sofa. "Nice sofa." He twisted around and took a look at the tufting across the back.

"You like it?" Nadia asked.

"I like the style." He stuffed the taffeta throw pillow behind his back. "You got a cup of tea for an old man?"

"Of course." Nadia winked at Mosey.

"You're supposed to say, 'you're not old.' "

"I don't know what good it'd do. You've convinced yourself otherwise." She handed him a cup with a slice of lemon. "Daddy, you ought to be *here*...working. I don't have your expertise or your knowledge of Hembree history."

"Are you saying I didn't train you well?" He squeezed the lemon into his cup.

"Like these paintings." She poured the tea. "I know they were probably part of the Bilyeu estate at one time. All you have to do is look at the frames to know that." She set down the pot and, approaching the smaller of the two paintings, ran her fingers along the ornately carved frame. "Obviously, the same process was used for the frames, and the motifs of the carving are the same." She paused and looked at her father. "Wasn't the frame that held the Fernanda portrait just like these?"

He turned to Mosey, tapping his forefinger against his temple. "See what I mean? She has a fine memory, this one."

"She does," Mosey agreed, "but she'll never believe she's up to your standard, Toni. You know that."

He shrugged. "It's difficult doing the same thing a family member has done before you. You must make your own way. I've always told Nadia that. But does she listen to her old father?"

Mosey became pensive. "It's amazing how many of us do that—follow in our father's footsteps."

Toni nodded. "Your generation, yes. Mine, not so much." His expression fell. "You take Arnold Bilyeu, for example."

"I thought Mr. Arnold was older than you, Daddy," Nadia said.

"He was, ten years, maybe, just old enough to go to

war, World War II. But my group was born during the war or soon after. Me? I was born in 1945. Arnold's crowd? They all went to war except Arnold and Kit. That picture you showed me"—Toni glanced at Nadia—"got me to thinking about the older men—Arnold, Kit, Amos, Tim, Colton…"

"You were friends with the poker players?" Mosey asked.

"Sure was. Well, maybe not friends so much as acquaintances. I wasn't around when they got started, but they kept that game going for years."

"You knew about the cellar, then," Nadia probed.

"Did you ever go down there?" Mosey cut in before Toni could respond.

"Once." Toni glanced at the paintings. "Kit asked me to give him a quote on those very paintings."

Nadia's mouth opened and closed. "I had a feeling about this."

Mosey stared at Nadia, eyes wide with surprise.

"You see—" Toni took a sip of his tea. "—these paintings did, indeed, belong to Arnold. Family heirlooms, as you suspected." He nodded at Nadia. "But Arnold had gotten himself into debt playing poker. Seems like it was poker." He paused to think. "I guess it could have been something else." He shrugged. "Anyway, the farm was doing well then. *That* misfortune came later." He arched a brow. "But Arnold was a ne'er-do-well, 'not fit to kill,' his daddy used to say, spent too much time knocking around with Kit, who wasn't much better. So Arnold took the paintings from the house and *pawned* them—actually, gave them to Kit with the understanding that Kit would hold on to them and give 'em back when Arnold could scrape together the money.

Until now, I never knew how it turned out. It wasn't any of my business. But now I must assume that Arnold was never able to redeem them." He rubbed his forehead. "No guessing about it. From what was left at the estate sale, if I had stopped to think about it then, I could have figured it out."

"Come now, Daddy. You must have wondered—"

"Of course, I wondered, but whom was I to ask? Ninon?"

"I see what you mean."

"You said Mr. Kit wasn't much better?" Mosey interjected.

He shook his head. "Never amounted to much, never made a farmer, which is what his daddy wanted him to be. He was the only son. But Kit had other aspirations, wanted to be a writer. Spent more time underground than above…in that cellar of his, reading, writing, playing poker with his buddies."

"Tell me something if you can," Nadia said. "What do you suppose Will Grayson had to do with any of this? You know he was found dead in the tool shed behind the Morris house."

"Yes." He sighed. "I read about it in the paper. Will went on working for the Morris sisters after Kit passed. But now that they're out at the Magnolia, I'm not sure why he'd be hanging around."

"It had something to do with these paintings," Mosey chimed in. "He must have known they were there."

"It sort of looks that way," Nadia agreed.

"Maybe Kit left the paintings to Will," Mosey suggested. "Peggy didn't seem to know anything about them. If she had, surely, she wouldn't have left them down there."

"Maybe Will knew they were there"—Nadia looked at Mosey—"and planned on going back to get them. But then somebody else who wanted them…"

"You're thinking what I'm thinking."

"But, girls," Toni interrupted, "you're jumping to conclusions. Will was a sick man."

"Yeah, Daddy, he was. And desperate to take care of business before he died."

"What business?" Toni asked.

"I don't know. But if Will was the only one who knew where the paintings were, and somebody he knew *wanted* the paintings…"

"I guess," Toni said, hands splayed.

"I'm wondering," Mosey proposed, "if maybe we shouldn't get in touch with Dave."

"Yes, maybe we should." Nadia looked at Toni. "David Senior sent his son here. Did I mention…? David Senior contacted Mosey about tracking down some casta paintings in Hembree, but looks like Lieutenant Olivera has done our work for us."

Toni nodded. "Have you spoken with Dave?"

"Briefly. We had lunch today, but he had an appointment. I imagine he'll drop by when he's finished. By the way, David Senior still has the Fernanda portrait. He mentioned he was surprised we hadn't paid him a visit."

"What for?" Toni asked. "I have no real interest in casta paintings."

"Nor do I."

"So, how'd y'all—?" Toni glanced from Nadia to Mosey.

"Good question." Nadia looked at Mosey. "How did

we?"

"Don't look at me. I got a call from David Senior. Rafael had given him my name."

"You don't suppose—" Nadia said.

"Suppose what?"

"—that David Senior somehow heard that you'd sold Morris House."

"Now, how would he know that? Besides, why would David Senior lie about it? He told me that Rafael had given him my name."

"Wait a minute," Toni turned to Nadia. "You aren't suggesting that David *knew* the paintings were there, are you?"

"He might have known. Mightn't he?"

"If he knew, why get *me* involved?" Mosey asked.

Nadia looked at Mosey. "You're the go-between. You sold the house. You must have had access to it. So David, knowing that, put you on the scent, anticipating you'd look for the paintings, find them, then offer them to him. He buys them. All very neat, all above board, nothing suspicious about it."

Toni shook his head. "Look, you're never going to figure this out, so why waste your time? Call Dave, get him over here, show him the paintings, and see how he reacts."

Nadia nodded. "Good idea."

"They aren't ours to show, not really," Mosey said. "Not sure how Olivera would feel."

"Who says Olivera has to know?" Nadia said. "But if you're concerned, we could just leave them there, wait till Dave shows up."

"You told Olivera you'd put them in the safe."

"Yeah, I guess I did."

Nadia and Mosey's caviling was rendered moot when the door opened, and Dave came in.

"Dave," Nadia exclaimed. "We were just…"

Dave looked past Nadia to Toni, extending a hand. "I'm Dave Morrell. You must be—"

"Toni Abboud." Toni stood and bowed briefly as he shook Dave's hand. "I know your father," Toni smiled, "but of course you know that."

"Yes." Dave took a step back. "I've heard him speak of you for years. He hoped you'd pay us a visit."

"Yes, he suggested that some years ago, but you know how it is, hard to get away from the shop."

"But you're retired now, aren't you?"

"Yes, for a couple of years, and who knows? I might surprise you when you least expect it."

"We'd be glad to show you the gallery any time."

"I understand you are here now looking for casta paintings."

"That's right."

Nadia glanced at Mosey, then Dave. "After you left for your appointment, we had a visitor."

"Oh?" Dave said.

"Our Chief of Police, Lieutenant Gus Olivera. Strangely enough, he brought us *those*." She pointed toward the paintings.

Dave, yet to take a seat, went over to the counter and, bending down, examined the lower portion of each painting. "My gracious. They're Cardosos, both of them." He looked up at Nadia. "Of course, they'll have to be authenticated."

"I suppose so," Nadia said.

"How did—?" He shook his head and frowned.

"Quite unexpected." Nadia might have hastened to

offer a more complete explanation but was more intent on watching Dave's reaction.

"Father will be thrilled."

Nadia's expression fell. "I'm afraid they may be, let us say, *encumbered*."

"How's that?" He frowned.

"Evidence in a police investigation." Mosey sighed.

Dave thought for a second, tapping his fingers against the counter. "Excuse me a moment if you will." He fished his cellphone out of his pants pocket. "I'm going to call Father. See what he recommends."

Dave moved toward the back wall, and while he consulted with David Senior, the others finished their last sips of tea.

"It's almost closing time." Nadia glanced from her dad to Mosey. "Shall we adjourn to the Tavernette?"

"Sure," Toni stood, "but shouldn't we put those in the safe?" He nodded toward the paintings.

"Dave may want a final look." Nadia glanced at Dave, who had stationed himself at the mantel on the rear wall.

Mosey leaned toward Nadia and, in a hushed voice, said, "Dave's appointment…who was it with?"

Nadia shrugged.

"I bet it was about *this*." Mosey eyed the paintings.

Nadia shrugged again, then glanced at Dave, who was walking back toward the front.

"Father says let it go, at least till the case is resolved."

Mosey sighed. "Case…? Olivera doesn't even know if he's got a case."

"What?" Nadia said, befuddled.

Mosey responded with a shrug. "I can understand

why the paintings were in the cellar. I can even understand why the cellar remained a secret. What I *can't* understand is why Mr. Kit just left them there. From all accounts, he could have used the money."

Nadia gave her father a questioning look. "Dad...?"

He shook his head. "Why would he? Doesn't make sense to me, either, unless he was saving them, holding them back for some reason."

"That has to be it," Dave said. "Otherwise..."

"I don't suppose"—Mosey turned to Dave—"that your father ever had any dealings with Kit Morris."

"Not to my knowledge, but I guess he might have. When did the man die?"

"Some years ago," Toni answered. "Must have been at least ten or more."

"And once Mr. Kit died," Mosey said, "seems like no one knew they were there. The sisters didn't know, I'm pretty sure. And we're only guessing that Will Grayson knew."

"That's right," Toni said. "I suppose someone around here might have known. If not Will, maybe one of the poker players."

"Of course, any of them might have known, but if they had—"

"Yeah...but wait a second." Nadia turned to her father. "You knew, didn't you?"

"At the time of the appraisal, yes."

"So, when Mr. Morrell was here years later, mightn't you have mentioned...?"

"No, my business with Arnold was confidential. I did, however, ask Kit after Arnold died if he was interested in selling the paintings, and he wasn't. My hands were tied. That's the way it is in our business. You often have to keep the secrets of your clients."

"So, you knew where more casta paintings might be, but you weren't able to tell Mr. Morell?"

Toni nodded, then sighed. "And I'm sure David would understand my position."

Dave looked at Toni and nodded.

"And as I was saying before," Toni continued, "tell Olivera what you know, and let him get on with it. Otherwise, you could be running in circles till doomsday."

"I suspect," Dave said, "that perhaps my other client, the man I saw this afternoon, might be interested."

"In buying the paintings?" Mosey asked.

"I believe so."

"Not to pry," Nadia said, "but if you could tell us, or if not us, Olivera…"

"I could, I suppose, but I'd need to speak to him first."

"Someone here in Hembree?" Mosey asked.

"Yes and no."

Mosey looked puzzled.

"He's here," Dave continued, "but he doesn't live here."

"I thought," Nadia said, "your father wanted the paintings for the gallery."

"He does, but he's had some inquiries."

"I see." Nadia stood and moved back toward the paintings. "There are a lot of unanswered questions, but I guess it all boils down to who wants the paintings and why."

"And how *badly* they want them," Mosey intervened. "Enough to…"

Nadia looked at Mosey. "Yeah, that's what I'm

wondering."

Dave, who had taken a seat on the sofa next to Toni, looked at Nadia, then Mosey. "You don't really think…"

"You're in a better position to know than we are," Mosey said. "How valuable *are* they?"

Dave looked at Toni. "What would you say, Mr. Abboud? When you purchased the Fernanda portrait, you must have had some notion of its worth. One Cardoso should provide some idea of the value of the others."

"I don't think that's it at all." Toni's eyebrows rose, then fell.

"What then?" Nadia said.

"I think it's the subject matter. As far as I know that's the best piece of extant evidence of Hershel Bilyeu's involvement—"

"You know about that, then," Nadia broke in.

"I suspected. When Kit asked me to assess them, they were no more valuable, as far as I could verify, than the Fernanda portrait I sold to your father." He glanced at Dave. "But the Fernanda portrait is more striking, more aesthetically appealing than either of those. They have historical value, of course, and any Cardoso would be worth a small bundle."

"I don't know, Toni." Mosey shook her head. "Most people wouldn't want them hanging in their living rooms. I know I wouldn't."

"I can't imagine that they would, but a museum, of course," he turned to Dave, "or a gallery like your father's…"

"I'd like to text Father a picture if that's okay," Dave looked at Nadia, "see what he has to say."

"Go ahead."

Dave made snapshots of the paintings and, after texting them to David Senior, said, "Once he's had a chance to actually see them, hopefully he can cast some light on the situation."

"Dave, by the way," Nadia said, "while you were on the phone, we were considering adjourning to the Tavernette. Would you like to come with us?"

Dave checked his watch. "I was hoping to fly back tonight."

"We can't convince you to stay the night? We'd be happy to put you up at the house," Toni offered.

"I'd love to, but I need to get back."

"Might save you some time in the long run if you could get this settled now," Mosey said.

"That's true." Dave looked over at the paintings, then back at Toni. "Sure you wouldn't mind?"

"Not a bit. We'd love the company."

Chapter Eighteen

*Abboud Antiques*
*Tuesday, 4:30 p.m.*

Mosey, having decided to pass on happy hour, took off on foot for McAllister Street, thinking she'd drop in on Lauren Wilson. She hadn't spoken with Lauren since Olivera had discovered the cellar and was feeling uneasy about that. Wouldn't hurt to call John Earle, see what he'd advise. So she took out her phone and made the call but, not getting an answer, left a message. "It's me, Mosey. You know the house I sold Lauren Wilson? They found a body in the tool shed. Crazy, right? And get this, Olivera discovered a cellar nobody knew anything about. I've heard of undisclosed defects but undisclosed rooms? Might I be liable? I'm over my head on this one. Give me a call, please, sir."

From across the street, she looked back at the shop. Nadia and Toni were locking up, and Dave, nearby, stood at the open door of his rental car. With a wave goodbye, she continued down Lee toward McAllister, one of her favorite streets since childhood. Something about the old houses had always appealed to her. Mae Baker's was the first house on the block—a quaint cottage with rockers spread out along the front porch. Across from Mae's was the Raineses' house, a sizable Victorian. She'd come that way the day before and, taking a look at the second story of the big Queen Anne, had noticed that the lights were turned on, suggesting Charlotte was around. She wondered if the Raineses had heard about Will's death. She was fairly sure Will had occasionally worked for them over the years.

A year ago, she would have needed a good excuse to open the wrought-iron gate at the front of the property. She might have even concocted a story before attempting to gain entrance to the imposing residence. But things were different now. As a real estate agent, she'd picked up valuable information on the people in the neighborhood, discovering a good bit about their strengths and weaknesses, financial and otherwise. So, intimidation wasn't holding her back. Still, she needed to get focused, figure out how to approach the subject of Will Grayson's death. She wasn't entirely sure he was on their payroll. Nonetheless, her faith in her conversational skills led her to believe she would come away with *something* and, with a little luck, maybe a clue or two about the old guy's demise. Folks on McAllister knew what was going on with their neighbors. In Hembree, in general, people made it their business to know.

She opened the gate and strolled along the smooth slate sidewalk to the entrance, then, lifting the brass knocker, let it drop with a thud. The wide veranda was furnished in natural rattan. On either side of the door, there was a pair of ample chairs with magazine-rack arms and pineapple feet and, farther along, a chaise lounge, strategically placed to face away from the sun. With no hanging baskets of ferns or summery palms, the somber décor blended seamlessly with the surrounding hues of winter. As Mosey waited to be invited in, she leaned against a post and breathed in the faint scent of the dusky green perennials that edged the porch.

The door opened at last, and Charlotte stuck her head out. She didn't look ready to receive a visitor. She looked drowsy, as if she'd just gotten up from a nap.

"Charlotte, I didn't wake you, did I?"

"Oh, heavens no." Charlotte swept a long strand of blond hair away from her face. "Who has time for a nap these days?"

"I know I don't."

"Would you like to come in?"

"Just for a minute. I don't want to intrude."

Charlotte ushered her in, and from the foyer, they entered the spacious living area, virtually unchanged since Mosey's visit the year before. She followed as Charlotte glided smoothly across the room, past an elegant grand piano and a cluster of dainty rosewood chairs. Stopping before a tall velvety armchair, Charlotte turned to Mosey and said, "Won't you have a seat?"

"Thank you." Mosey sat and rubbed her fingers along the black velvet upholstery. According to Matthew, he'd been sitting in one of those same velvety chairs on the night of Delaney Crump's murder. And, who knows? Maybe he *had* gotten that part right. But as Mosey had proven, his version of the events wasn't exactly as he'd reported. In fact, one small flaw in his story had prompted Olivera to reopen the case.

Lost in thought, Mosey was startled when a voice called her name. She wheeled around just as Matthew descended the stairs.

"Will you join us, Matt?" Charlotte said. "I was about to offer Mosey a drink."

"I'll get the drinks. You ladies continue with your conversation."

"Matthew," Mosey extended her hand, "it's good to see you. It's been a while, hasn't it?"

He shook her hand and responded with a wry smile. "Yes, it certainly has. What have you been doing with yourself, Mosey?"

*Ha!* came the voice of Ellis Frye. *I'd love to hear the answer to that one!*

"Shh," Mosey mouthed.

Matthew gave her a sideways glance, then strode over to the long console and, picking up the ice bucket, continued on through the foyer toward the kitchen.

Mosey had realized—finding herself in the company of both Raineses—that it wasn't actually Charlotte with whom she wanted to speak. Charlotte was a newcomer to Hembree and wasn't much older than she. But Matthew, closer in age to the deceased gardener, likely knew him, just as he would have known the older members of the poker-playing gang, her granddaddy included. How odd that the reappearance of a photograph from the forties had somehow awakened her interest in Hembree's *old boys*. Matthew hadn't figured in the photograph, but his older brother, Colton Raines, had... Hmm.

Once Matthew had left the room, Mosey was about to say to Charlotte, "Matthew's looking well," which is what people often said about older people. But Matthew wasn't all that old. Sixtyish? Still, even an elusive reference to the couple's age difference might come off as a slight, so instead, Mosey remarked, "It's good seeing y'all again. It really has been a while."

"Yes," Charlotte replied dryly.

"You know you have a new neighbor down the street, Lauren Wilson. Have you met her? She's just settling in at Morris House."

"No," Charlotte said, still at the console, "can't say I have."

"She's the new hire in psychology at Blanchard. She's young, younger than I, in fact."

"Where's she from?" Charlotte asked.

"Pennsylvania."

"Huh."

"She seems okay with Hembree, though I'm sure it's been sort of a rude awakening."

Matthew's return stopped Mosey's revelation in its tracks. "Would you care for a martini, Mosey?" He set the ice bucket and tray on the console. "Or would you prefer something else?"

"No, actually, I'd love a martini."

He unscrewed the top of the shaker and poured three drinks. He offered a glass to Mosey, then Charlotte.

Charlotte accepted and turned to Mosey. "What was that you were saying before?"

"You mean about Lauren? Yeah, it was awful. They found Will in the tool shed at the back of the property."

"What do you mean 'they *found* him'?" Matthew gaped. "Was he drunk?"

"No." Mosey took a sip of her martini. "I'm sorry to say he was *dead*. Just yesterday morning. So, you haven't heard."

"No, we *haven't*," Charlotte said. "What happened?"

"They're still sorting it out. Eads and Olivera, I mean."

"Surely they don't suspect foul play, do they?" Matthew said.

"It's not clear. The circumstances are suspicious."

"What circumstances?" Matthew came closer.

"It could have been that somebody was trying to hide the body. It was found behind a stack of paint cans. They're waiting on the coroner's report, so I heard."

"That's dreadful." Charlotte set her martini on the coffee table and sat across from Mosey. "Poor Will…such a kind soul."

"He worked for the Morrises at one time. Did he ever work for y'all? He worked for people up and down McAllister."

"Yes, he did odd jobs for us, mostly during the summer," Matthew answered. "Haven't seen him in a while." He took a sip of his drink and set it on the table.

"They say he was ill…stomach cancer," Mosey added.

Matthew grimaced, then sighed. "I guess that's not too much of a surprise. I tried to get him to go to AA meetings, but he wasn't much interested."

"Yeah," Mosey said. "He didn't take good care of himself. Thing is, the coroner isn't sure if it was his illness or something else."

"Like what?" Matthew asked.

"I don't know. Olivera is looking into it. He did a search of the premises. I just happened to be at Nadia's shop when he showed up with some paintings he found in an alcove in the cellar. By the way, did you know Morris House has a cellar? Kinda strange for around here, isn't it? I didn't know—never suspected—and I was the one who sold Lauren the house. Beats all."

"Come to think of it," Matthew said, "I was in that cellar once…long, long time ago. My older brother Colton played poker with Kit and the rest of 'em."

"My granddaddy, too." Mosey glanced at Charlotte,

who, silent, seemed to be lost in thought. "I'm sorry, Charlotte. We must be boring you to tears with all this talk of old Hembree."

"If people around here didn't talk about old Hembree, what *would* they talk about?" Charlotte rolled her baby blues at Matthew.

Apparently unaffected by her mild chide, Matthew laughed and headed to the console. As he opened the shaker and poured in more ice, he turned to Mosey. "Did you say Olivera found some paintings in the cellar?"

"He did—casta paintings. Two of them."

"Indeed," he responded, eyebrows raised.

"Come to think of it, I think Nadia mentioned that you had a couple of them yourself."

"That's right. I thought you and I looked at them that day."

"No, I don't believe we did," she quickly added, hoping to spare him the embarrassment of specifying *which day*. "You showed me your clock collection."

"I remember. And you said you liked Mother's little rose clock. That's right." He speared a couple of olives and dropped them in his drink. "Care for one of these, Mosey?" He gestured toward the dish of kalamatas.

"No, thanks."

"These paintings Olivera found…"

Mosey perked up.

"You say they were in an alcove?"

"Uh-huh, behind a bookcase. By the way, I don't suppose your paintings would be Cardosos, would they? Mateo Cardoso, I believe is who he said."

He cocked his head. "No, a French artist, Henri Bonneville. But you're familiar with Mateo Cardoso's work?"

"Not so much, but I've heard Nadia mention him. They—her dad, actually—bought and sold a Cardoso some years ago. Bought it from Arnold Bilyeu and later sold it to a dealer from New Orleans."

He picked up an olive and popped it in his mouth. "Cardoso lived and worked in New Orleans."

"Yes, and I suppose that explains the dealer's interest."

"I wonder if Olivera would mind if I took a look at them."

"I could ask."

"I would appreciate that." Matthew, coming back in their direction, topped off Charlotte's glass. "Mosey, would you care for another?"

"Thanks, Matthew, but it's getting late." She smiled and, getting up from her chair, set her empty glass on a coaster on the coffee table. The conversation didn't seem to be going anywhere. Besides, she didn't really care much about Mateo Cardoso's casta paintings except for their possible bearing on the case. She wanted to know what Matthew knew about Will Grayson, but that subject had somehow fallen through the cracks. She sighed and looked at her watch. "I'd better get on with my walk. I'm hoping to pay Lauren a visit."

"Another time, then." Charlotte, getting up, accompanied Mosey to the door.

"Thanks, Charlotte." Mosey pushed back the screen and stepped out onto the veranda.

"And Mosey," Matthew appeared behind Charlotte, "you won't forget to ask Lieutenant Olivera…"

"I won't forget."

As Mosey closed the gate, her gaze drifted across the street to the grand house with the flight of stone steps.

Waite House it was called. She'd sold it herself after she'd helped Olivera solve the case of the owner's murder. The apprehension she had once felt upon looking at the house had completely disappeared now that the case was solved and the house was sold. She genuinely hoped the Raineses had moved on as well—as it seemed they had.

With little time to dawdle, she hurried along the street. The sun was barely beginning to set, and she needed about half an hour to catch up with Lauren and make it home before dark. As she approached the last dwelling on McAllister, she spotted Lauren's car in the drive. "Oh, good," she muttered, "Lauren's home." She pushed back the gate, and as soon as she entered the property, something—like a glimmer of light—caught her eye. To the right, around the area of the thicket, a light had flashed and gone out. "Wonder what that was." She walked in the direction of the thicket, but hearing a rustling in the bushes, hesitated. "Probably just a bird or a squirrel." At the edge of the trees, she stopped and carefully scanned the thicket. The wind had settled down, and the branches were scarcely moving. Then, catching sight of a shiny object on the ground close by, she bent down to see what it was. She was going to pick it up, but a swishing sound came from the undergrowth, and just as she stood, a tall figure loomed out of the darkness, arm raised. "No!" she screamed and dropped to the ground.

Chapter Nineteen

*McAllister Avenue*
*Tuesday, 6:00 p.m.*

When Olivera pulled up at Morris House, Mosey Frye was stretched out on the ground. She was conscious, apparently, given that she was reaching for the top of her head. Lauren Wilson, a few feet away, was aiming a gun toward the thicket.

"Over here, Lieutenant," Wilson shouted.

"Oh, my God!" Springer reached for his gun.

"Hold on, Springer." Olivera held up a hand.

"What in the name of—?" Springer broke off.

"Reagan, call 911. Get an ambulance over here." While keeping an eye on Wilson, Olivera hastened toward Mosey.

"Step out slowly," Wilson instructed. Adhering to her command, a man dressed in dark attire, a mask over his face, came out of the thicket.

Olivera drew his gun. "Handcuff him, Springer."

"Hands behind your back." Springer pulled the suspect into the clearing and handcuffed him. While reading him his rights, he guided him toward the squad car.

Mosey sat up.

"Don't get up." Olivera squatted on the ground beside her and checked her head. "You've got a nasty gash." He turned to Reagan. "Bring the first-aid kit, and did you call 911?"

"Yeah, Lieutenant, they're on their way."

"Good, this wound looks sort of bad." He pulled out his handkerchief and held it to the top of her head.

"Ouch!" Mosey cried. "You're about as gentle as Robert." She tried to get up but fell back to the ground.

"Hold on," Olivera urged. "The paramedics are coming."

"I don't need a paramedic," she huffed.

"Mosey," Wilson intervened, "listen to Lieutenant Olivera."

Olivera glanced up at Wilson. "You want to tell me what happened?"

"Isn't it obvious?" Wilson dropped to her knees beside Mosey.

"Humor me."

"I saw something in the bushes," Mosey said. "There was something on the ground, and I reached to pick it up."

"I don't suppose you saw who hit you."

Mosey shook her head.

"It was *that* guy, obviously," Wilson said.

"You stay put." Olivera cautioned Mosey, then standing, turned to Wilson. "You see anything?"

"I was in the house, in the kitchen. I heard a scream, grabbed the gun, and headed out the front door. He was standing over her. He must have heard me and ducked into the thicket. I yelled out, 'Stop or I'll shoot.' He stopped, and you know the rest."

"Did you recognize him?"

"Yes, I think I did."

"Who?"

"Paul Krueger."

Olivera sighed and glanced toward the squad car. "Tell Springer to check for identification," he instructed Reagan.

Following Olivera's orders, Reagan directed his steps to the squad car where Springer was shoving the suspect into the back seat. In a swift motion, Springer handed over the suspect's wallet to Reagan, who flipped it open and called back, "It's Paul Krueger."

"Tell Springer to hold on," Olivera called back to Reagan. "We'll wait here for the paramedics."

"I don't need a paramedic," Mosey insisted.

The sound of a siren pierced the evening air, rendering her insistence moot. As they waited, the setting sun cast an eerie glow over the unsettling scene before dropping behind the horizon.

"Mosey—" Olivera paused, realizing he'd been calling her Mosey, not Ms. Frye, as he usually did. "—the guy who allegedly assaulted you is Paul Krueger. Name ring a bell?"

"Yeah, it rings a bell. That's the guy—" Mosey turned toward Wilson, who was still kneeling at her side. "—the guy you told me about, the para…"

"Paraphiliac."

"So, he *was* the guy you saw," Mosey said.

Wilson nodded. "Sure looks like it."

"We'll get this sorted out at the station," Olivera said, "but you, Mosey, are going to Delta Infirmary."

Shortly thereafter, the first-aid squad pulled up, and Reagan, alongside two paramedics pushing a stretcher, came in their direction. "What we got here, Lieutenant?" one of the paramedics asked.

"Gash on the top of the head." Olivera looked at

Mosey. "I'll speak to you at the hospital."

"It's no big deal," he heard her say as they lifted her onto the stretcher. He turned to Wilson. "I'll have to take that firearm." He pulled a plastic bag from an evidence kit.

"I didn't fire it, Lieutenant."

He sighed. "Gun, please, Dr. Wilson."

Complying, she dropped it in the bag.

"Reagan, we need to look for the weapon. Search around the immediate area. See if you can find anything…a bottle, tree limb, whatever. Likely it'll have blood on it and fingerprints, so be careful when you bag it."

"Sure, Lieutenant."

"I need to speak to Dr. Wilson. I'll only be a minute."

Olivera followed Wilson in through the front door. When she switched on the foyer light, he said, "You've got electricity, I see."

"Finally," she exclaimed. "They came this morning. Have a seat." She pointed to a folding chair in the middle of the room.

He sat, then got up and walked to the window that faced the right side of the lot. "Perfect view of that woodsy area."

"Or, if you're out there" —she pointed— "you'd have a perfect view of my living room."

"So, that's what you think. Krueger was doing his voyeur thing."

"Of course."

He returned to the chair but, before sitting, looked at Wilson, who had perched on one of the lower rungs of the ladder. "Wouldn't you prefer the chair?"

She shrugged. "I'm okay."

"So," he began, then paused, reaching for his notepad and pen, "let me make sure I understand how this played out. You were inside." He turned to a fresh page and looked up. "Where exactly?"

"The kitchen."

"And you heard a scream."

"Right."

"Then?"

"I came in here for the gun." She nodded toward the mantel where he'd seen the gun the day before.

"I didn't expect you'd be needing it, but looks like it came in handy."

She nodded.

"Then you went outside—by way of the front door?"

"Yes."

"Because?"

"I could tell from the scream it'd come from that direction." She nodded toward the front.

"What did you see?"

"Well, first, Mosey, lying on the ground. Then I saw the guy."

"He was running away?"

"Starting to move away, but he hadn't gotten very far. He was no more than a couple of yards from where she was lying."

"And?"

"I yelled, 'Stop or I'll shoot,' and he stopped, then ducked back in the thicket."

"Did you recognize him right off?"

"No, but, of course, I had it in my head that it might be Krueger. I've been thinking that all along, but when

Grayson's body was found and then the cellar…"

"Yeah, I know what you mean. It hasn't been very clear, has it?"

"You don't know what to make of it either, I take it."

"No, I don't. We're gathering evidence, but the circle seems to be widening." He looked down at his notepad. "Tell me what you can about Krueger."

"I don't really have much to tell, other than what I told you yesterday. He was a post-doc at Rutherford, under my supervision. I suspected he had some mental issues."

"Paraphilia."

"Yes."

"Can you be more specific?"

"Are you familiar with paraphilia?" she asked.

"In broad strokes."

"It's not uncommon. There are several types, and some are more serious than others. I thought he might be a voyeur."

"Seems like he might." He thought for a second. "Did he bother you before?"

"Not me. One of his students. She claimed she'd seen him hanging around outside her dorm. She *thought* she'd seen him looking in her window but wasn't sure. It's hard to identify—"

"Yes," he interrupted. "I imagine it would be."

"Lieutenant, this sort of thing happens to women more than you think, but they rarely report it."

"*You* reported it." And, indeed, Wilson *had* reported it, first at Rutherford and then to him. Sad to say, his initial reaction to her complaint had been about as lukewarm as the other guy's—the psychology chair's.

"Yes, I did. But that first time, I might *not* have reported it if I'd been the victim. People don't take you seriously…"

He sat bobbing his head, then glanced over at the window. It was dark now. "Dr. Wilson, if I were you, I'd get some curtains up at those windows."

"You would? Men think about such things?"

He closed his notepad and tapped it on his knee. "Probably not."

"I didn't think so."

"One more thing." He paced toward the ladder, where Wilson was still perched, and then back toward the fireplace. "You told your supervisor about the incident with the student."

"That's right…Dr. Davis, the chair. You called him, right?"

"But Davis didn't do anything. Why not?"

"No hard evidence. The girl wasn't sure it was Krueger."

"But surely he must have called Krueger in, questioned him."

"He did, and Krueger denied it. Claimed the student had it in for him because he'd given her a low grade."

"And you didn't feel comfortable after that."

She nodded. "When administrators don't take you seriously…"

"Did anything specific happen that made you feel uncomfortable?"

"Specific? To me it felt specific. Hard looks, frowns, snubs, sarcasm, that sort of thing. I can't point to anything easily quantifiable if that's what you're getting at. But I wasn't imagining things. His behavior made me fearful, and I'm not one to wait around until…"

"What?"

"Until something horrific happens."

He stopped pacing and looked at Wilson. Her face was flushed, and she'd pulled in tight like a frightened animal. He'd been giving her the third degree, as if *she* were the suspect. But Krueger was the suspect, and she'd held him at bay with a gun until he and the guys could get there. "You know"—a faint smile hovered around his lips—"that was some good police work you did, Dr. Wilson."

She relaxed, took a breath, and stood up from the ladder. "Thanks, Lieutenant. I guess tonight we worked our first case together." She looked at him and smiled, and when he held out his hand, she shook it. Her smile broadened. "Sorry to have brought a bad element to Hembree," she added.

"I'll get your gun back to you right away. Just need to check the registration and examine it for prints, so I can fill in a few blanks on a form."

"No problem, but I would like to get it back as soon as possible."

"We'll rush it." He looked at his watch. "I tell you what, I need to get over to the hospital, check on Ms. Frye and see what she can tell me. Suppose we meet at the station in about an hour, hour and a half?"

"Sure," she agreed. "If you don't mind, please text me when you're ready. I'll keep working around here till you need me."

"Okay. I want you present when I question the suspect. We can put you in a room with a mirror. You can watch, offer an opinion."

"Certainly."

Olivera showed himself out and headed to the squad

car. Springer and Reagan were leaning against the front fender. "You find anything, Reagan?"

"Sure did." Reagan reached into the evidence box and lifted out a bag. "Piece o' hardwood. Spot of blood near the tip."

"You see anything else?"

"A cigarette butt, still warm, and this." He held up a bag with a squashed can.

Olivera took the bag. "A beer can looks like. I guess he was smoking cigarettes, drinking beer, and getting his jollies."

"Is this the same guy—?" Springer asked.

"Sure is," Olivera cut in. "The one Wilson suspected, Paul Krueger." Olivera bent to look at the suspect in the back seat. "Let's get this guy to the station. Put him in lockup. You read him his rights, didn't you, Springer?"

"Sure did, Chief."

"Okay. So I'm going to stop by the hospital, check on Ms. Frye, see if I can get a statement."

"You coming in after that, Chief?" Springer asked.

"Yeah, I'll be there shortly. Wilson, too."

Chapter Twenty

*Delta Infirmary*
*Tuesday, 6:30 p.m.*

As Olivera entered Delta Infirmary by the back door, Eads McGinnis was coming out. "Dr. McGinnis. Didn't expect to find you here this late."

"Nor I you," she responded. "What's up?"

"I'm going to check on Mosey Frye. Somebody conked her over the head at the Morris place. The ambulance squad brought her in."

"I hope it's not serious." Eads turned and headed back in, following him along as he walked toward Receiving.

Reaching the ward clerk's desk, he stopped. "Bonnie, I need to check on Anne Moseby Frye. She was brought in about half an hour ago."

"The doctor is with her now, but if you want to wait…" She glanced toward the waiting room, where Robert and Nadia sat looking rather glum.

"Sure, I'll wait. It won't be long, will it?"

"I can't tell you that."

"Well, I'll wait as long as I can."

Robert and Nadia got up and met Eads and him at the entrance to the waiting room. "Lieutenant," Robert said.

"Have you spoken with Mosey?" Olivera asked.

"Briefly. She called me on the way here. Some guy attacked her."

"From what we can surmise so far, he was in that woodsy area next to the house. He hit Mosey over the head with a chunk of wood. I don't suppose you know what she was doing there."

"I do," Nadia chimed in. "We were at the shop. Then Daddy, Dave Morell, and I left to go to the Tavernette, but Mosey wanted to stretch her legs. She took off on foot for Morris House, and we went on to the Tavernette."

"What time was that?"

"Well, we were locking up for the day. Must have been about five."

"And an hour later—" Olivera paused for a second. "—she gets hit over the head."

"You know Mosey, or maybe you don't. She could have easily stopped somewhere along the way."

"I called her about five thirty," Robert said. "She hadn't gotten home yet, hadn't called or texted. I thought it a little strange that she didn't return my call."

"Well, we should get some answers soon." Olivera took a deep breath and let it out.

"She has a lesion on the top of her head," Nadia said, "but otherwise she seems okay."

"Did either of you speak with her after they brought her in?"

"I did," Nadia said. "She complained of a headache."

"Do they suspect a concussion?" Olivera asked.

"Nothing indicates it so far, but they want to keep her overnight, and, of course, she won't hear of it."

Olivera looked at Robert. "So, you'll be taking her

home?"

"I will and watching her like a hawk."

"Good luck with that." He smiled and headed toward the door, where Eads was waiting. "I'd better get to the station. Lauren Wilson is coming in. I want her there when I question the suspect."

"You do?" Eads asked.

"She knows him."

"*Knows* him." She gave him a look of disbelief.

"This is the guy she told me about, the one from Rutherford, remember?"

"My word! So, he *did* follow her here."

"It seems that way." Olivera placed his hand in the small of Eads's back and guided her away from the waiting room. "Hold on a second." He stepped back to the door. "Robert, I'll call later. I need Mosey's account of what happened, and I'd like to speak to her tonight if she's up for answering a few questions."

Robert nodded, and Olivera joined Eads again in the corridor. "So, as I was saying, I bet what happened is Mosey, after she stopped wherever she stopped, hurried on to Morris House, saw something, went to investigate, and this guy, this Paul Krueger, stepped out of the bushes and hit her over the head."

"Huh." Eads gave Olivera a discerning look. "You sound, well, not entirely sympathetic."

He shook his head. "Of course, I'm…" He stopped.

"You're *not* sympathetic," she insisted.

Strangely, under the penetrating gaze of Eads, an expert at deciphering the truths of corpses, he suddenly found himself devoid of strength, as if *he* were the lifeless body. Utterly disarmed, how could he respond except with complete honesty? "Okay, okay, you're right. I'm not *entirely* sympathetic. Not that I would want any harm to come to her…or anyone else, for that matter."

"You think she had it coming," Eads said with a tone of disdain.

"No, no, no. *Not* that she had it coming. But, you know, sometimes a lesson learned is a good thing."

"As long as the person learning the lesson—"

"Don't say that." He raised a finger to her lips. "Hush, don't say that," he repeated. Then, in the dim hall between Emergency and the morgue, Olivera did what he'd been wanting to do for weeks—no, months, actually. The slightly emotional eruption in both him and Eads, triggered by their first real clash, brought a particular yearning to fulfilment. Lowering his hand from her lips, he looked into her eyes and kissed her, first gently, then passionately. She didn't resist—he wasn't sure whether out of shock or mutual longing—but he soon found out. For when she withdrew his arms from her waist, she didn't step away but, taking him by the hand, led him toward the door at the end of the hall.

That evening, Olivera was a little late getting back to the station, but Springer was still there waiting, having already processed the suspect, who was in the holding cell at the back. "What took you so long?" Springer asked.

Olivera checked his watch. "It hasn't been that long. I had to stop by Delta Infirmary, check on Ms. Frye. I told you that."

"She have anything to add?" Springer asked.

"I didn't get to question her. They were stitching her up. I'll try to see her tonight if she's up to it. Robert expects they'll be releasing her soon."

"Huh. It looked like a serious wound to me."

"It probably looked worse than it was. Lots of blood."

"Yeah, well, if they're letting her leave—"

"No word yet from Dr. Wilson?" Olivera cut in.

"Not yet."

"She's supposed to be here. I want her here when I question Krueger. Well, it's not that important. I think I'll go ahead."

"You want me in there?" Springer asked.

"No, wait for Wilson, and when she gets here, take her into the observation room. I want her to hear what he says. But go ahead and start the camera."

"Will do, Chief."

Olivera's cell phone buzzed. "It's a text from Wilson." He tapped his forehead. "Dang! I was supposed to text her and let her know I was here." He shook his head and sighed. "I'll go ahead and set up. Bring Krueger in as soon as I open the door. And when Wilson gets here, you two slip in *quietly*. I don't won't him to know he's being watched."

Olivera gathered up the folders Springer had prepared and, after pouring himself a coffee, headed to the interrogation room.

Meanwhile, Springer unlocked the holding cell and went in. "Chief's here," Olivera heard him say. "He wants to ask you a few questions." He led him into the room.

Olivera rose and gestured for Krueger to take a seat. Then Springer left closing the door behind him. "We're recording this. Do you mind?"

Krueger shook his head. "Why should I mind? I haven't done anything."

Olivera looked closely at the man. At Morris House, he'd gotten no more than a quick look. He was young, fair-complexioned, clean-shaven, like the professors at Blanchard more or less. He wore a striped shirt and a loosely fitting jacket, classic chinos, and oxfords. Except for the ski mask he'd been wearing when they'd dragged him out of the bushes, he might have been any instructor headed to the classroom. "Why were you wearing a ski mask if it was business as usual?"

"Oh, that." Krueger shrugged. "Just a joke."

"Not my idea of a joke." Olivera lifted his brow.

"I know Lauren. Ask her. She'll tell you."

"How do you know her?"

"We were at Rutherford together."

"And you were here to—"

"—pay her a visit."

"I see. So, she was expecting you?"

"Course not. That would have spoiled the fun. You must know what it's like. In your day, didn't schoolmates play pranks on one another?"

That stung. In *his day*, indeed. He breathed deep, then took a sip of coffee.

"I wouldn't mind a cup of that, if you've got any," Krueger said.

Olivera hoped Wilson had slipped in and was catching all this. Sociopathy *par excellence*. Hmm. What to ask next? He had a feeling that no matter what he asked, Krueger would have an answer as annoying and falsely innocent as the ones he'd given so far. Olivera lightly tapped the table, then looked him in the eye. "I hear you've been relieved of your services. Your post-doc has been terminated, no?"

He didn't squirm as Olivera had hoped, just smiled

and shrugged. "It wasn't my cup of tea, Lieutenant. Rather boring work. I left of my own accord."

"Indeed, and have you found another job?"

"Not yet, but I'm not in any hurry."

Olivera quickly assessed where the interview was going and decided to try another approach. "Tell me. You know, I'm guessing you've been around—well, I don't really know how long you've been preparing to give Dr. Wilson a surprise visit, drop in unexpectedly— but I was wondering. Did you happen to witness any of the shenanigans at her place? She's had us out to the house a couple of times. First time was yesterday morning. You didn't happen to see anything, did you?"

Krueger frowned. "What if I did?"

"Well, if you had information valuable to the investigation—"

"Ha," he smirked, "you're offering me a deal."

"I suppose you could say that—if you did, in fact, see something."

"Maybe I did."

"Like what?"

"You're referring to the old guy."

"That's right."

"I saw that."

"What exactly?"

"He was there, at the side of the house. Then another guy showed up, they argued, the old guy dropped down. Then the younger guy, well, I didn't see exactly. Maybe he checked the guy's pulse, whatever, then picked him up and carried him off. A little while later, the young guy left, sort of went running off toward the street."

"You didn't hear what they said, didn't get a good look at either of them? Must have been dark still."

"I got a good enough look. It was early but not dark. The old guy was sort of grubby, like a homeless person. Very thin, staggered around. The young guy was about my height, well-built, well-dressed."

"You think you could pick him out of a line-up?"

"Maybe. I didn't see him up close."

Olivera closed his folder and stood. "You may have been our only witness to a murder."

"Wait, murder?" he said, showing surprise.

It was the first time Olivera had seen *genuine* emotion on Krueger's face. "Yes." He nodded. "But then there's this other matter. You know you assaulted the blonde woman who came to pay Dr. Wilson a visit. We'll have to see if she's going to press charges. In the meantime, you'll be staying with us." Olivera approached the door. "I'll be right back. I'll see about getting you a coffee." He left the room, closing the door behind him, then opened the door to the observation room, which was dark so as to allow spectators to watch the interrogation. "I suppose you caught that," he said to Wilson, who was sitting in a straight-back chair pulled up to the window. Springer was standing behind her.

"I might have expected as much." She swept her hair back from her face, twisted it to one side, and let it flow over her shoulder. "He's not going to admit to anything that will place him in disfavor. He will always want to be in control. Was what he said helpful, I mean about Will Grayson?"

"Yes, it was. Who would have guessed that Paul Krueger would lead to a break in the case?" He sat in the chair next to Wilson. "Seems clear now what happened to Grayson. So"—he tapped the folder he was holding against the palm of his hand—"now it's a matter of finding this guy, a young man about Krueger's size. No wonder you thought it was Krueger."

"Yes, I suppose, between the two of us—Krueger and me—we ought to be able to identify the man. Doesn't sound like Grayson was murdered, does it?"

"No, it doesn't, and I can't think of any reason Krueger would have to lie about what he saw, can you?"

"No, to the contrary. The value of his testimony is his get-out-of-jail-free card, is it not?"

"I don't know. I imagine Ms. Frye will press charges. I'll be speaking to her a little later."

"How *is* Mosey, by the way?" Wilson asked.

"She was getting her head stitched up when I left the hospital. She's probably home by now."

Chapter Twenty-One

*Mosey and Robert's House*
*Tuesday, 8:00 p.m.*

It was getting onto eight o'clock when Olivera knocked on the door to Mosey and Robert's house. He had driven past it numerous times but had never actually gone in. However, having visited quite a few Victorians in the historic district, he had a rough idea of what to expect. Robert answered and warmly invited him into the living room. He took a quick glance around and realized that his assumptions were fairly accurate. The ceilings were impressively high, the windows reached from floor to ceiling, and the wooden trim added an elegant touch. And like the other homes he had seen, the furnishings were rather hefty—large armoires, consoles, and the like.

There, by the crackling fireplace, Mosey sprawled lazily on the sofa. She propped herself up and, instead of flashing him the usual smile, said with a sigh, "Lieutenant…I understand you've got the guy in custody."

"How are you feeling?" he asked.

"Oh, I'm okay. Have a seat." She motioned toward the armchair next to the sofa.

"I'm not taking Robert's spot, am I?"

"No, you're good."

"I won't stay long. I appreciate your seeing me. I

just wanted to ask a couple of things. But first, what did the doctor say about your injury?"

"He wants me sitting up, staying awake, in case I have a concussion. I'm sort of surprised I passed out. I've taken hard knocks on the head before."

"You have?"

"Horseback riding when I was a kid."

Robert came back into the room. "So, this guy—"

"Paul Krueger's his name." Olivera stood.

"Keep your seat," Robert said.

"He's not from around here," Olivera sat back down, "but Dr. Wilson knows him. I don't suppose you've spoken with her."

"Yes, she called to check on Mosey. Said the guy worked with her at Rutherford."

"That's right. I'd already contacted the college, found out he was no longer there. Dr. Wilson suspected from the start it could be him. But as it turns out, it probably *was not*."

Mosey rose off her pillow. "Not Krueger?"

"He was the one who assaulted you. That much we know. But Krueger claims he actually witnessed the altercation that might have preceded Will Grayson's demise. He's given a description of a man, a young man he saw arguing with Grayson yesterday morning."

"And you believed him?" Robert asked.

"Not sure what to believe, but his story makes sense and matches Dr. Wilson's. It's hard to imagine how he could have been aware of the details if he hadn't been there, hiding in the thicket."

"Yeah." Mosey nodded. "I see what you mean. So, you've got the guy in custody, but you still don't know who—"

"—killed Grayson, if in fact he was killed. Or how he and Grayson happened to be at Morris House."

"Huh. "So, you think this voyeur—I suppose you could call him that—might be willing to cooperate?"

"Looks that way, if we make it worth his while. And that's one thing I wanted to ask you about. Are you going to press charges?"

"You mean I have a choice?"

"Actually, yes, you and Dr. Wilson, too. If nobody presses charges—"

"—he walks away scot-free?" Robert said.

"Well, yes, if no one presses charges." Olivera turned to Mosey. "But…if you want to pursue it, I suggest you contact a lawyer, see if it's worth it to you. You may prefer to ask for a restraining order and compensation for damages."

"Yeah…I think I ought to speak to Carlotta before I decide one way or the other. How long have I got?"

"There's no rush. Check with Ms. Humphrey. In the case of third-degree battery, the complainant has a year, maybe more. She'll have to check the 2010 Arkansas Code."

"And you say Lauren might press charges?"

"For voyeurism, which would be a much lesser charge, a class A misdemeanor."

"Do you think it would stick?" Robert asked.

"I don't know. Given what Krueger claims…"

"What *does* he claim?" Mosey asked.

"According to him, he was just pulling a prank. He'd come to see Lauren, no harm intended. In the case of voyeurism, hiding near the dwelling wouldn't be enough."

"Not enough!" Mosey exclaimed.

Olivera shook his head.

"Well, if that be the case…"

"Talk to Ms. Humphrey." Olivera stood. "I'll hold him as long as I can."

Robert got up and walked with Olivera to the door. "You'll let us know, should you release him."

"Certainly, and sorry to disturb." Olivera looked at Mosey, then Robert. "She'll be okay?"

"Yes, I think she's more concerned about her appearance than the cut. They shaved off quite a bit of hair."

"It'll grow back." Olivera smiled, put on his hat, and stepped out.

Reaching the bottom of the steps, he pulled out his cellphone and tapped in Eads's number. "Eads, it's Gus."

"Did you talk to Mosey?"

"Yeah, just leaving her and Robert's place. I don't suppose you'd want to grab a drink somewhere. I know it's late, but I thought we might run over the evidence."

"Sure, it's not that late. I'm in my car, close to the Square."

"Shall we meet at the Tavernette?"

"Yeah. See you in a bit."

When Olivera got to the Tavernette, Eads had already taken a corner booth and was sipping a mojito. "It's mojito night, half-price." She raised her glass. "You want one?"

He sighed and slid in next to her.

"Lieutenant, so close?"

He grinned. "Do we really care?"

"This is a very small town." She took another sip. "Don't wanna set the tongues to wagging."

He got up and moved across from her, waving to the

bartender as he did. "Bring me a draft, please."

"Beer, eh?"

"It feels like a beer day. I've been up since five."

"So early?"

"I couldn't sleep. Trying to sort out this business…"

"Yes, and by the way—"

"You found something?" he asked.

"Yes."

"You didn't tell me."

"We were otherwise occupied."

"Which reminds me. We can't let *this*, I mean, you and me, get in the way of—"

"Of course, not," she cut in.

"Whew!" He laughed. "I'm glad that's settled." He laughed again.

"You are terrible."

He continued laughing. "So—" He put on a half-serious face. "—what was it you found?"

"It was more what I *didn't* find. I finished the autopsy, went over Grayson's clothing, checked his nails, and so on. There wasn't the slightest sign of an altercation. No grass stains, bruising—which would have shown up by now. He wasn't dragged. If someone carried him to the shed and placed him on the floor, it was done gently."

"Hmm. I suppose that jibes with what Krueger had to say."

"Krueger?"

"Yeah, he claims he saw the whole thing. Grayson apparently met someone at Morris House…a young man, tall, well-built, nicely dressed. He and Grayson talked, Grayson collapsed, the man checked his pulse, then picked him up and carried him off, evidently to the shed."

"And Krueger witnessed the whole thing?"

"Yep. Moreover, the evidence and Wilson's statement corroborate what he had to say."

The bartender arrived with Olivera's beer. "Start a tab for you, Lieutenant?"

"Sure." Olivera lifted the glass. "You care for something, Eads?"

"No, I'm good." She took another sip of her mojito. "So, I suppose you now need to find this *other* person."

"Do I?" He sipped his beer.

For a second, she seemed to be tossing it around in her head. "I see what you mean."

"The so-called *crime* may have vanished. No murder. Voyeurism, possibly. But I doubt it would stick. Third-degree battery if Mosey presses charges."

"Huh." She crinkled one eye, then the other, as if envisioning one scenario, then the other. "There's *more* to this," she said, apparently convinced.

"Yeah, possibly. You have to wonder what Grayson and the other guy were doing there, why he—the other guy—didn't report the death. And then there's the cellar, the hidden alcove, and the paintings, which, apparently, have stirred up quite a bit of interest. Come to think of it," he cocked his head, "this fellow from New Orleans— I met him at Nadia Abboud's shop this afternoon—fits the description. Young, tall, well-built, nicely dressed…"

"Wait a minute. What cellar, what alcove?"

"When we were examining the crime scene, we found a door flat on the ground under the porch. It led to a cellar—a rather odd-looking place if you ask me. Wilson knew nothing about it. We went back over there to check it out and found an alcove hidden behind a bookcase, which contained, strangely enough, a couple of old paintings. Casta paintings. Ever heard of them?"

She nodded. "I saw an exhibit in New Orleans some years ago."

"The two were by the same painter. Mateo Cardoso, early nineteenth century. Nadia Abboud was able to fill me in." He paused to sip his beer. "You know there seems to be a connection between the Bilyeus and the paintings. Nadia's father, Toni—he was at the shop, too—purchased one at Arnold Bilyeu's estate sale and sold it some years later to David Morell. He owns a gallery in New Orleans."

"That's where the exhibit was," Eads broke in, "at the Royal Street Gallery. The owner's name was Morell."

"You don't say. Morell's son is here, Dave Junior." He shook his head. "I'm going to need a *map* to figure this one out."

She opened her purse and, pulling out an index card, laid it on the table in front of him, then handed him a pen.

"Hey, that's convenient." He picked up the pen, ready to start sketching the crime scene, but before he could even make a mark, something caught his attention. Two men approached the bar, and one, the younger of the two, ordered a Bloody Mary and a martini. Olivera looked at Eads and discreetly pointed with the pen toward the bar.

Eads looked, then turned back, mouthing, "Bilyeu and DeGroat."

Olivera nodded.

"What are *they* doing here?" she whispered.

"Working on the Summer House."

"Maybe you should pay them a visit."

He frowned but, after thinking about it, whispered back, "Not a bad idea."

"Go over there." She tilted her head toward the bar. "Tell them."

He considered her suggestion, then shook his head. "I'd rather surprise them."

Her eyes widened as she nodded approvingly.

Chapter Twenty-Two

*Mosey and Robert's House*
*Wednesday, 9:00 a.m.*

Mosey's stitched-up scalp didn't hold her back for long. She was up by eight the following morning and, by nine, was seeing Robert off to school. "How long before classes start?" She washed the last of the breakfast plates and set it in the drain.

He pulled his cellphone out of his pants pocket. "Let me see." He tapped the screen. "One week exactly, Wednesday, January 13."

"Reckon Lauren will show up for the general faculty meeting today?" Mosey leaned over the sink and peeked out the window. The clouds had parted, and the sun, letting in a little blue, was flickering across the neighbor's white picket fence.

"I would think . Why not?"

"She's got a lot going on." She turned to face Robert, who had slipped on his overcoat and was checking his pockets for his keys.

"Well, she'd better be there. A no-show wouldn't be good. Everyone's expecting her."

"Like who?"

"Like everyone—the dean, the department chair, her colleagues in social sciences…"

"Yeah, I guess so." Mosey sighed. "I was thinking

of going back over there. You know they discovered a cellar we knew nothing about."

Robert had picked up his briefcase but dropped it on the table. "Mosey"—he gave her a hard look—"don't you set foot on that property. And do not under any circumstances go snooping around *under* the house. That's trespassing, for crying out loud."

"Don't get so worked up. I'm not going to do anything dangerous…or illegal."

"Oh, yeah? You don't think. You just plow right in."

"I do not." She walked toward the door and, picking up his briefcase, draped the strap over his shoulder.

He shook his head and groaned, "Mosey, please. Take the day off. Let yourself heal."

"I'm okay. Go on to work." She gave him a little push. "I'll see you this afternoon."

Robert kissed her on the check and left by the kitchen door.

Once he was out of the driveway, she grabbed up her jacket and headed down the steps. Though the sun was out, the sky was still looking overcast. Would she need an umbrella? Nah. Her jacket had a hood. She got in her truck and cranked the motor but, instead of pulling out, sat idling in the drive. She had an uneasy feeling, like, well, she didn't want to be seen. It wasn't that she cared so much about her partially shaved head, it was more like she knew she shouldn't be out and about "in her condition." But that was dumb. She wasn't bedridden or anything. She just had a little cut on her scalp. She glanced at herself in the rear-view mirror and raked her bangs from side to side, then checked her lipstick. She took out a tube and added a layer of glimmering peach, then pulled up her collar and slipped on her tam. "Ouch."

The wound was sore. She carefully fitted the hat over the bandage. "There now, I look perfectly fine."

*Yeah, perfectly heedless. You heard what Robert said.*

"Yeah, and I wasn't the only one, obviously. Daddy, do you have to be such a snoop?"

*As I live and breathe, child! You are the most hypocritical individual who ever drew breath.*

Oh, Daddy, stop exaggerating.

*I'm not exaggerating. Besides, you have no business going back over there.*

"Over where?"

*Kit Morris's.*

"I'm not going to Kit Morris's. I'm going to Shepherd Realty, and anyway, it's not Kit Morris's. It's Lauren Wilson's, and I am perfectly welcome to go over there if I want." Mosey cast her eyes toward the seat beside her, not that that there was anything to see, but the voice seemed to come from that direction. "By the way, I don't suppose you were ever in the secret cellar."

*Of course, I was in the cellar, and there's nothing* secretive *about it.*

"So, how come it was never mentioned? I sold a house that had a cellar, and I didn't even know."

*Those sisters of his forgot all about it. They never went down there.*

"What was it—a man cave?"

*Yes, as a matter of fact, that's exactly what it was, a place Kit and company could get away from the womenfolk.*

"And why the hidden alcove?"

*Now, I don't know about that.*

As the voice began to fade, Mosey hurriedly asked

one last question. "And the casta paintings, what about them?"

No answer.

She soon came to Shepherd Realty, parked, and got out. Saffron was already there and—wonders never cease—John Earle was there, too. She pushed through the door, unbuttoned her jacket, and hung it on the rack in the corner. "Morning, everybody." She started to take off her tam but left it on. "How are you, John Earle?" She approached the stool where he was sitting.

He twisted around. "The burning question would be *how are you?* Now ain't that right?" His straight-line half-smile spread into a full grin.

"You heard, then," Mosey said.

Saffron laughed. "The whole town has heard. You think you can go screaming through town in an ambulance—"

"Oh, hush," Mosey cut in. "It wasn't that big a deal. I could have gone to the emergency room on my own steam."

"So, why didn't ya?" John Earle asked.

"Olivera insisted."

"You're never gonna learn, are ya?" He twisted back around and looked at Saffron, who was shaking her head *no.*

"Well"—Mosey smirked—"it's a good thing *somebody* in this town has got some gumption."

John Earle and Saffron broke into laughter.

"I'm not kidding. Look at all the weird stuff—the cellar, poor old Will's demise, not to mention a paraphiliac in town—what about that?"

John Earle looked back at Mosey. "What's a paraphiliac?"

"A voyeur, well, this one's a voyeur. He's the one who hit me over the head."

"I thought voyeurs—" Saffron waved her fingers in the air. "—were sort of…"

"Creepy?" John Earle interjected.

"That, too, but *bashful* is what I was thinking."

"Well, this one wasn't bashful," Mosey said.

"This guy—what was his name?" John Earle asked.

"Paul Krueger," Mosey said.

"I heard he's a *friend* of Dr. Wilson's."

"Not a friend." Mosey shook her head. "They worked together at Rutherford."

"So, he's a shrink?"

"He's in psychology."

"Psychologists for the most part," Saffron asserted, "*are* crazy. "Didn't you know that? They go into psychology hoping to heal their own fevered brains."

"I didn't know you held such a low opinion of the field—my major, by the way," Mosey said.

"The two psychologists I know of, Lauren Wilson and Paul Krueger, are not the most stable individuals."

"Lauren's okay," Mosey said.

"She's nice enough, but that woman…she needs to get her head screwed on straight."

"It's not her fault that guy followed her here."

"Maybe not, but everything out of the ordinary that's happened around here lately involves her."

"Her and Mosey." John Earle broke into a laugh.

"Now that you've had your little joke"—Mosey glared at John Earle—"can we get down to business? What about the cellar? You never called me back."

"I did too and left a voice message."

"Oh, I guess I haven't checked my messages since

last night. So, what did you say?"

"I can't see you'd have any liability issues, given the owners made no mention of a cellar. And besides that, I can't see why Dr. Wilson would mind."

"Yeah, I guess not. So, you didn't know about the cellar?" She looked at John Earle.

"Well, I guess it skipped my mind. At one time that cellar had a bit of a reputation. It was a hideaway for all sorts of shenanigans, back around the time of the war."

"I guess your father was part of that."

"Daddy was too much of a businessman to squander his money on gambling and liquor."

"Huh."

"But he did have a few stories to tell."

"Really?" Mosey asked.

"Yeah, mostly about Kit and Arnold."

"What about Colton, Matthew Raines's older brother? He was one of the regulars, showed up in some of the pictures we found, didn't he, Saffron?"

"Who you talking about?" Saffron looked up from her paperwork.

"Colton Raines, Matthew's brother."

"I have no idea."

Mosey turned back to John Earle. "You must have known him."

"Not really. He's been gone from here a good long while."

"What'd he do?" Mosey asked.

"For a living? Good question. I don't remember hearing any mention—"

"I wonder if he's rich like Matthew," Mosey cut in.

"Why such an interest in Colton Raines?" John Earle asked.

"He's the only one of the poker players I don't know. Grandaddy, Mr. Kit, Mr. Arnold, Eads's grandfather…"

"Whatcha talking 'bout?" he asked.

"The poker players in the photograph. We found a bunch of old photographs in some of the drawers at the Morris place."

"Oh." John Earle shrugged and, standing, walked his stool back to the kitchenette. "I got to run, ladies. Mosey, don't worry about the cellar. If Dr. Wilson has any concerns, I suppose we could have it checked out."

"Okay, that makes me feel better, but before you go, tell me something. You know anything about casta paintings? That's what they found in the cellar—besides a bunch of old books."

"Old books?"

"Yeah, according to Olivera, it's full of books, floor to ceiling. The paintings were hidden in a secret compartment behind a bookcase."

"Casta paintings," he repeated. "Yeah, I've heard of 'em. Seems like my grandparents might have had a few. Daddy got rid of 'em, didn't want 'em in the house."

"Unsightly things, if you ask me," Saffron said.

"Not all of them," Mosey said. "That one of Fernanda de Lobos was quite stunning."

"True."

"You remember it?" Mosey looked at Saffron.

"I saw it in the shop, when Mr. Toni still had it."

"Yeah, that's where I saw it." Mosey paused, then continued. "You know it's funny about those snapshots. The guys in uniform—they all looked happy. Hard to believe something, well, untoward was going on."

"Well, who knows." John Earle said. "Not that it

was anybody's business."

"The sisters didn't go down there, before or after Mr. Kit died. I wonder if they knew something or suspected something. And all those pictures Kit left behind. You should have seen Miss Eleanor's and Miss Peggy's faces when I laid them out on the table in the sun parlor. It was like, 'What the devil are *those* doing here?' "

"Mosey, don't go stirring things up, for God's sake," John Earle said. "Everybody's got pictures they'd just soon get rid of." He put on his hat and headed out. "See you ladies later."

"Saffron," Mosey said, "I'm going over there. I want to see that cellar with my own two eyes."

"If you say so. But leave me out of it."

"What's the matter? You scared of a little old cellar?" Mosey perched on the edge of Saffron's desk. "Nothing's down there but some moldy old books."

"Watch out for perverts." Saffron got up. "I'm taking an early lunch."

"Early lunch? Where are you going?"

"Never you mind. I got a little business to take care of."

"Whatever." Mosey waved goodbye to Saffron and, getting up, walked toward her office. "I guess I'd better check my messages and open my mail while I'm here."

She had no more than settled in front of her computer when she remembered she needed to speak to her step-aunt Carlotta. She picked up the phone and called Dot. "Dot, it's Mosey. How you doing?"

"Good, but what about you?"

"My lord, you've heard, too?"

"Carlotta mentioned it to me this morning. Are you

okay?"

"I'm fine. It's just a cut. They stitched it up. I didn't have to stay overnight. They wanted me to, but I couldn't see the point. I feel fine."

"No concussion?"

"My head was harder than that stick, ha."

"You be careful, Mosey. Head injuries don't always manifest right away."

"Listen, Dot, I was thinking about dropping by. Is Carlotta there?"

"She is. You want to talk to her?"

"I'd rather drop in if you think—"

"She's got some appointments after lunch, but you could probably talk to her now. Hold on."

Mosey held the phone till Dot came back on the line.

"Come on over. She's free."

"Perfect. I'll be there in ten."

Mosey got in her truck, wheeled around the corner to the square, and parked in front of Frye, Frye, and Humphrey. Taking the stairs, well, not by two this time, she ascended slowly to the second floor, gave a quick knock, and opened the glass door. "Dot?"

"Mosey? Let me see your head." She scooted back from her desk and stood.

Mosey took off her tam and angled the top of her head toward Dot.

"They shaved it," Dot gasped. "Looks inflamed to me. You better watch that. Are they going to change the bandage for you?"

"They didn't say anything about that. Just told me to come in next week to get the stitches out."

"Well, keep it clean, and if I were you, I'd get Robert to change that bandage. Or go over to the pharmacy.

215

They'll change it for you."

"Don't worry about it. It's okay. Is Carlotta ready for me?"

"Yes." Dot sat back down. "Go right in."

Mosey knocked on the open door. "Hi. Thanks for seeing me on short notice."

Carlotta motioned for her to come in. "Mosey, I'm so sorry about your little accident."

"How'd *you* hear, by the way?"

"The police dispatcher."

Mosey raised her brow. "I swear. The whole town knows."

"It's nothing to be ashamed of." Carlotta grinned. "We all get conked over the head sooner or later."

Mosey threw up her hands. "Carlotta, not you, too." She sat in the upholstered chair nearest Carlotta's desk.

Carlotta laughed. "Mosey, get used to it. Your reputation precedes you. How many incidents does this make?"

Mosey sighed and, propping her chin on her fist, looked over at Carlotta. "I guess there've been a few."

"But now that I see you're okay, I can relax." She joined Mosey at the low round table and, sitting in the chair next to hers, gave her a pat on the shoulder. "I'm glad you dropped by. How can I help?"

"I talked to Olivera last night. He suggested I speak to you about pressing charges—or not."

"Yes, that *is* an issue in cases of third-degree battery when no real harm is done, and I'm assuming—"

"Well, harm? I'd say there's no *real* harm, except for the emergency room bill."

Carlotta chuckled. "You could ask for damages, see if we could settle out of court. It'd save us some time and money. You don't know the guy, right?"

"No, I don't know him, but Lauren Wilson, the new owner of Morris House, knows him. They worked together. She quit her job and came here *because* of him. She turned him in to the department head."

"What for?"

"She suspected paraphilia. She didn't go into it very deeply, but I suppose she thought he was a peeping Tom."

"And maybe he is." Carlotta looked concerned.

"I'm not so sure now. Olivera isn't convinced. He wasn't sure it'd stick if Lauren pressed charges. The guy was in her yard at least twice…the morning they found Will Grayson in the tool shed and yesterday evening. But she never actually saw him peeping in the window. So, that's what I'm here for. Should I press charges for battery?"

"You certainly could. You have an airtight case. I guess it depends on what you want."

"Maybe we should ask Olivera to do a background check."

"Yes, that's where I would start. And there's no rush. There is, however, another consideration I should mention. The possibility of retaliation."

Mosey's eyes widened. "Ooh…I don't like the sound of that."

"If the guy is the least bit paranoid," Carlotta continued, "he might want to get you back. If you don't press charges, it's unlikely you'll hear from him again. Those are the statistics. Retaliation is a real possibility. And it sounds to me like this guy could have a screw loose. Coming all the way from Philadelphia—"

"How'd you know that?"

"It was in the paper." She reached for the folded newspaper on the table. "You didn't see it?"

"No, I didn't see it."

Carlotta opened the paper to the second page. "Didn't say much"—she pointed to the article—"but it did give his name and so on."

Mosey took the paper. "Tabb Wilson." She read the name of the reporter who covered local news. "Great."

"He doesn't have much to report on in Hembree, poor fellow."

Mosey scanned the short article and, folding the paper, laid it back on the table. "As you were saying?"

"Yeah, the fact that he came all the way down here to rattle Wilson... Sounds like that was what he was up to."

"Maybe."

"If he wanted to do serious harm," Carlotta continued, "he would have gotten in and out as quickly as possible. But hanging around the house off and on for at least two days, I don't think he was up to anything serious."

"I see your point. But why, then, did he hit me over the head?"

"*Ask* him."

"No, thanks. I don't want to lay eyes on him."

"You didn't see him?"

"No, not really. I got a quick look before he hit me, but he was wearing a mask."

"He might have panicked. That happens sometimes. He probably was more afraid of you than you of him."

"Ha. That's what they say about snakes. I didn't even know he was there, or I would have called the police."

"Yeah, I suppose there are some unanswered questions, but I'm sure Olivera will get to the bottom of it."

"Let me ask you about something else if you don't mind. You know anything about the Morrises? I mean, that house is the *real mystery* if you ask me. When Olivera was checking around the yard after they found Will Grayson's body, he found a cellar, and in the cellar—get this—a secret compartment with two paintings."

"What sort of paintings?" Carlotta tilted her head. "Are they worth anything?"

Mosey nodded. "I would say yes, but what do I know? We could ask Toni Abboud. He appraised them at some point. But, if they're valuable—and I think they must be—why didn't Mr. Kit display them or sell them instead of sticking them in an alcove? I'm sure he could have used the money. And here's another thing. According to Toni, the paintings belonged to the Bilyeus."

"*Them* again!" Carlotta shook her head. "You know it hasn't been that long since I gave the Bilyeu files a thorough going over, but I guess I could take another look. After Ninon's death, I thought Hembree had seen the last of that family, but you know her cousins, A. B. and Cecil, are back in town. They've started work on the restoration."

"Of Larkspur?"

Carlotta nodded. "And I guess they'll be in and out of here for a while."

"Where are they staying?"

"The Tavernette, where else?"

"Hmm. I guess I don't really know them well

enough to approach them, though I did handle the transfer of the property."

"If you approached them, what would you say?"

"Good question."

"Look, if you think the paintings are at the heart of this—whatever *this* is—get Nadia involved. She and Toni ought to know…if there's anything *to* know."

"They *are* involved, actually. They've already seen the paintings. I guess I need to get back to Nadia. You know, for once I thought I'd sold a house without complications, but it's turning out to be the most perplexing of the lot."

"You could back away, leave it to Olivera."

"Yeah, and maybe I will. Thanks, Carlotta." Mosey smiled and, getting up, moved toward the door. "I appreciate your help."

"So"—Carlotta stood—"give what I said some thought, and if you decide you want to press charges, I'd be glad to help you with that."

"Thank you. I kinda doubt I do, but I'll let you know."

On her way out, passing Dot's desk, Mosey stopped and gave Dot a quick hug. "Thanks, Dot."

"Was Carlotta able to help?"

"She surely was. Carlotta always has good advice."

"Take care of yourself, Mosey."

As Mosey left, she glanced back at Dot and smiled again, hoping to give her some reassurance. "I'll be okay. Don't worry."

Chapter Twenty-Three

*Police Station*
*Wednesday, 9:00 a.m.*

Olivera took his time getting to work. Tuesday had been a long day, and he'd wanted to get a full night's sleep before tackling the Grayson case. It was around nine when he arrived and, passing reception, tipped his hat to Ms. Hill. "It's nice to have you back. You have a good vacation? Where was it you went?"

Ms. Hill looked up from her computer. "Thanks, Lieutenant. We didn't go anywhere. A 'staycation,' I think they call it."

"That's the best kind." He chuckled and walked on toward his cubicle. He waved to Springer and Reagan but didn't stop to chat or to pour himself a cup of coffee. He was intent on settling in and getting something down on the index card Eads had given him the night before. He fished in his pocket for the card but before sitting down, glanced over at the evidence board he and Springer had cleaned off earlier in the week. So far, there wasn't much on it, just a picture of the Morris house and tool shed. Remembering the photograph Eads had given him at the morgue, he felt in his breast pocket and retrieved the picture of Grayson stretched out on the floor of the shed. He thought for a moment. What he really wanted to know was *who* put him there and why he'd failed to report the death. Who leaves a body to rot in a tool shed? It seemed to him that hiding the body was a fact that couldn't be ignored. So, how was he going to find this *other man*, as Eads had called him. The procedure itself wasn't all that complicated, but whether it would produce the desired results was an altogether different matter. First, he ought to go back to the shed, go over it with a fine-tooth comb. Then he'd interview his only suspect, Paul Krueger, and see if he could provide a better description of the man he'd seen in Wilson's yard.

"Come in here a second, Springer," Olivera called out.

Springer came to the door. "What you need, Chief?"

"A picture of Paul Krueger, and I'm going to question him again before we let him go."

"Let him go?"

"I seriously doubt Wilson or Frye will press charges."

"Why not?"

"Wilson doesn't have much of a case for voyeurism. Krueger was in the woods near the house, but that's as far as it went, at least that's all he's admitting to, and she never saw him at the window."

"Huh."

"Frye's going to talk to Carlotta, but I can pretty much guess what she's gonna tell her."

"What's that?"

"Not worth the time, plus, the possibility of retaliation… Well, you get the picture."

"We're letting him go, then?"

"Not quite yet. I'll give it a few hours."

"You want the mug shot?"

"Yeah, for the evidence board."

"I'll get it for you."

"And, while you're at it, a cup of coffee."

Springer left the cubicle, and Olivera scooted up to his desk. He glanced down at the blank card before him and, picking up a pencil, sketched in the house, the yard, the porch running along the side of the house, the tall stretch of latticework below the porch, the tool shed, and the edge of the thicket.

Springer set the mug on Olivera's desk and craned to see the card. "That's pretty good, Chief."

"Thanks." Olivera reached for the mug, held it between his palms for a second, then set it down. "What do you reckon his motive was?"

"Whose motive?"

"This other guy, the one Krueger saw."

"*Claimed* to see," Springer corrected.

"Good"—he smiled at Springer—"very good."

"We only have his word for it, don't we, Chief?"

"Exactly. So, suppose we search the area again. We'll start with the tool shed, see if we can come up with evidence to support Krueger's story."

"But we already looked."

"We did"—Olivera nodded—"but now, taking what Krueger had to say into consideration, I'd be willing to take another look. We miss stuff, do we not?"

"Yeah, we do." Springer nodded. "You want to head over there now?"

"Not quite. I need to think through some things."

Once Springer had left, Olivera tacked the mug shot on the board under *Suspects*, though he didn't think of Krueger as a suspect really. "In fact," he muttered to himself, "*witness* might suit him better." He picked up the card, flipped it over, and made a rough sketch of the cellar. As he did, it occurred to him that the suspects and witnesses were for the most part *dead*, like Grayson, who seemed to be the last in a series of victims caught up in something more, something Olivera was barely beginning to catch sight of. He had no idea what this bigger scenario was or when it might have started, but he had a feeling about it. And to help fill in the missing pieces, he would need to depend on those who were still around…sideliners mostly, like the Morris sisters. He needed to get over to the Magnolia and find out precisely what they knew. Eads's father, Mosey Frye, Nadia and Toni Abboud… They, too, might know something pertinent to recent events that had been set in motion maybe around the time of the war…or even earlier than that. The blessed casta paintings were nineteenth-century, *por Dios!*

He took a couple of sips of coffee and, leaving the index card on his desk, got up and reached for his hat. "Springer."

"Yeah, Chief." Springer peeked over the top of the partition.

"I'm running out for a bit. I oughta be back in an hour or so. In the meantime, I'd like you and Reagan to go back to Morris House. Start with the tool shed. See if you can find anything at all that seems like it might not belong there."

"Anything that seems like it don't belong there."

"Yes, and bag and label anything you find."

"Sure thing, Chief."

That taken care of, Olivera went directly to the morgue. His conversation with Eads the night before had been truncated by the appearance of A. B. Bilyeu and Cecil DeGroat. He wanted to find out if she had anything else to say about the autopsy, i.e., if Grayson's body had anything more to tell.

When he arrived, she was hunched over her microscope. "Morning." He was tempted to slip his arm around her waist or kiss her on the cheek. But he stopped himself, having decided that *this* was not going to get in the way of *that*, or vice versa. He'd said it, and she'd apparently agreed.

"Morning, Lieutenant."

"How's it going?" He hung his hat on the corner rack and joined her at the counter.

She looked up. "I wouldn't be surprised if Grayson was poisoned."

"Poisoned?"

"I found some residue on his face, not sure what it is, but I've read about this sort of thing."

"What makes you think he was poisoned? Couldn't this residue be something else?"

"Yes, but given that I haven't found a specific cause of sudden death…"

"He didn't have a heart attack or a stroke?"

"When a person dies of a heart attack, there are certain things you expect to find, like a blood clot in the coronary arteries or an enlarged heart, a breakdown of the vessels."

"And I suppose you haven't found any of that."

"Nothing."

He paced away, stopped, and looked back. "No sign of a stroke, either?"

She answered with a shake of her head. "No sign of an ischemic stroke, no bleeding in the tissue, no tumor."

"And this residue?"

"I'm curious to see what it is. I saw a case once, in

medical school, of a person who died from exposure to sarin. It's a nerve gas. It's been around for a while. The Germans invented it."

"You mean like…for extermination?"

"No, it was developed as a pesticide, 1938. That's not to say—"

"—that in the wrong hands…"

"Right."

"So, how can you know?"

"I'll send off blood and tissue samples."

"How long will that take?"

"I'll see if they can let us know right away. If someone around here has sarin in his possession, we'd want to know."

"What are you thinking?" he asked.

"It's dangerous. There was an incident in Japan not long ago."

"I remember." He paced silently along the counter and, at the end, stopped with his back to Eads.

"What's the matter?"

"References to World War II. The photographs, now this poison. I wonder if it started then, this…"

"What?"

He turned around. "This morning at the station, I was working on my *map* of the crime scene, and suddenly it occurred to me that this situation—not sure *what* to call it—is somehow rooted, let's say, in the distant past, before either of us was born."

"Okay, so—"

"Will Grayson's connection with Morris House goes back to Kit Morris's time. Kit evidently took a bunch of pictures of his World War II buddies, but he didn't go to war. Arnold Bilyeu, either."

"Was Grayson in any of the pictures?"

"I don't think he was born yet. He might have been in some of the later pictures."

"But you think Will was left holding the bag, so to speak?"

"Holding *what* bag?"

"Taking care of unfinished business."

"Yeah, something like that. We've gotten some indications that something illegal was going on in that cellar. Toni Abboud thought so. Gambling…and he was asked to go over there once, to appraise the very paintings we found in the alcove. Since the paintings once belonged to Arnold, and Arnold, it's been established, was hard up for money, I wonder if he let Kit have them to cover a debt."

"Well, let's suppose that's true, that Arnold passed the paintings to Kit in payment of a gambling debt. That doesn't explain why, after Arnold died, Kit didn't sell them or—"

"Yeah," Olivera said, "especially since Kit was apparently hard up, too." He shrugged. "I keep coming to a dead end. Too bad the person who could tell us is dead." He glanced toward the gurney. "But you know what? That could give us motive. Somebody killed Grayson to shut him up."

"That's one possibility, but here's another. Somebody might have killed him to get him out of the way."

"Yeah…out of the way, so *they* could get the paintings."

"Or maybe the paintings had nothing to do with it."

"Yeah, I guess we have no *real* proof…"

"We don't. We only know that Grayson was at the

house at an unusual time of day and the presumed assailant was there, too. Grayson ended up dead. The presumed assailant hid the body and ran off without reporting the death—"

"—or taking the paintings."

"Wilson's presence," she continued, "would have likely put an end to that if, in fact, that was his intention."

"And now the paintings have been discovered and taken away. So now what?"

She shrugged. "I don't know. I suppose you could set a trap for him, use the paintings as bait."

He leaned back against the counter. "That's not a bad idea, not a bad idea at all. I wonder if Nadia Abboud could be convinced—"

"—to provide a trap for an art thief?"

He raised his brow. "Might be worth a try."

"I don't know. Sounds dangerous." Eads frowned. "Maybe you should wait till the toxicology report comes back. If this guy has access to sarin…"

"Yeah"—he shook his head—"I see what you mean. I suppose I could run it by Nadia."

"My guess is she's going to balk at the idea. Now, Mosey, on the other hand…"

He chuckled. "I wonder how she's doing."

"I saw her on the Square this morning."

"Indeed. I wonder if she's spoken with Carlotta."

"She was near there. I wouldn't be surprised."

"Maybe I should speak with Carlotta."

"Yeah, maybe Grayson had a will. I sort of doubt it, though. He probably never set foot in a law office."

"Maybe he didn't have a will, but I wonder if Kit Morris mentioned him in *his* will."

"My guess would be he left everything to his

sisters."

"More likely. It wouldn't hurt to ask, though. But you know, I think I'll start with the sisters."

"Go gently."

"I will—you know that."

She smiled.

Chapter Twenty-Four

*Magnolia Nursing Home*
*Wednesday, 10:00 a.m.*

Olivera found himself back at the Magnolia Nursing Home, and as he strolled across the gravel lot toward the entrance, his mind wandered to the first time he had visited last November. It was Mosey Frye who suggested he seek Martin Eldridge's advice concerning the incident that had occurred at Sunny Banks. That visit turned out to be more beneficial than he had expected. If only he could manage to achieve something similar now...

As he ascended the steps of the beautiful old building, he paused to experience the emptiness of the landscape. With the growing season soon to begin, he could imagine lushness all around, but now, it was a vast plain of barrenness with little more in sight than a few deciduous trees, ochre grass, and tilled rows with puddles of water gathering in the low spots.

Entering the nursing home, he removed his hat, then crossed the soft carpeting to the receptionist's desk. "I'd like to speak to the Morris sisters, Miss Eleanor and Miss Peggy, please ma'am."

"Are they expecting you, Lieutenant?"

"No, I'm sorry," he said demurely. "But I was in a bit of a rush. I didn't call ahead."

"Let me see if they are in their room." After a quick

phone conversation, she turned back to him. "They'll be down in a minute." Then with a smile, she added, "In the meantime, if you'd like to take a seat in the sun parlor…"

"Don't mind if I do." He smiled and nodded. Evidently, he'd managed to garner a little favor with the staff, maybe even proved himself not the ogre they'd originally taken him for.

Accepting her suggestion, he crossed the wide foyer to the sun parlor and sat in one of the chairs near the floor-to-ceiling windows. With light beaming in through the lace curtains, he leaned back and soaked up the warmth of the mid-morning sun. A clatter rose behind him, and he looked around. Guests had begun to stir, some returning to their rooms from the dining hall, others making their way to the recreation room. Some few passed with walkers or in wheelchairs, but most were able to navigate the corridors on their own steam. An African American man, quite old but with bright eyes and a cottony head of hair, stopped at the receptionist desk. "Ms. Cane," he heard him say, "I'm expecting my niece today."

"Saffron coming by?" she asked.

"She is, and let me know when she gets here. I'll be in the rec room most likely."

"Not to worry. We'll track you down."

He rolled away from the desk and down the hall. Must be Saffron's great uncle, Olivera thought, recalling having seen him at Eugene Brown's funeral back in the fall. Another familiar face soon appeared, and this time Olivera stood and waved his hat. "Mr. Eldridge, sir…"

Stout and well-dressed, the tall gentleman squinted in Olivera's direction. "Lieutenant Olivera," he said in a husky voice.

"That's right."

"Keep your seat." Eldridge slowly moved toward him, pressing his cane into the soft carpet with each step.

"I spend too much time sitting." Olivera ignored Eldridge's courtesy, and, walking in his direction, met him halfway.

"Don't we all." Eldridge chuckled. "You aren't here on business, are you?"

"I suppose I am."

"Not any of my people, I hope."

"Actually, it might be." Olivera grinned. "Lot of you Hembree folks seem to be related to one another."

"Yeah, that's what they say, but you'd be hard-pressed to find any Eldridges around here. They've all gone to Vicksburg, Mississippi."

"But aren't you related to Carlotta Humphrey?"

"Yeah, by marriage." He rubbed his forehead. "Now, how is that?"

Out of the corner of his eye, Olivera caught sight of two women he presumed to be the Morris sisters, one tall and angular, the other short and round. They'd paused at the opening into the sun parlor. Neither spoke, just stood, apparently waiting for a cue from him. He excused himself and approached the younger of the two women. "Ma'am, I'm Lieutenant Gustavo Olivera of the Hembree Police Department. You must be Miss Morris."

"I'm Peggy Morris, and this is my sister Eleanor."

"I'd like to speak with you briefly if that'd be all right."

"Of course. Shall we wait over there?" She motioned toward the opposite corner of the room.

"Yes, ma'am. I would appreciate that. I'll be just a second."

Meanwhile, Eldridge drew near, stopping a few feet away. "So, it's Miss Eleanor and Miss Peggy you've come to see. Ladies." He greeted each with a slight bow. "I see you've made the acquaintance of our new Chief of Police."

"No, we have not," the older sister huffed.

"I haven't had the pleasure till now." Olivera turned to Eldridge. "And, if you'd excuse me, I wouldn't want to keep these ladies waiting."

Eldridge graciously took the hint and walked on, but seemingly unable to resist one last gibe, stopped and said with a chuckle, "I'd be careful what I told him if I were you."

"Now, then"—Olivera passed over Eldridge's little joke—"please have a seat. I appreciate very much your willingness to see me, and I will keep this as short as possible."

While the sisters made themselves comfortable on the settee, he sat in one of the single chairs on the other side of the table.

"I know what you've come about," the younger sister said.

"This one!" The older sister's eyes flashed toward the ceiling. "You'd think she was a psychic, always trying to figure things out before they happen."

Olivera laughed. "I could use a good psychic. This case I'm working on—"

"The Grayson case, you mean?" Miss Peggy Morris chimed in.

"That's right!" Olivera feigned surprise.

"If you think we know anything about that," Miss Eleanor Morris said, "just 'cause it happened at our old house…"

"Well, it's not really that. I believe you ladies moved out some time ago, didn't you?"

"Yes, and none too soon before it came down on top of us." The elder sister's tired gray eyes rolled up as her thin lips turned down.

"I wasn't aware—"

"Not aware?" Miss Eleanor gasped. "You've been to the house, haven't you?"

"Yes, ma'am, a few times."

"Before it's over, you'll know the place as well as we do," Miss Peggy said with conviction.

"I doubt that, but I could use your expertise on a couple of matters, this cellar, for instance. I believe Ms. Frye may have spoken to you about that?"

"Yes, Mosey was here," Miss Eleanor said and then stopped. "Peggy, when was that? Was that yesterday?"

Miss Peggy nodded, then turned to Olivera. "Mosey bought us the nicest album for our old photographs, some we'd left back at the house."

"Yes, she mentioned that."

"You've spoken with Mosey?"

"Yes, ma'am. She's been helping Dr. Wilson get settled. I spoke with her about the cellar, and she thought you might have some idea—"

"That cellar was one big headache," Miss Eleanor cut in. "Kit convinced Daddy he needed a little privacy, a place he could write undisturbed. He wanted to be left alone, that's for sure, so he could carry on with his drinking buddies."

"Eleanor, you're being harsh. Kit *did too* use the cellar to write. You *know* he did."

"When he wasn't gambling or drinking."

Olivera cleared his throat. "It'd be helpful if you

could give me some idea how Mr. Grayson fit in. Was he a friend of your brother's?"

"*Friend.*" Miss Eleanor paused, as if searching for a different word. "Birds of a feather, those two. Will Grayson was as work-shy as Kit."

"Eleanor" —Peggy frowned—"how dare you speak ill of the dead."

"Huh! If you ask me, they got away with it long enough."

"It?" Olivera asked.

"Gambling." Miss Eleanor nodded. "Illegal gambling."

"Tsk, tsk, tsk." Miss Peggy shook her head and looked his way. "A harmless game of poker among friends. My sister didn't approve, but I didn't see anything wrong with it."

"*Friends*, my hind foot," Eleanor interjected.

Olivera looked from one to the other, uncertain whom to believe.

Miss Eleanor shook her finger at him. "It didn't stop there. Don't you believe it."

"Where?" he asked.

"There at the house." She tilted her head.

"Hmmm," Olivera began, "I suppose the other men—"

"Other men, nothing," Miss Eleanor cut in. "Arnold Bilyeu, that's who."

"You mean Arnold Bilyeu of Larkspur Plantation?" She nodded.

"It's been quite a while since your brother and Mr. Bilyeu passed on. But Mr. Grayson's death... I don't suppose there was any connection—or was there? You see, I find it strange that he was at your house, your former house, and apparently, as has recently come to light, there was some other man there, too, at the time of Mr. Grayson's death. I don't suppose you would know if Mr. Grayson had any enemies around town, people he might have fallen out with?"

"Why, Arnold, of course," Miss Eleanor said.

"Eleanor," Peggy said gingerly, "Arnold Bilyeu is dead. Ninon, too, poor soul. All the Bilyeus are gone."

"Not all." Miss Eleanor glared at her sister before turning away.

Miss Peggy placed her plump fingers to the side of her mouth and whispered. "My sister didn't care for Arnold, but you mustn't listen to her."

He acknowledged her apology for her sister, then glanced from one to the other. "To get back to my question, you think Mr. Grayson was not a fan of the Bilyeus?"

"A fan of the Bilyeus?" Miss Peggy said. "Well, who knows. There might have been some bad blood, maybe some business deal gone wrong. I don't know."

"Up to no good, I'm thinking," Miss Eleanor added. "Always down in that cellar…"

"But I have to wonder," he interjected, "how all of that, so long ago, could have had anything to do with Mr. Grayson's death."

Both sisters sat shaking their heads. Neither seemed to know anything specific about an alleged riff between Kit and Arnold, but while one sister was certain it hadn't amounted to a hill of beans, the other was maybe even more certain it had. "One more thing. I don't suppose you know anything about the paintings we found in the cellar. They were hidden in an alcove behind a bookcase. I've heard them referred to as *casta* paintings."

Miss Peggy cocked her head. "*Casta* paintings."

Miss Eleanor shrugged.

"I snapped a photograph, if you wouldn't mind taking a look."

Miss Peggy bent toward him as he brought out his cellphone. Once he'd found the picture, he held it up for her to see. "These are the two paintings we found."

"Oh, my," Miss Peggy said, "yes, I remember Kit once telling me about some paintings he'd received from Arnold. Valuable, very valuable. And I asked him, 'How valuable?' And he said, 'That depends.' Then I asked him what it depended on, and he said, 'However much he's willing to pay.' 'Who?' I asked, and he said, 'Arnold's cousin'—I think he said *cousin*."

"So, he—your brother—hoped to sell them to one of Arnold's relatives?"

"Oh, yes. That's why he held on to 'em. Arnold was going to pay a good price to get 'em back. But Arnold died. That's when the cousin popped up."

"You wouldn't happen to remember his name, would you?" He looked at Miss Peggy, then Miss Eleanor.

"No, Lieutenant, I don't remember the man's name." Miss Peggy's eyes rolled up as she slowly shook her head.

"And you, Miss Eleanor?"

"I have no idea who she's talking about. I never met any cousins of the Bilyeus."

Olivera allowed the conversation to end there, as the sisters were looking a bit fraught and he didn't want to rattle the receptionist, who'd been hovering at the end of the reception desk, eyes flicking regularly in their direction. So he thanked the ladies, bid them farewell, and left, feeling a little more knowledgeable about the Morris past, though this new knowledge had come tinged with uncertainty. The paintings, it seemed, were a bone of contention between Kit and Arnold. Besides that, there was the matter of the cousin—which cousin he didn't know—who, according to Miss Peggy, had involved himself in the sale, which, evidently, hadn't gone through.

"All these old families," he muttered as he crossed the lot to the squad car. He couldn't quite put his finger on it, but he had a feeling something big had gone down in Hembree, something of which decent folks, like Mosey Frye and Nadia Abboud, hadn't the vaguest clue. Or had they? Were they living in a *swamp* of sorts? Not real, like the one their ancestors had drained. A figurative swamp… He shuddered to think.

A puff of wind blew up, and he quickly got into the squad car, cranked the engine, and turned on the heat. But before he pulled out, he paused a moment to ponder his next move. He could drive back to town, stop by Morris House to see if Springer and Reagan had anything to report. Alternatively, he could head over to Larkspur—it wasn't so far away—to chat with Bilyeu and DeGroat about the lead he'd just gotten on a cousin of theirs, interested perhaps in the casta paintings. He didn't have much to offer in the way of evidence, and he was likely to get more cooperation if he had something concrete to show them. Uncertain what to do, he opted to call Springer first.

"I'm out at the Magnolia," he said to Springer, "about to head over to Larkspur, but before I do that, I wanted to check with you guys, see if you've come across anything of interest."

"As a matter of fact, Chief, we ran across a little…well, not sure what it is. You want me to send you a picture?"

"Sure. You say you don't know what it is?"

"It's a piece of metal, gold, I'd say. Looks like it might have come off something."

"Send the picture."

"Hold on a second."

Springer and Reagan mumbled back and forth and, together, managed to decide on the best shot. "You get that, Chief? Looks to me like a piece of a cufflink."

"Yeah, could be. It's about the right size. Have you dusted it for prints?"

"Not yet, we just found it."

"Where'd you find it?"

"Lying in the grass near the porch."

"So, maybe this guy, in doing whatever he did, like moving the body or whatever, lost a part of a cufflink."

"But, Chief, for pity's sake, who wears cufflinks, especially so early in the day?"

"Very few, would be my guess."

"Some rich dude maybe."

"Yeah, I would think. Good work, Springer, but don't stop. See if you can find something more. Footprints or handprints would be particularly helpful or anything that might carry DNA. In fact, I'd like you to take that item you found to the morgue as soon as you finish at the house." Olivera clicked off and sat staring at the snapshot. It did look like part of a cufflink, and if he could connect it to DeGroat, he might be on his way to solving the case. He thought he'd seen DeGroat wearing a tie pin with a similar design, the sort of thing you might see on a coat of arms. It occurred to him, however, that he wanted to be sure of the evidence before he approached him. And who better than Nadia Abboud to fill him in on the heraldry of the local gentry. He texted her the picture, then phoned. "Ms. Abboud?"

"This is Nadia Abboud."

"Olivera here. I just sent you a text."

"Hold on. I'm on the landline. Let me grab my cell."

After a short silence, she came back on the line. "I've got it. What was it you wanted to know?"

"This was found near Morris House, just now. I've only seen the picture, not the object itself, but it looks like part of a cufflink, and I wondered if the design might be a symbol used, for example, on a coat of arms."

"That's possible, I suppose. It might also be a slider from a bracelet or necklace."

"I see."

"If I could see the object itself, I think I could tell."

"I'll bring it by, but in the meantime, what about the design? Does it look familiar?"

"Yes, of course. That's a gammadion."

"Gammadion?"

"Four capital gammas connected to form a kind of cross."

"Might it be associated with a family, say, a local family?"

"Maybe. I could certainly check. I have a couple of books on heraldry here at the store."

"Thank you, Ms. Abboud. That would be *very* helpful. Would you mind if I drop by?"

"I'll be here until lunchtime."

Olivera checked his watch. "I'm out on Little Smith. Let's make it after lunch if that's okay."

"No problem."

Chapter Twenty-Five

*Abboud Antiques*
*Wednesday, 1:00 p.m.*

Nadia, Toni, Mosey, and Dave had arrived at the shop and were putting their heads together, when Toni, who'd spent the better part of the morning jotting down recollections on sticky notes, held up a lavender note and waved it in the air. "You see this?"

Mosey and Dave turned to look. Nadia, closing the file drawer she'd been rifling through, rounded the counter and perched on the arm of the tufted sofa. "Whatcha got, Daddy?"

"This." He handed her the note.

" 'Colton Raines,' " she read, " 'the only remaining member of the original poker group, left Hembree under somewhat mysterious circumstances.' " She looked down at her father. "Okay, so why do you think he left?"

"Search me. Nobody seemed to know. He just left. Took his son with him. Hollis was his name."

"Seems strange for a person to leave without some sort of notice or explanation."

"Exactly. But Colton did. Said he was moving to New Orleans."

"So, did he?" Dave set the album he'd been working on for Mosey on the tray top table.

"I have no idea. I think the last time I saw him was

at the Tavernette. Some of us got together for a send-off."

"Didn't offer any explanation at the send-off?" Dave asked.

"That's what I've been trying to remember. He was a little dodgy about that. Said he was ready to try his hand at something different—business, maybe—and figured New Orleans was a better place to be."

"Did he leave a forwarding address?" Mosey asked.

"I don't think so, but I remember he had a little address book, passed it around, and we all wrote down our addresses and phone numbers. He wanted to stay in touch."

"And did he?"

Toni shook his head. "Not with me."

"Hmm," Mosey said. "Surely he stayed in touch with his brother, one would think."

"His brother?" Dave asked.

"Yes, Matthew Raines."

"I don't know that he did," Toni said. "Matt didn't seem to know much more than the rest of us."

Mosey, who had been working on the Morris sisters' album with Dave, flipped back to the first pages where she had placed the December 1945 pictures of the poker players. "Is this the guy you're talking about?" She slipped a picture out of its pocket and passed it to Toni.

Toni lifted his glasses and gave it a quick look. "That's Colton."

"Let me see that," Nadia said. "Not a bad looking guy."

"May I see?" Dave asked.

Nadia passed him the photograph.

"Looks like an athlete."

"Athletic, yes, tall, thin guy," Toni said. "All the Raineses are like that. Hollis, too. The spitting image of his daddy."

"I think I've seen this man," Dave said.

"In New Orleans?" Toni asked.

"In the shop, just the other day."

Mosey glanced at Dave. "In *your* shop?"

"Yes, I spoke to him briefly. Father was talking to him before he went to answer your call."

"What were they talking about?" Nadia asked.

"Father didn't say, and I didn't ask. But it'd be worth a call to find out."

"Please do."

Dave pulled out his cell and, strolling toward the back, phoned his father.

Mosey looked at Nadia. "What are you thinking?"

"It's a long shot, but if the old group has anything to do with this business, well, I mean, who's left? Arnold and Kit are gone, your granddaddy, Eads's granddaddy. Nobody's left but Colton Raines."

"But Raines has been gone from here for quite some time. You remember him?"

Nadia shook her head. "Not really."

"Yeah, unlikely we'd have paid much attention, him being older. Seems like I remember hearing about him, vaguely."

Dave returned to the group. "Father says the man didn't give a name at first, which seemed a little suspicious. But when Father sort of pushed him into saying who he was, he said he was Hollis Raines."

"Oh, my," Mosey said. "So, not Colton but his son. The Morris sisters pointed him out to me. Said he was close in age to Colton's brother, Matthew."

"Did your father tell you what they spoke about?" Nadia asked.

"He was interested in the same paintings another client had come to see, the Mateo Cardoso collection, including, of course, the painting of Fernanda de Lobos. The other client was a Mr. Philpot. Father greeted him when he came in and showed him through the gallery. Meanwhile, this other guy, Raines, came into the gallery and was looking around on his own. Father went to take your call." He glanced at Mosey. "I checked on him while Father was on the phone, but he didn't have much to say. But now Father says he thought he was a little odd, seemed to have knowledge of some missing Cardosos but wouldn't say exactly what he knew."

"Likely *those* missing Cardosos." Nadia nodded toward the paintings.

"What makes you say that?" Dave asked.

"How many missing Cardosos can there be?"

"I don't know, but I imagine Father knows."

"Your father has actually seen Cardoso's records, no?"

"Yes, and he couldn't account for some of the paintings listed on the inventory."

"So, if Raines was curious about the same missing paintings, it makes sense he would have dropped by the shop to speak to your father."

"Yes, but what piques my curiosity was the guy's manner. According to Father, he didn't come right out and say what he wanted. It was as if he had—"

"—information he wasn't prepared to share?"

"Yes, exactly."

"Well," Mosey said, "given that the paintings were once part of the Bilyeu heirlooms, it makes perfect sense."

"How's that?" Dave asked.

"Well, the Bilyeus, some of them at least, played their cards close to their chest."

"Except for Ninon," Nadia said.

"Right. The rest of them, well, they kept hidden what they didn't want the world to know."

"Which was?" Dave asked.

"Evidently," Mosey said, "Hershel and Fernanda absconded with certain valuable items when they left New Orleans. A bejeweled dagger and a couple of dueling pistols along with an old apothecary were found buried at the hermitage after Arnold's only heir—Ninon, also known as Sister Clare—was murdered. Of course, you read about the homicide, right? I believe we talked about that yesterday."

Dave nodded.

"As I believe we mentioned yesterday, the heirlooms were passed down from one Bilyeu to the next but never mentioned in the wills. It makes sense, then, that the paintings—"

"But wait a minute," Nadia cut in. "Unlike the pistols and dagger, the paintings weren't stolen."

"That's right," Toni said. "The Cardosos were all commissioned by either Bilyeu himself or Fernanda's father, so why would they want to hide them?"

Nadia looked thoughtful. "Maybe it wasn't the paintings themselves exactly. Maybe it was the subject matter."

"Right," Dave said, "what the paintings might have revealed about the family. I think Father was on to that, too."

Nadia approached the paintings, still propped

against the counter. "This first one—" She examined the composite. "—may or may not contain a Bilyeu, but this second one likely features Hershel Bilyeu and a Haitian priestess. If this is Bilyeu, then it's obvious why he wouldn't have displayed it in his home. It points indirectly to his criminal past, his violation of the Code Noir. But suppose *this* one—" She moved back to the composite. "—is just as revelatory, only…"

"Only what?" Mosey asked.

"To us it isn't obvious, but to someone better acquainted with the Bilyeu history…"

"Like who?"

"Raines, for one," Toni said.

"You think Colton would have been aware…?" Nadia asked Toni.

"Possibly. The families were acquainted for a long time."

"And Kit must have known," Mosey said.

"This is beginning to make sense," Nadia said. "Suppose Kit and Colton were privy to Arnold's secret. Kit, however, a more loyal friend, *kept* the secret, even held onto the paintings when it was to his advantage to sell them. Colton, on the other hand—"

"Colton," Mosey cut in, "must not have known where the paintings were hidden, nor did Arnold and Kit *want* him to know."

"Why not, I wonder," Dave said.

"Well, obviously they didn't trust him. They thought he might exploit them for his own selfish purposes."

"You mean blackmail?" Dave asked.

"Possibly," Nadia said.

"So, what's in them that the Bilyeus wouldn't have wanted known?" Mosey asked.

"This one." Nadia pointed to the composite. "We aren't entirely sure. But this other one" —she pointed toward the suspected portrait of Hershel and the priestess— "is rather damning, don't you think?" She looked at Dave.

"Not necessarily, unless, of course, you know the history of Hershel's collusion with the priestess. But the composite..." He approached the composite and bent down in front of it. "I wouldn't be surprised if one of these vignettes holds a clue."

"And how are we going to figure *that* out?" Mosey asked.

"I bet David Senior could figure it out. What do you think?" Nadia turned toward Dave.

"I imagine so. He's become an expert on the iconography of casta paintings. If there's something there, there's a very good chance he'll see it and know what it means."

"Then I think it's pretty clear what needs to happen," Toni said. "Either David has to come to Hembree or you guys—" He looked at Nadia, then Mosey. "—have to go to New Orleans, take the paintings with you."

"Good luck with that first option," Dave said. "Father hasn't traveled in years."

"Nadia, Mosey, you ladies up for a road trip?"

"Well, sure," Nadia said, "but what about the shop?"

"I'll keep an eye on things."

"I'd be happy to take you back with me," Dave said.

"Hmm," Mosey said, "I don't see how we can turn that down."

"What about Olivera?" Nadia looked at Mosey. "You think he'll let us take the paintings with us?"

"Good question. I suppose if we could convince him it's vital to the case."

"It's worth a try, and if he refuses, I guess we could take a couple of snapshots, send them back with Dave, though I'm not sure photographs would be adequate. The first step would be to authenticate the paintings, wouldn't you think?"

"Heck if I know. You're the art dealer."

"Not quite, but I imagine Olivera knows even less than we do about old paintings." Nadia glanced at the mantel clock on the back wall. "Come to think of it, he said he was dropping by the store after lunch."

"He is?"

"Yeah, he wants me to take a look at something they found at the crime scene."

"Speaking of lunch," Toni said, "shall we call an order into the Tavernette?"

"You folks go ahead," Nadia said. "I'll wait for Olivera. He should be here any minute."

No sooner had Mosey, Toni, and Dave left the shop than Olivera arrived. Nadia, hearing the roar of a car engine, looked up just as Olivera peeped in. She was next to the counter, still studying the paintings he'd dropped off the day before.

"Afternoon." He removed his hat and hung it on the rack by the door.

"Lieutenant."

He pulled a plastic bag out of his coat pocket and laid it on the counter.

"I was just studying this painting," she said, "looking for clues."

"You find anything?"

"Nope, but I think I know who could. David Morell

Senior. His son says he's developed a good bit of expertise on the iconography of casta paintings."

He cleared his throat. "You don't say."

She walked around behind the counter, then picked up the plastic bag and held it up to the light. "I think you're right. Looks like part of a cufflink. And that's a gammadion, for sure."

"Were you able to connect the symbol to any of the local families?"

She shook her head. "Sorry, but I've been so caught up in this other business. It completely slipped my mind." She approached the bookshelf on the wall behind the counter. "Here"—she lifted a thick tome—"we should be able to find something in here." She plopped it down on the counter and opened it to the index.

"I'm not familiar with the word *gammadion*, " he said, "but the symbol itself is certainly common enough."

She looked up. "Yes and no."

He tilted his head, evidently perplexed at her answer.

"It depends on how the letters are facing." She paged through the book till she came to a diagram, then turned the book around for him to see. "See these?"

He studied the two symbols she indicated. "This one looks like a mirror image of this other one."

"Good way to describe it. This one"—she pointed to the image on the left—"is a fylfot, and this one is a gammadion."

"Never heard of either. They look like swastikas to me."

"And they are, but the Nazi symbolism is rather late. Fylfots and gammadions appeared in the British Isles before the arrival of the Romans. The Romans adopted them, as did the Anglo-Saxons later on."

"Hmm. I didn't know that."

"That's how they came to be used in heraldry."

"I was thinking whoever wore this"—he picked up the bag to take another look at the object—"might have some sort of Nazi connection."

"Maybe he did, but there are other possibilities. This one—" She tapped the diagram of the fylfot. "—appears in the catacombs in Rome and on church bells in England, stained-glass windows and chalices, too. It was also the symbol of the Norse god Thor." She closed the book, and after pushing it back onto the shelf, reached for another. "Let's check out the heraldry of some of our locals." She thumbed through the book, stopping at each of several family crests, none of which contained anything that remotely resembled a fylfot or gammadion. She looked up at him and sighed. "Sorry, Lieutenant."

He glanced at the object. "Dr. McGinnis couldn't find a traceable print."

"But someone must have a matching cufflink, and chances are it was custom made. You might check with the local jewelers."

"Yes, I guess that's the next step."

"By the way, before you go, I wanted to ask you about the paintings. As I mentioned before, Dave Morell's father knows a good bit about the iconography of casta paintings. If you would permit us to take them down to New Orleans, he may be able to come up with an explanation for their, well—"

"—why they were hidden? What secret…?"

"You see, *we*—Mosey and I—figure the paintings must be at the center of this. Whoever was there on the morning of Grayson's death must have gone there because of the paintings."

"That's a leap, don't you think?"

She dropped her head. "Yes, I guess it is, but everything we know about the house, the family…seems to be related to—"

"—a time in the past? Something related to Kit?"

"Yes, and Arnold Bilyeu," she added, "who was Kit's friend or his enemy."

"About that." His eyes narrowed. "I got the same impression from the Morris sisters. It was hard to make out exactly what Kit was to Arnold. The older sister seems quite convinced they were not friends."

"Yes, I suppose there's no way to resolve that, at least for the time being, but we've been able to put together a scenario of sorts. You see, Daddy knew Kit and Arnold. He also appraised the paintings after they had been taken to Kit's cellar. He thinks Arnold gave the paintings to Kit in payment of a gambling debt. Pawned them, let's say, in hopes of getting them back. But Arnold died, and Kit, by default, got to keep them yet didn't display them or sell them, though he was hard up for money. We also think another one of Kit's and Arnold's friends, Colton Raines, who was one of the poker players, might have had an interest in the paintings. Dave Morell recognized Colton in a picture, one of the snapshots the sisters left at the house. His son Hollis showed up at David Senior's gallery just the other day."

His eyes widened. "That's quite a bit you've been able to pull together."

"Yes, quite a bit, but how much of it is true or relative to the crime, we don't know."

"That's often the way it is in the beginning, isn't it? Hard to sort out the facts from the suppositions, but you have to work with whatever you've got, and in this case, hard facts haven't been easy to come by." He picked up the bag with the cufflink and slipped it into his coat pocket.

Nadia, meanwhile, mustered up her courage to press the question she had raised before. Though it felt a little awkward—no, a lot awkward—she said, "So, Lieutenant—" She paused. "—if you would allow us to take the paintings to New Orleans, Morell *might* be able to tell us why Arnold didn't want them displayed."

He looked down at the paintings, then up at her. "Then you're convinced these paintings point to some sort of…family secret or something?"

"Maybe. This one"—she pointed not to the composite but to the other painting—"discreetly substantiates what *you* learned from Rafael about Hershel's criminality, the concoctions he and the priestess administered to Hershel's house servants."

He nodded, then paced away from the counter before turning back toward Nadia. "But this other one. You think it may suggest something else, some *other* family secret?"

"That's what we're hoping."

"Well, you would have to sign some papers, but yes, by all means, if you are willing to do that, I'd consider it a favor."

She breathed a sigh of relief. "Dave flew up here in the company plane, and he's willing to fly us to New Orleans tonight or tomorrow. You're okay with that?"

He nodded. "As I said before, I'd consider it a favor."

"Okay, then." Nadia smiled. "We'll do it, and we'll let you know what David Senior has to say. I'll give you a call soon as we find out anything."

"Thanks for checking on the cufflink."

"No problem. I'm sorry I couldn't give you an answer."

He retrieved his hat from the hat rack and opened the door but then turned back.

"Did you forget something, Lieutenant?"

"Not exactly, but I was wondering if you might take this with you, too." He pulled out the bag with the cufflink. "David Morell deals in jewelry, does he not?"

"Yes, he does. Are you thinking the piece was made in New Orleans?"

"Yes."

"Huh." She stopped to think for a second. "I believe I know where you're going with this. You think this person, whoever was at Morris House, isn't from around here. You think he might be from New Orleans?"

He smiled. "Yep, that's what I'm thinking." He laid the bag back on the counter. "It's a long shot, but it seems like a few people of interest have a New Orleans connection."

"I'm not sure whom specifically you have in mind, but, yes, I get your point."

Chapter Twenty-Six

*Morgue*
*Wednesday, 2:30 p.m.*

Olivera had swung by the lab earlier that day to collect the cufflink fragment Springer and Reagan had found at the crime scene. But now, he felt the need to go there again. He glanced around at the antiseptic walls, the gurney, the counter—the only parts of the antiquated morgue that smacked of anything modern or scientific. He sniffed. He didn't like the smell of it, but he felt more at home there than at any of the other places he'd visited that day. That classy shop of Nadia Abboud's was easy on the senses, but he never felt comfortable there. All that posh stuff—throw pillows, porcelain vases, scented sachets—seemed to stand in the way of reality. The morgue, on the other hand, had a way of stripping away the cobwebs, allowing him to see things as they were.

"Eads," he said, getting her attention.

"Lieutenant." She looked up, startled.

"Sorry. I called you *Eads*, and I promised myself I wasn't going to do that, not here."

"I wasn't expecting you, that's all. Not again, not so soon." She pulled the sheet over the cadaver and stepped back from the gurney, then brushed a wisp of dark hair from her face and slipped off her gloves.

"Nor was I expecting to be back, but I've just come

from Nadia Abboud's shop. I went over to drop off the evidence I picked up earlier. She's in agreement, by the way. It's likely part of a cufflink with an engraving of a gammadion or a fylfot, but she couldn't connect it—the symbol—with any of the old families, any with *abolengo*."

"*Abolengo*," she repeated.

"Lineage." Rarely did a Spanish word displace an English one in his vocabulary, but that word, *abolengo,* came to mind more readily than *lineage*, which had never seemed quite appropriate. It seemed more British than American, maybe because Brits were aristocratic, and Americans, not so much. But Spaniards, oh, yeah. Some he knew were all about *abolengo*.

"So, you must have decided that some of our *old families* are involved."

"Yes," he nodded, "I guess I have."

"And how is that?"

"Well," he paused, "seems to me all the evidence points in that direction, don't you think? Morris House, a hidden cellar full of old books, an old typewriter, a secret alcove, old paintings. Besides that, Grayson did yard work for the Morrises and Raineses and maybe others up and down McAllister. And then the cufflink, gold…" He stopped pacing and faced McGinnis. "Doesn't it seem that way to you?"

She laughed. "I didn't mean to put you on the defensive, Lieutenant. You're probably right, but it'd be worth remembering that Grayson wasn't *one of them*. He was just a sad old guy, coming to the end of his life, a life that amounted to very little. Well, maybe not to him, but to the hoi polloi of Hembree. Hard to believe any of them gave him a second thought."

"The elite, you mean?"

"Right, the Hembree elite." She chuckled again. "Sounds a little ridiculous, doesn't it?"

He chuckled, too. "Yeah, it does." He took off his hat and tossed it onto the hat rack. "Well, I guess what it comes down to is that I don't have much to go on." He sat on the stool next to her desk and mindlessly picked up a bottle of water, unscrewed it, and was about to take a drink.

"Here." She moved in his direction. "Let me get you a fresh bottle."

He set it back on her desk and accepted the bottle she brought from her desk drawer. "Thanks." He unscrewed the top and took a drink.

"Understand," she said, "I'm not suggesting that any of your suppositions are incorrect. I just think that you need something to tie this death to the Morrises or the Bilyeus."

"Or the Raineses," he added.

"The Raineses? Matthew and Charlotte?"

"Well, not *those* Raineses probably, though I think Grayson was in their employment from time to time."

"What other Raineses are there?"

"Colton Raines and his son Hollis."

"Oh, yeah."

"You know them?"

"I know the names. Colton was a friend of my grandfather's. Well, I heard my grandfather speak of him."

"Really?" He picked up the bottle and took a sip.

"Hmm. I haven't thought about that in a long time."

"Whatever you can remember might be helpful. People seem uncertain about this guy Colton, who, apparently, doesn't live here anymore."

"Where does he live?"

"New Orleans."

"Yes, I think Granddaddy might have mentioned that. Raines was part of the old crowd, but he left Hembree—the only one of the group who left."

"Do you know what he did—for a living, I mean?"

"I'm not sure. I believe the Raineses were entrepreneurs."

"Wealthy?"

"Matthew, yes. Not sure about Colton. Daddy would know."

"I'll give him a call—or *you* call him, if you don't mind."

"Now, you mean?" she asked.

"I'd really like to get to the bottom of this."

She pulled out her cellphone and placed the call. Meanwhile, he restlessly paced over to the opposite side of the room, fiddling with things on the counter until she finished her conversation.

"Daddy says Colton Raines got into some trouble…some sort of swindle concerning a mining venture in Louisiana. Bilked some unknowing investors."

"One wasn't Arnold Bilyeu, was it?" He walked back toward her.

"As a matter of fact."

"Gosh, how'd they keep that quiet?"

"Not sure, but I can imagine Arnold, proud man that he was…"

"Yeah." He rubbed his chin. "So now this Raines fellow—"

"—has found another chance to stick it to the

Bilyeus."

"Does seem like some kind of ongoing feud. I wonder if Matthew Raines is aware of his brother's shenanigans."

"How could he *not* be?" Eads laid her cell on her desk and took a seat.

"Did Colton do jail time? Sometimes they don't."

"Daddy wasn't sure."

"I'm thinking that Colton Raines is still in New Orleans and possibly up to no good. Dave Morell claims he saw his son at the Royal Street Gallery this week, and apparently, he'd gone there to look at the casta paintings."

"Okay, so let's pretend that Colton and Hollis are involved. But how?" she said, hands splayed. "Neither could have been the man at Morris House when Grayson died...or was killed."

"That's true." He sat on the folding chair next to Eads's desk. "Both Wilson and Krueger described the guy they saw as young."

"So if the Raineses were involved, they must have had a partner."

"*Or*...maybe Grayson *was* their partner. They might have sent Grayson to the house to retrieve the paintings and the other guy, the young guy, tried to stop him."

She nodded. "Makes sense." She paused. "Oh, my."

"What is it?"

"If Colton and Hollis are somehow involved and their first attempt to get the paintings failed, who is to say they won't try again?"

"And being in New Orleans, if they try anything..."

"Hmm. Maybe you ought to let Morell know."

"Yeah, and Nadia," he added. "They're flying the

paintings down there today." He reached for his phone. "And you know something else?"

"What?"

"This puts a new spin on this *other guy*."

"The young guy?"

"He could have gone over there to prevent Grayson from carrying through with the plan."

"I still can't figure why he didn't report the death."

"Unless he didn't know that Grayson was dead."

"You think he was still alive?" she asked.

He nodded. "Hold on a second. I'm going to see if I can catch Nadia before they leave." When Nadia didn't pick up, he left a voice message asking her to return his call as soon as possible. "So"—he glanced at McGinnis—"who might have wanted to stop this theft from taking place?"

"At the house, you mean?"

He nodded.

"Well—" She stopped to think. "—either someone who wanted the paintings for himself or someone who didn't want the Raineses to have them."

"Like who?"

"Someone who stood to gain something…or to lose something."

"Yeah?"

"Like the Bilyeus."

He patted his knee pensively, then stood. "A. B. and DeGroat."

"Aha, that fits, DeGroat being young."

"Young, nicely dressed, and just the type to wear a pair of gold cufflinks."

"You'd have him dead to rights if you could connect him to the cufflink. But wait." Her expression fell.

"What's the matter?"

"I was just thinking, he didn't really do anything, did he? Well, not necessarily."

"Even if he didn't, maybe he could clear up this business, tell us why he was there, why Grayson was there."

"Yes, maybe he can."

"Darn."

"What?" she asked.

"I left the cufflink with Nadia. She's going to see if David Morell can identify the owner. We figure it's custom made."

"You have the picture, though."

"And I guess it'll have to do."

"Are you going to approach DeGroat?"

"I think I must, before he leaves town. I don't relish the conversation."

"Without anything to place him at the scene of the crime…"

"If there was a crime," he said. "This keeps happening, doesn't it?"

She nodded. "Little ol' Hembree hasn't produced any clear-cut murders of late." Her expression fell.

He laughed. "Aren't you the bloodthirsty one?"

"Hey! No more than you."

He laughed, leaned over the desk, and kissed her.

Chapter Twenty-Seven

*Royal Street Gallery, French Quarter*
*Wednesday, 9:00 p.m.*

On a Wednesday night in January, amblers through the French Quarter had settled down to a steady flow. The sharp, hollow sound of horse hooves in sync with the rumbling of carriage wheels rose above the noise of the passersby. David Morell dragged his sign into the shop and locked the door. His son had called to let him know he'd be home by nightfall and would be bringing Mosey Frye and Nadia Abboud with him. Morell set the sign in the corner of the front room and carried the easel into the gallery. He brought in another easel from the storage room and set it alongside the first, both positioned near the portrait of Fernanda. Soon after he'd finished closing up, a knock came at the door. Must be Dave, he thought. "I'll be right there," he called, walking back toward the entrance. Seeing it was his son and the others, he unlocked the door and welcomed them in.

"Father," Dave said, "this is Nadia Abboud. I'm sure you remember Nadia. And Mosey Frye. I believe you spoke with Mosey on the phone."

Morell nodded politely to the ladies. "I feel like I already know you, but I'm delighted to see you here. Too bad Toni couldn't come."

"He would have loved nothing better," Nadia said as

she followed Dave into the shop, "but someone had to watch the store."

"Of course. Another time. And soon, I hope. Neither of us is getting any younger."

"You look the same to me, Mr. Morell," Nadia said.

"Oh, come now." He chuckled. "How many years has it been?"

"Twenty? But some people don't age, and you seem to be one of them."

"That's all the flattering I can take for one night." He smiled broadly. "Can I offer you something to drink? I have a bottle of champagne cooling in the back." He motioned toward the gallery. "I figure we have reason to celebrate." He then eyed the large parcel Dave had propped against the ring display. "I see you've brought the paintings."

"We have," Dave said, "and we're depending on *you* to help us decipher this, uh, perplexing situation, shall we say?"

"Perplexing?"

"Didn't Dave fill you in?" Nadia glanced at Dave.

"Well, I wasn't sure how much I should disclose," Dave said.

"But before we get into all that," Morell said, "Mosey, Nadia, can I take your wraps?"

Nadia and Mosey slipped off their coats, as did Dave.

"And let's carry the paintings into the gallery," Morell suggested. "I've set up a couple of easels."

They entered the gallery, and while Dave put away the coats, Morell brought out the bottle of champagne, corked it, and poured four flutes. "Mosey and Nadia," he offered each a flute of champagne, "I appreciate this fast turnaround on the paintings. I never anticipated—"

"Nor did we." Mosey accepted the flute. "It wasn't *us*. It was Lieutenant Olivera, the Hembree chief of police, who actually found them, in an alcove in the cellar of an old house."

"An alcove, you say?"

"Are you familiar with Morris House on McAllister?"

"I can't say that I am."

"It's at the end of the street, a dilapidated old place."

"And this alcove…how did the lieutenant run across it?"

"A body was discovered in the tool shed," Mosey said.

"My goodness."

"It's complicated," Mosey sipped her champagne, "but to get to the crux of the matter, Olivera brought the paintings to the shop, hoping Nadia might be able to fill him in on their value."

"I knew, of course," Nadia said, "they were casta paintings and by the same artist who painted the portrait of Fernanda, but more than that…"

"What it boils down to—" Dave came back into the room. "—is that the victim, Will Grayson, had no business at the Morrises', especially so early in the morning, unless he'd gone there on some important errand. Another man, a young man, was spotted in the yard around the time of Grayson's death. The lieutenant, in looking for motive, began to suspect that the paintings might be at the heart of it. He thinks Grayson could have gone there to retrieve the paintings and the other fellow stopped him."

"Does he have anything, this lieutenant, to tie

Grayson to the paintings?" Morell asked.

"Not really," Dave replied, "though Grayson was a friend of the man who once lived there, now deceased. Kit Morris was his name. I don't suppose you knew him."

"Kit Morris," Morell repeated pensively. "It doesn't sound familiar." He shook his head. "No, I don't think so."

"You know, before we continue with this, I would like to propose a toast." Dave lifted his champagne flute. "To Mosey and Nadia, for completing for you, Father, what has been a life's work." He nodded to the women. "We are forever in your debt."

Mosey smiled, lifting her flute. "We're thrilled to have played a small part in this remarkable undertaking of yours, Mr. Morell." She glanced at the paintings, still in their wrappings.

"I couldn't have put it better," Nadia said. "And we were very lucky to have them literally fall into our hands. If it weren't for the death of poor Will Grayson, they might have never seen the light of day."

"Speaking of which," Morell said, "have you wondered how they ended up concealed?"

"We can't be sure," Mosey said, "but—"

"Hold on a second, Mosey," Dave cut in. "I'd like Father to see them first." He and Morell carefully unwrapped the artworks and positioned them back on the easels. "As you were saying…"

"Well, we can't be certain all of this is true, but we've concocted a scenario of sorts. Kit's poker buddies—this was back around the time of World War II—used the cellar for their weekly poker games, which continued on for, well, I'm not really sure how long…maybe decades. That much we *do* know. You see, my grandfather was one of the regulars. We also know that Arnold Bilyeu *pawned* the paintings, so to speak, left them with Kit in payment of a gambling debt. Toni actually appraised them for Arnold some years later, assuming he might be ready to sell them, but it never happened. After Arnold died, they remained with Kit. He didn't sell them, either, though he certainly could have used the money."

Morell, who had been gazing at the paintings, looked at Mosey. "So, I guess the question is *why* have they been hidden from the world for so long."

"We're hoping," Nadia said, "that with your knowledge of iconography, you might be able to see something we can't."

He pulled out a pair of reading glasses and scrutinized the smaller of the two paintings. "This one, according to Cardoso's invoice, is titled *Portrait of Hershel Bilyeu at Work in His Apothecary*."

"The name of the woman isn't mentioned?" Dave asked.

"No" —Morell glanced at his son— "though if I am permitted to purchase the painting, I would certainly include it in the caption. The names of *castas*, a term I don't care for, are frequently omitted."

"Why is that?" Mosey asked.

"These paintings are all about class, though sometimes they have been mistakenly thought to be more about race," Morell explained.

Mosey, appearing a bit confused, said, "Wait, does that mean they *aren't* about race?"

"Yes and no. The culture that was responsible for their existence sought to set parameters, you could say, for interactions among the classes. If you were born in Spain, you were a *peninsular*, in other words, at the top of the social ladder, but if you were born in America, you were a *criollo* and had a slightly lower standing in society. A person's rank was established at birth and, oftentimes recorded as such in the church registry at the infant's christening. None of this was taken lightly. A person's rights were often determined by status."

"So, what about Bilyeu's status?" Mosey asked.

"He's portrayed here as an aristocrat"—Morell looked back at the painting—"but he wasn't from Spain. The Bilyeus were French Bourbon, and the painting's iconography suggests that."

"Would you mind being a little more specific?" Mosey said.

"Of course. Take a look at Hershel's clothing and the objects in the room. Only a person of his status, a distinguished Frenchman of considerable means, would have been able to afford such an outfit or the other accoutrements you see here."

"And the woman?"

"Haitian, likely a freed slave and therefore a casta."

"So she's a casta, he's not, and yet they are together."

"That was often the point, to show how people of different statuses related and, through the depiction of that relationship, make a sort of *pronouncement* to the viewer of the painting. *If you associate with a person of this ancestry, you might expect*—"

"Sounds rather prejudicial, does it not?" Mosey cut in.

"Indeed"—he arched a brow—"but the so-called enlightened people of the time tended to think that way."

"What about the other painting?" Nadia asked. "I'd be especially curious to know if you see anything there that the owner wouldn't have wanted others to know."

Morell examined the composite scene by scene. "There's a lot of information here, sixteen separate depictions. Generally speaking, composites are sequential, and after looking at a few of these, you'll notice that, in the first scene, you'll find the epitome of aristocracy and in the last, the complete opposite, the person to whom society has granted no status whatsoever. Here we have a man, a *peninsular*, from all indications" —he gestured toward the central figure in the first vignette— "in the company of a woman, his wife we might assume, who also appears to be a *peninsular*. Their child, however, is not." He paused. "Interesting."

"What do you see?" Dave asked.

"The painter has labeled the little girl" —he pointed to the child, who was no more than a toddler— "by writing the word *mestiza* below her cradle. I've seen this sort of thing before. In this case, it might indicate that the child was the product of a so-called private birth."

"Private?" Mosey asked.

"Yes, private," Morell continued, "meaning that one of the parents, though not a biological parent, claimed the child as his or her own."

"The biological mother or father was of a different status, then," Nadia concluded.

"Yes, that's right."

"So, who *were* these people?" Dave asked.

"I can't say for sure," Morell said, "but there is an interesting clue here. You see the brooch the wife is wearing?"

Mosey and Nadia drew near the painting. "Yes,"

Nadia said, "I noticed that when I was studying the painting back at the shop."

"If you look at the portrait of Fernanda de Lobos," Morell turned toward the painting that hung on the wall nearby, "she is wearing an identical brooch."

Nadia inhaled deeply. "This first vignette, then, implies that Fernanda was of mixed blood?"

"Fernanda?" Mosey shot him a puzzled look.

"We're assuming the woman with the brooch is Fernanda's mother," Nadia explained. "She could have passed the brooch to her daughter, who is wearing it there." Nadia nodded toward the portrait as Dave walked over and switched on the light above it.

"How beautiful," Mosey exclaimed.

"You've seen it before," Nadia said.

"Yes, but it's been years. Stunning."

"I would say the star of the collection," Morell said. "Strictly speaking, it isn't necessarily a casta painting, though I've always considered it one."

"Or maybe it *is*," Mosey said. "Maybe Cardoso was trying to make a point."

"I wonder if Cardoso might have actually painted in the brooch to suggest just that," Dave suggested. "Despite what the people of the time would have considered a hindrance, Fernanda de Lobos rose to the level of a *peninsular*."

"Yes and no." Nadia looked at Dave. "She was beautiful and quite distinguished, but—"

"True," Mosey cut in, "but Cardoso was not privy to Fernanda's...well, he wouldn't have known about the heirlooms. All that happened *after* he painted the portrait."

"That's right." Nadia nodded at Mosey. "When

Cardoso painted the portrait, she wouldn't have yet committed the crime she was later known for, namely, the theft of her father's heirlooms."

"Well," Mosey said, "I think I'm beginning to get the picture. Pardon the pun." She snickered. "Arnold didn't want the paintings seen because of what they revealed about his ancestors."

"And that was substantial"—Nadia glanced at Mosey—"considering that Fernanda and her descendants wouldn't have been able to inherit, given their casta status."

Mosey approached the composite and stood gazing at one vignette after another. "We know what this first vignette suggests, but what about these others? Who knows? Each one may have something to say about the Bilyeus—or some other family."

"True," Morell said, "and, if you like, I'd be glad to look at all that. But it would take some time. How long might I keep them?"

"I promised Lieutenant Olivera I'd give him a call," Nadia said, "and if you want, I'd be glad to ask."

"Yes, and please let him know that when all this is straightened out, I would like to purchase both of these."

"But *from whom* is the question. My guess is that they belong legally to the Morris sisters, but I imagine a case could be made for their belonging to Arnold's family. And the New Orleans Bilyeus being his next of kin…"

"That sounds like a matter we might take up with Carlotta," Mosey said.

"Carlotta?" Morell asked.

"Carlotta Humphrey, my step-aunt," Mosey clarified. "She took over the family law firm when my father died. The Bilyeus are old clients of ours."

"Well, I would like to approach the rightful owner, whoever that might be, as soon as you know."

"And in the meantime," Nadia said, "please do continue to study the paintings. Whatever you can decipher…"

## Chapter Twenty-Eight

*Police Station*
*Wednesday, 4:00 p.m.*

Olivera sat in his cubicle staring at the evidence board and feeling frustrated. He'd contacted every person he could think of who might help speed up the progress of the case. Even so, it was still stuck, going nowhere in particular. He focused his attention on Krueger's mug shot. He was holding him in custody, waiting for Mosey or Lauren to press charges. But neither had. He'd also considered driving out to Larkspur to question DeGroat regarding his whereabouts on the morning of January 4. But having handed over the cufflink to Nadia, he'd decided to hold off till she returned, thinking she might come up with a name for the designer if not the customer.

As his eyes scanned the board, he couldn't help but feel underwhelmed at the meager amount of evidence. The mug shot, the snapshots of the tool shed and the thicket where Mosey had been attacked. What else did he have except for the cufflink? Aha! He sat up in his chair. The poison, sarin, as Eads had called it. He picked up the phone and punched in the number of the morgue. "Uh, Dr. McGinnis," he cleared his throat, "Olivera here."

"What's up?"

"It totally skipped my mind—the sarin. Know any more about that?"

"I spoke with Hayes over at the feed store. Likely he'd know if any farmers in the area use it as a pesticide."

"And do they?"

"No, not sarin. But they do use a common type of organophosphate."

"Uh, excuse my ignorance, but what is that?"

"Man-made chemicals for killing mammals and insects. Sarin is one, but it's dangerous and mostly used in warfare, as a weapon of mass destruction. The less deadly organophosphates are used in agriculture, including home gardens."

"So, Grayson, in his work, might have come in contact with a…what you said."

"Organophosphate. Yes, he might have. In fact, I would say it's likely. And one more thing. It's a common self-harm substance."

"Self-harm, eh?"

"So, I guess we can't rule out suicide, but it looks to me like the smear on the face was probably accidental. I found a spot of it on the top of his right hand. He might have gotten some of it on him, then touched his right cheek, which is where I found the first bit."

"Hmm. Doesn't sound like—"

"No, it doesn't," she agreed.

"Well, we'll keep it in mind."

"You could ask DeGroat if they're using organophosphates at Larkspur."

"Ha, that ought to rattle him. Suppose he says yes? What then?"

"Good question. And I suppose he might. Even if he doesn't drive a tractor, he probably pays the bills."

He chuckled at the thought of DeGroat perched on a tractor. "I'll catch you later. I think I'll drop by the Tavernette, see if any of the older locals know anything." He placed the receiver on the hook and got up from his chair. "Hey, Springer."

"Yeah, Chief."

"I'm going out for a spell. Running over to the Tavernette. If you hear from Nadia or Mosey, ask them to call my cell."

"Sure thing, Chief."

He slipped on his sports jacket and headed through the front office, waving his hat to Ms. Hill.

"You have something for me, Lieutenant?" she inquired.

"Not really. I doubt I make it back today. I have a few things to handle," he replied.

"Okay, then. See you tomorrow."

The Tavernette was two short blocks away, and he paced it quickly, hoping to get ahead of the happy hour crowd. As luck would have it, he arrived in time to get a seat at the counter and, waving at the bartender, called out, "Clinton, a lager when you can."

The bartender placed a coaster in front of him. "Short or tall?"

"Short. And, by the way, are any of the ladies around—Ruby or Miffy?"

"They're both here. Shall I call them for you?"

"No, I'll catch them in passing." He twisted around, hoping to spot Ruby or Miffy—or Ms. Tisdale would have done in a pinch—but no one was around, except A. B. and DeGroat, at a corner table in the dining room. Once his beer had arrived and he'd taken a few sips, he paid the bill, and, picking up his glass, headed into the dining room. DeGroat, who was sitting at a table against the wall, caught sight of him and mumbled something to A. B., who, without turning around, finessed a glance in his direction.

"Hello, gentlemen." He approached. "Mind if I join you for a moment?"

"Not at all." DeGroat rose and pushed back a chair. "Have a seat."

"Thanks." Olivera placed his beer on the table and sat across from A. B. "Looks like we beat the crowd."

"Indeed, we did," A. B. said. "You off work so early, Lieutenant?"

"I would prefer not to be, but this case I'm working on is dragging."

"What case is that?"

"Will Grayson. Did you know him?"

"Vaguely, not personally."

"I read about it in the paper," DeGroat said.

"I thought he died of natural causes," A. B. said.

"Maybe he did. It's not clear. He was a sick man. Stomach cancer."

"That's what I heard." He picked up his glass and wiped away the dampness with his napkin. "So, you think there's more to it?" He looked at Olivera.

"The circumstances suggest there might be."

"Circumstances?"

"You have to wonder what he was doing at Morris House at that hour of the morning. He didn't work there anymore. The house, in fact, had been sold to Dr. Lauren Wilson, the new forensic psychologist at Blanchard. Then"—he raised his brow—"we discovered the house has a secret cellar."

"Secret," A. B. said, surprise in his voice. "There's

nothing secret about it, Lieutenant."

"You were aware—?"

"Course I was." A. B. gave a half frown.

"Seems the new owner didn't know. I suppose you knew about the poker game, too?"

"Half the town must have known—" A. B. chuckled. "—though the chief of police pretended not to. Ha!"

"Interesting. Those were different times."

"Maybe not as different as you think." A. B. took a sip of his drink.

Olivera ignored A. B.'s insinuation. "Guess I missed the fun."

As A. B. was sipping to the bottom of his glass, Ruby arrived. "Can I get you another mojito, Mr. Bilyeu?"

"You surely can." He pushed his glass in her direction. "Cecil, you want another?"

"Sure." DeGroat placed his glass on her tray.

"Lieutenant, would you care for something?" A. B. asked.

"No thanks. I'm good."

"Two mojitos, then." He looked at Ruby and smiled as she picked up his glass.

"I'll be right back with those."

"You know, in those days," A. B. continued, "Arkansas was dry. Why, most of the country was dry, and gambling was strictly forbidden. Course, we had it a little easier in New Orleans, but around here, people had to make their own entertainment. Kit Morris kept that game going for a good twenty years or more, and my cousin Arnold never missed a game, so I hear."

"Never missed a game." Olivera casually lifted his beer.

"Arnold was a consummate poker player. Not that good, but he loved to play—win or lose. Loved to gamble."

"I heard he racked up some debts."

"You did, did you?" A. B. gave him a probing look.

"Yes, I did." He knew it was risky to speak of a dead family member's financial affairs, but given his current state of disgruntlement, he was ready to go for broke. "There's a theory, not sure it's much more than that," he continued, "that Arnold settled a dept with Kit Morris, something about a painting, two paintings, actually."

A. B. turned to his nephew. "Never heard him speak of that, did you, Cecil?"

"Can't say that I did." DeGroat shrugged and looked away, apparently reluctant to make eye contact with either his uncle or Olivera.

Olivera, increasingly emboldened, stared unabashedly at DeGroat. "I thought you might."

"Why is that?" DeGroat glanced at Olivera.

"You're a lawyer, aren't you?"

"I am."

"Somebody must be dealing with the finances." Olivera gave the table a couple of pats with his palm.

"My uncle Emile looked after things for Ninon for a while after her father died. But as far as finances are concerned, I'm sure any debts would have been paid."

Though he wasn't about to take DeGroat at his word, Olivera nodded and responded in a friendly manner. "I'm sure everything must have been settled when Ninon died…or before. *But those heirlooms…*" He took a sip of his beer. "It's always bothered me that valuable items like the dagger and the dueling pistols were passed from one Bilyeu to the next with no mention whatsoever in the wills—except for Ninon's, of course. I wonder what Internal Revenue might have to say about that."

Neither DeGroat nor A. B. responded. It seemed as if he'd caught them red-handed and anything they said—without first consulting with Carlotta—might put them in jeopardy if they weren't in it up to their necks already.

Finally, A. B. spoke. "Lieutenant, can I order you another beer?"

Olivera looked down at his empty glass. "I guess another wouldn't hurt."

A. B. waved at Ruby. "Miss, please bring the lieutenant another beer when you bring the mojitos."

"Sorry about that, Mr. Bilyeu," Ruby said. "I'll bring those right away." She picked up the glass and hurried away toward the bar.

"Now then," A. B. said, his bottom jaw nervously shifting back and forth. "Let's get to the bottom of this."

"Of what?" Olivera said naively.

"Obviously, something is amiss with the finances," A. B. responded. "Why don't you just put your cards on the table?"

"For all I know, the finances are fine. What's worrisome to me is those paintings."

"Paintings?" A. B. exclaimed, a hint of color tinting his cheeks. "Exactly which paintings are we talking about?"

"You *must* know," Olivera responded coolly. "They belonged to the Bilyeus."

"I assure you, Lieutenant—" The portly gentleman lifted up slightly on his elbows. "—I do not know."

"The casta paintings." Olivera thought A. B. seemed rattled, and it didn't look like pretense to him. But it

277

could be. He found the man hard to read.

"Casta paintings." A. B. cast a hard stare at his nephew.

DeGroat, throwing out a hand, stared back at his uncle. "I have no idea what he's talking about."

To Olivera's amusement, DeGroat's defensive gesture allowed a cuff to slip from his coat sleeve, and Olivera reached for the flaring cuff. "Mr. DeGroat, you're missing a cufflink."

DeGroat glanced at his sleeve. "So I am."

"It wouldn't be a *gold* cufflink, would it?"

"Might be." DeGroat checked his other cuff. "Yes, I guess so."

"Engraved with a fylfot?"

He didn't react.

Olivera took out his cellphone and tapped the Photos icon. "Today...over at Morris House...Sergeant Springer ran across a cufflink or a piece of one." He tapped on the photo Springer had sent him and handed the phone to DeGroat. "I don't suppose..."

DeGroat looked, then handed the phone back to Olivera.

"Let me see that." A. B. reached for the phone and, after eyeing the photograph, turned his attention to DeGroat. "Your momma gave you those cufflinks if I'm not mistaken." He handed the phone back to Olivera.

"Yes, she did," DeGroat said, "and now I've lost one. A pity."

"You want to explain to me," Olivera said, "what you were doing at the Morris property? We could head over to the station if you prefer."

"No, I would *not* prefer." DeGroat glared at Olivera.

"Well?"

DeGroat glanced at his uncle, who seemed every bit as curious as Olivera. "If you must know, I went over there to see if I could reason with Will Grayson."

"About what, pray tell?" A. B. asked.

"I thought I might be able to talk some sense into him, but he was hell bent on following through with his plan."

"What plan?"

DeGroat glanced from A. B. to Olivera and, ignoring his uncle's question, said, "I can promise you this, I didn't harm him in any way. He collapsed on me, and I carried him into the shed at the back of the property. When I left, he was alive."

"Well, he didn't live for long," Olivera said. "When we found him, he was dead, hidden behind a bunch of old paint cans."

DeGroat cocked his head. "I didn't see any paint cans."

Feeling a tad flummoxed, Olivera shook his head and sighed. Either DeGroat was telling the truth, or he was the best blamed liar he'd run across in a while. How could he have carried Grayson into the shed and deposited him on the ground without at least *seeing* the cans? Even if he hadn't placed them around the body, surely he would have noticed… "I'll be honest with you, Mr. DeGroat. I just don't see how that could be. How could you not see—?"

"Well, it was dark in there," DeGroat cut in. "I offered to call a doctor, but he insisted I leave him there. He didn't want to see a doctor."

"So you just left?"

DeGroat nodded. "I assumed he might be living there in the shed."

"Let's back up a minute." Olivera, who'd been basically winging it, pulled out his notepad and, after wiping up a circle of moisture, set it on the table. He looked around for Ruby. "I wonder what's taking her so long."

"I was wondering that myself," A. B. said.

Olivera stood and, spotting the bartender, waved. The bartender signaled and Olivera sat back down. He glanced at DeGroat. "Let's go back to your reason for going to Morris House."

"Grayson was blackmailing me—well, us, actually—but I didn't want my uncle to know."

A. B. frowned at his nephew.

"Grayson claimed he had evidence of something the Bilyeus wouldn't want known, and if we didn't pay up, he would make sure the word got out."

"Did he say what?"

"No. He said he'd tell me later, at the Morrises' on McAllister. He told me to meet him there at six a.m. sharp and to bring the money."

"How much money?" A. B. asked.

"Ten thousand."

Olivera raised his brow. "That's a nice sum, not exorbitant, but… Did you take it with you?"

"No, of course not."

"Wise," Olivera said.

A. B. knuckled DeGroat on the arm. "Why in tarnation didn't you say something?"

He looked at his uncle. "Like I said, I was hoping I could talk some sense into him."

"Convenient he dropped dead, well, not immediately," Olivera said sarcastically.

"I did *not* kill the man," DeGroat blurted.

"Not saying you did," Olivera said calmly.

"And what makes you think somebody killed him? According to the paper, he could have died of natural causes."

"Yes, maybe he did. Your story sounds plausible to me. Uh-huh. It could have happened just that way…except for the paint cans."

"I'm telling you, there *were* no paint cans."

"When we found Grayson, there were paint cans stacked in front of the body, between the body and the door. I seriously doubt he put them there himself."

"Maybe he did. Maybe he didn't want anybody to see him."

"Hmm." Olivera rolled his eyes around, as if were searching for an answer in thin air. Then, thinking out loud, he said, "He was in the shed, feeling too bad to get out of there, maybe heard someone coming and stacked the paint cans in front of him. I suppose it could have happened that way." He looked at DeGroat.

DeGroat shook his head. "All I know is that he wasn't dead when I left him, and I didn't see any paint cans."

"And this alleged blackmail scheme of Grayson's. Any idea what he was talking about?"

"He wouldn't say."

"Any idea why he chose Morris House as a meeting place?"

"Not really, although he gave me to understand that his so-called *evidence* was there…inside the house, I suppose." DeGroat shook his head. "Or who knows. It could have been in the shed or the yard. Or maybe there *wasn't* any evidence."

"Did you know the house is occupied?"

"Well, I assumed. There was a car parked in front."

"Dr. Lauren Wilson lives there now, just moved in. She bought it from the Morris sisters, Kit's sisters. Kit Morris was a friend of Arnold Bilyeu."

"Yes," A. B. interjected, "I knew Kit."

"And you, Mr. DeGroat, did you know him?"

"Before my time."

"Not really," Olivera said.

"Well, before my time in Hembree."

"But Emile surely would have known him," Olivera said.

"Maybe he did. I don't remember him ever mentioning him."

The drinks arrived, and Ruby dispensed them with apologies. "I am so sorry." She placed mojitos in front of A. B. and DeGroat. "These are on the house, gentlemen. Your beer, too, Lieutenant.."

Chapter Twenty-Nine

*Tavernette*
*Wednesday, 5:00 p.m.*

Olivera was getting answers. But, *diablos*, not the ones he expected. DeGroat had copped to meeting Grayson at the house, even owned up to carrying him to the shed. But he had confessed to nothing criminal. Even more worrisome, neither Bilyeu nor DeGroat knew anything about the casta paintings. Surprising, right?

Just as he was leaving the Tavernette, a streak of lightning opened up the sky. He hovered under the awning as rain pelted the sidewalk, splattering his pants legs and shoes. His cellphone buzzed. "Springer?" he said as he answered.

"Yeah, it's me, Chief. You won't believe this."

"I'd believe anything about now. What you got?"

"Dr. Wilson called again. She wants us back over there soon as possible."

"Something happen?"

"Well, yeah." He sounded distressed. "She had somebody out to trim up the thicket, and—"

Lightning struck again, and Olivera moved closer to the entrance. "What?"

"A tombstone, he found a tombstone."

"In the thicket?"

"Yeah!"

"Gather up the gear and pick me up in front of the Tavernette."

"What you want us to bring, Chief?"

"The usual, and a couple of shovels." Olivera dropped his phone in his pocket and was about to re-enter the foyer when A. B. and DeGroat came out.

A. B. pulled up his collar. "You need a lift, Lieutenant?"

"Thanks, but Springer's coming to pick me up."

"I thought you'd finished for the day."

"As did I, but you never know in this business."

A. B. chuckled. "We'll be seeing you, Lieutenant."

DeGroat whipped out an umbrella, opened it, and held it above his uncle's head. They hurried to the curb where a car had pulled up. The driver stepped out and courteously opened the door for A. B.

Within a few minutes, Springer arrived in the van. Olivera got in and, fetching a handkerchief from his breast pocket, wiped the rain from his hands and face.

"Reagan—" Springer looked back."—pass the chief a towel, would you?"

Reagan reached in the back for a towel. "Here you go, Lieutenant."

"Thanks." As he ran the towel down his sleeves, he turned to Springer, "Did you let her know we're coming?"

"Yeah, I did. They'll be waitin' for us on the porch—her and Frank Ferguson."

"Good, I'd like to expedite this quickly as possible."

"Why's that, Chief?"

Olivera shook his head. "Frustration."

"I know what you mean. I figured by now we'd know somethin', but the evidence so far don't amount to much."

"Not at all clear to me where this is going," Olivera said, surprised to hear the words come out of his mouth. He wasn't usually so frank with the sergeants. He wasn't sure why, maybe some macho thing he'd picked up as a kid. "By the way, you guys see Bilyeu and DeGroat get into a car back there?"

"Yeah, I did," Springer said.

"They were in the Tavernette." He looked at Springer.

"You learn anything?"

"Yeah, but not sure it was helpful. Just slammed another door."

"What door?" Reagan asked.

"That cufflink belongs to DeGroat." Olivera twisted around. "And he admitted being at the Morris house, admitted talking to Grayson."

"Good grief," Reagan exclaimed. "That don't sound like nothin' to me."

"He claimed that when he left him, Grayson was still alive and there weren't any paint cans stacked around."

"What the heck was he doing there?" Reagan asked.

"Grayson was blackmailing him, or so he claimed." Olivera turned back around.

"Well, that sure speaks to motive," Springer said.

"Yeah, it does, but he sounded convincing to me. And when I tossed out a question about the casta paintings, neither he nor A. B. knew anything about them."

"Chief," Springer said, "you're not taking their word for it, are you? You know they'd lie to cover their hides."

"I can't disagree with you there."

"You placed DeGroat at the scene of the crime."

"If there *was* a crime," Olivera added.

"That again?"

"Dr. McGinnis hasn't come up with any evidence of homicide. Grayson could have died of natural causes, for all we know."

Springer sighed and said nothing.

The rain was slacking off, and Springer turned down the windshield wipers, which had been on high speed since Olivera had gotten in the van. "I know what you're thinking." Olivera glanced at Springer. "But she's been right before, don't forget."

Reagan scooted toward the front seat. "She darn well has. She nailed it with that other dude."

Olivera looked back at Reagan. "Ashby?"

"Yeah, Ashby."

"Sure did."

As the threesome continued their wrangling about what had happened and what hadn't, they soon arrived at Morris House, and Olivera looked toward the porch. "There they are. Better park close to the thicket, close as you can."

Springer stopped the van at the curb. Olivera got out and motioned to Wilson, who waved him over. She was standing next to Ferguson, who was wearing work clothes and a baseball cap flipped backwards.

"Lieutenant, you know Frank Ferguson?" She and Ferguson came to the edge of the porch.

"Course. What'd you find, Mr. Ferguson?"

"I was thinning out some trees, the smaller ones over yonder." He gestured toward the trees. "And just as I pulled up the trunk of a dead elm, an old tombstone fell out."

Olivera was already aware of the situation, but even

so, his heart skipped a beat. "A tombstone."

"Yeah. Looked like a tombstone to me, like you see in really old cemeteries."

"Is that all? You didn't see anything under it?"

"I didn't really look."

Olivera eyed the thicket. "Can you show me what you saw?"

Ferguson came down the steps, and Olivera expected Wilson to follow, but she didn't. He glanced back, just as the screen door closed. "Reagan," Olivera called, "bring the cones. And might as well bring the shovels, too."

"Not sure you'll need to do any digging," Ferguson said. "The tombstone came right up with the root ball."

While Reagan hung back, setting cones along the edge of the thicket, Olivera and Springer followed Ferguson in among the trees. Ferguson patted the trunk of the toppled tree—an elm, a rather small one. The root ball, well-exposed, balanced above a deep hole. A rustic gravestone was tangled in the roots along with the lid of a casket. A small skull—about the size of an infant's head—and the top half of a skeleton dangled within the lid. Olivera shot a beam into the casket where the other half of the skeleton lay.

Springer removed his hat and held it over his heart. "Couldn't have been more than an infant." He sighed.

"You stay here, Springer," Olivera said. "I've got to give Dr. McGinnis a call." He took a few steps and turned back. "Mr. Ferguson"—he beckoned—"I'd like to get a statement."

"Sure, Lieutenant."

He and Ferguson walked out onto the lawn. The rain had stopped, and Wilson was back on the porch, still in overalls and with a jacket draped over her shoulders.

Olivera advanced to the edge of the steps and looked up at Wilson. "I need to contact the coroner, and then I'd like to speak to you and Mr. Ferguson." He walked up on the porch. "But first I think I'll give Robert Ellison a call. He's helped with this sort of thing in the past."

"This sort of thing?"

He nodded. "Excuse me a second." He walked past Wilson toward the far end of the porch and, stopping under the light, tapped in Ellison's number at the college. "Robert, glad I caught you."

"Lieutenant, I was closing up shop for the day. What's up?"

"I wonder if you could drop by Morris House. We've come across something that warrants a consultation."

"What'd you find?" Robert asked.

"Frank Ferguson was clearing out a thicket on Dr. Wilson's property and unearthed what looks like an old grave."

"Grave? You mean—"

"There's a tombstone dislodged by a tree," Olivera cut in. "Looks like when the tree fell, the root ball came up." He cleared his throat. "A small skeleton, an infant, I'm thinking…"

"Good lord."

"I'm about to call Dr. McGinnis, but I would like to get your opinion, yours and Dr. Jessup's if he's around."

"I'll find him, and we'll be right over. You're at Morris House?"

"That's right." Olivera clicked off and phoned McGinnis. "Dr. McGinnis."

"Lieutenant."

"I'm at Morris House."

"Again?"

"Yeah." He turned away and lowered his voice. "Looks to me like the skeletal remains of a child—"

"Where?"

"Frank Ferguson found an uprooted tree, or maybe he pulled it out of the ground. Not sure exactly what he said. But there was an old gravestone tangled in the roots, and I guess the root ball must have pulled up, well, what was left."

"My word."

"Yeah, looks like the skeleton of a small child, no more than an infant, uh, would be my guess."

"I'll get my gear and be right over." She clicked off.

While they waited for McGinnis and the others, Olivera, Wilson, and Ferguson went into the house. She scooted a couple of folding chairs in front of the fireplace, and once they had all seated themselves, Olivera asked a few perfunctory questions. "I don't suppose either of you would have any thoughts about how this, uh, *burial* came about." He looked from one to the other, and both shook their heads. Olivera didn't press it, not expecting to learn anything relevant to the actual burial from either of them. "Mr. Ferguson, you didn't happen to notice any markings on the tombstone, did you?"

"To tell you the truth, Lieutenant, I didn't really look."

"I don't suppose so. And you, Dr. Wilson, did you see the stone?"

"Not up close. My first thought, well, maybe not my first, but soon I realized…"

"You didn't want to contaminate the site?"

"Yes, that's what I was thinking."

When a knock came at the front door, Olivera stopped his questioning. "That'll be Dr. McGinnis, I imagine."

"I'll get it." Wilson said.

He heard her open the door and invite McGinnis in. Then McGinnis said, "Actually, could you ask Lieutenant Olivera to step out?"

He went to the door.

"Lieutenant, I'd like to see the site while we've still got some daylight." She glanced at her watch. "Sunset in fifteen."

"Sure, let's get over there. I left Springer at the site."

They walked to the thicket and made their way toward the grave. With a nod, she acknowledged Springer, who'd remained close to the site, and setting her case on the ground, she retrieved a camera and light. "Hold this for me, would you, please, Springer?" She handed him the light, and he switched it on.

He positioned it several feet from the root ball. "Is that good?"

"A little higher. I want to start at the top and move down." She took the first picture. "Okay, a little lower." She took a second shot. "That's good. Now the cavity." Springer aimed the light toward the hole. "Now let's get the area around the tree."

After she and Springer had covered the stretch of ground around the uprooted tree, Olivera said to McGinnis, "You see anything...footprints?"

"Yes, but I doubt they can tell us anything. Whatever evidence was here is long gone." She returned the camera to its case. "That'd be my guess."

"Of course, but still—"

"Still what?" she asked, looking up.

"Nothing." His eyes remained fixed on the broken remains of the child.

"I'll run some tests. We'll get something, but identification is less likely in the case of an infant."

"Ellison and Jessup are on their way."

"Good. Their equipment is better than mine."

"Yeah."

Chapter Thirty

*Morgue*
*Wednesday, 7:00 p.m.*

Around seven o'clock, Olivera and McGinnis entered the dimly lit morgue. Inside, surrounded by darkness, he fumbled for the light switch as she wheeled the dolly with the evidence toward the gurney. The eerie ambiance added an extra layer of unease to the nerve-racking experience at Morris House, where they had completed the exhumation initiated by the toppled elm. In stark contrast to its typical serene and solemn atmosphere, the morgue now resembled a foreboding chamber, with mysterious shadows lurking along the walls.

He helped McGinnis lift the body bag containing the skeleton onto the sheet. Then, gesturing toward the small casket, "What about this?" he asked.

"Just over there." She nodded toward the table on the other side of the gurney.

He placed the casket on the table. "And this?" He eyed the gravestone, wrapped in semi-transparent packaging.

"You can put that on the table, too."

She tossed the jumpsuit she had worn at the site into a bin and, putting on her lab coat, returned to the gurney. After pulling on latex gloves, she began her visual inspection of the bones. "I suppose we're looking for the usual—age at death, sex, ancestry of the individual?"

He nodded and went over to the gurney. "With an infant—" He paused, not sure what to ask, given his limited experience with corpses of infants.

"With an infant, it's not the same," she said, breaking into his thought.

"I suppose not."

"Past thirteen, sex becomes obvious in most cases, but with an infant? We have no idea if this is a baby John or a baby Jane."

"So, I suppose…DNA?"

She nodded.

"Can you tell the age?" he asked.

"Just so happens," she looked at him over her readers, "I read an article about this the other day." She pointed toward the small jaw bone. "Even infants have teeth below the gums. *Teeth germs*, they're called. And once you've identified the neonatal line, you can estimate age within a day or two."

"Didn't know that."

She looked up again and, with a wry smile, said, "It's becoming more and more difficult for a victim to conceal its identity, not that baby Jane or John would want to. I suspect this child would like very much for us to know who it is and how it died."

"What makes you think that?"

"Well, wouldn't you?"

"Possibly." He sighed and raised his brow.

She pointed toward the bone at the back of the skull. "Given the shape of the occipital bone and the length of the femur," she pointed to the larger of the leg bones, "I'm confident this is the skeleton of a newborn."

"Meaning?"

"It wasn't stillborn or aborted, which is often the case—"

"—considering the body was concealed."

"Yes, apparently," she added. She scanned the entire skeleton, then said, "I don't see any sign of trauma."

"So murder is unlikely?"

"No, I wouldn't say that. There are other ways."

"Suffocation?"

"Possibly."

"Poisoning?"

"That, too."

"Do you suppose we'll ever know?" he asked.

"Ever?"

"I mean…"

"If you mean can the remains tell us that?"

He nodded.

"Doubtful. There isn't much to go on." She moved from the gurney to the table where he'd placed the casket and gravestone. "But if you think of the larger scenario, infanticide seems unlikely." She slipped off her gloves and put on a fresh pair.

"Because?"

"Someone buried the child clandestinely, yes, but the body was placed in a casket and a stone set on the grave. Murderers don't do that, do they?"

He studied her face. She didn't seem to be speaking rhetorically. She was asking for his thoughts on the matter. Too bad he didn't have much to offer. He'd worked more homicides than he cared to remember but not infanticides. He tilted his head and, echoing her words, said, "Do they?" He stood tapping his fingers on the cool surface of the table. "I suspect they don't, unless the perpetrator knows the child and plans to get rid of it as soon as it's born, maybe has mixed feelings about it…doesn't want to kill the child but feels like—" He stopped, eyes glancing from side to side. "—for whatever reason, he must."

"For what reason?"

"Well, think about it. Why might a person kill an infant?"

She sighed. "Hard to imagine."

"I knew a case once." He walked away from the table. "It involved a woman in California. She wasn't from there. I don't remember where she was from, but she'd been raped by a white man. She wasn't white. I'm not sure what her ancestry was. She didn't want to abort the child, though she knew she wouldn't be able to keep it. Her family would have disowned them both. So she went through with the pregnancy, delivered the child herself, and left it at an old gravesite. A few days later, a group of archaeologists on a field trip found it and took it to a hospital. Miraculously, it survived."

"What happened to the woman?"

He stopped to think, glancing up at the light above the autopsy table. "The judge was lenient. She was given community service."

"That's surprising."

"Not if you had witnessed the trial. She was remorseful. As remorseful as a person *could* be. It was obvious she was horribly torn between what she wanted to do, which was to keep the child, and what her people would have insisted upon if they'd known, which was to avoid any stain on the family honor."

She inhaled and shook her head. "Amazing what people do in the name of honor."

He moved back to the table, stopping in front of the casket. "In this case, the evidence suggests it, doesn't it? A desire to give the infant a proper burial and yet the need to conceal the burial, and birth, too, from others. Whoever *buried* the child didn't want it known she'd *had* the child. But she didn't want it entirely forgotten, either. Otherwise, why place a marker on the grave?"

She shook her head. "You've got me there. Why mark a grave if you want the person who is buried—?"

"Exactly, why?"

She eyed the casket and the stone, then looked at the clock on the wall behind the gurney. "It's almost eight. I haven't had dinner. You suppose we could take a break, continue this later?" She removed her readers, revealing dark circles under her eyes.

"You're tired," he said, "you've had a long day."

"Haven't you?"

"I guess I have. It's been so busy, I haven't stopped to think."

"Maybe you should." She approached and placed her hand in his. "Let's get out of here."

He kissed her on each cheek, then her lips. "Before we go…"

"Yes?"

She hadn't stepped away, and he took that as a sign he might continue. He kissed her again and opening her lab coat, stretched his arms around her waist. His cellphone buzzed. "Hold on."

She stepped back.

He looked at the screen. "It's Hugh Jessup." He answered. "Olivera here."

"Lieutenant, we wanted to pass along what we've found so far."

"And what's that?"

"Couple of things. We've run some tests and looks like the age of the bones would put the death about mid-twentieth century."

"So, fifties, sixties approximately?"

"Right. The images we got of the skeleton aren't telling us much about ancestry. The victim, assuming it was a victim, was too young to show characteristics one associates—"

"Yes," he interrupted. "Dr. McGinnis has concluded the same."

"But there was hair," Hugh added, "and from the sample we tested, we're seeing a possibility of mixed ethnicity."

"Huh," Olivera said, "an infant casta, you're saying."

"What's that?"

"I was just drawing a connection to that *other* business, the casta paintings we found in the cellar at the house."

"Yes, Robert mentioned something."

"Ms. Frye, in fact, is in New Orleans as we speak."

"That's right…she and Nadia."

"And Dave Morell. Get Robert to fill you in." Olivera covered the speaker and turned to McGinnis. "It's all starting to fit together," he whispered. "About time, wouldn't you say?"

"What was that?"

"I was passing on what you were saying to Dr. McGinnis. By the way, you had something else?"

"No, that was it. Time of death, mixed ancestry. I doubt we can get much more unless you want us to try for DNA."

"Can you get results faster than the morgue?"

"Maybe. We aren't equipped here, but I know someone who is. I guess I could call in a favor if you think it's important."

"Well, I doubt they'd find much in the data banks."

"I don't know," Hugh said. "I'll ask. I suppose it's possible the data from a relative of the deceased might be there."

"Yes, which could be decisive. So, please, if you don't mind—"

"I'll try, and I'll let you know."

"Thanks, Hugh. And one more thing, I don't suppose Ms. Frye has been in touch."

"Hold on a second." Hugh said something to Robert, then came back on the line. "Not yet."

"Nadia said she'd give me a call. I suppose I'll have to wait. Thanks, Hugh. And thank Robert for me." He clicked off and dropped the phone in his pocket.

"Sounds like we have approximate time and ancestry," McGinnis said. "I'd say that's good progress," she rubbed her chin. "And possibly motive."

"How you figure?"

"What you were saying about the woman in California." She slipped off her lab coat and tossed it in the bin. "If you think about it, around mid-century in Hembree, among the elite—"

"Why the elite?" he cut in.

"The gravesite. McAllister is a fashionable street, has been since the town was founded." She tapped her finger against her chin. "How do you think it would have set with the Hembree upper crust if one of their own had given birth to a so-called casta?"

"Not well, you're implying?"

"Trust me. Not well at all."

"I thought that sort of thing was common in the South."

"Well, nowadays it's apparent that it was, but back then, as obvious as it must have been, people seemed to have been in denial."

"Huh." He paused, looking at the skeleton. "And with a blackmailer around—"

"A blackmailer?" she asked.

"Will Grayson."

Her brow shot up. "You think he knew—?"

"Maybe not at the time. But according to DeGroat, Grayson had some sort of evidence, probably at Morris House. Maybe he knew about the gravesite. Maybe he even knew who the child's parents were. Or—" He paced around the gurney. "—maybe he didn't know about the paintings but knew about this."

"So, you're saying the Bilyeus—?"

"Could be the Bilyeus. The paintings were theirs. Maybe this child…"

They moved toward the door, and Olivera reached over and flipped off the light. "We'll figure it all out tomorrow. Let's get out of here."

Chapter Thirty-One

*Morell Home, French Quarter*
*Wednesday, 10:30 p.m.*

Nadia and Mosey were delighted to spend the night
at the Morell home in the French Quarter. "What a
beautiful room." Nadia glanced over at Mosey, who was
already fluffing the bed pillow and preparing to slide in
between the pale blue silk comforter and sheets. "You
going to bed already?"

"I'm exhausted. Aren't you?"

"Not really. I imagine you're feeling the effects of
your little accident. You think it's too late to ring up
Olivera? I promised I'd give him a call."

Mosey looked at the clock on the wall. "It's late, but
I somehow doubt Olivera has called it a night. Go ahead,
phone him."

"I suppose what David said could be important to
the case, though I'm not sure how."

Mosey yawned. "Let Olivera figure it out for a
change."

"Don't tell me you've lost interest." Nadia sat on the
twin bed across from Mosey.

"No, but all these pieces of the puzzle—the
paintings, the Bilyeu family history, the Morrises, poor
dead Will—it's all a bit mind-boggling."

Nadia looked closely at her friend. "You feeling

okay?"

"You mean my head?" Mosey got out of bed and walked to the vanity mirror. "It looks okay to me." She brushed the hair away from the bandage. "A little sore."

Nadia grabbed her cellphone from the nightstand. "Get back in bed before you catch cold. I'll phone Olivera, and if he doesn't pick up, I'll leave a message." She tapped in Olivera's number.

"Ms. Abboud, that you?"

"I hope I didn't wake you."

"Not at all. Actually, I just got home, well, not long ago."

"We're in New Orleans. We just made it back from the gallery, and as promised, I wanted to give you a call."

"Did Mr. Morell have any insights about the paintings?"

"Well, he hasn't had much time to study them, but he did notice something that could be relevant to the case. It's a little complicated."

"Go ahead, I'm listening."

"He identified the paintings as Cardosos. Both show up in the artist's inventory, which doesn't make it definite, but it's a start. The smaller of the two is called *Hershel Bilyeu in His Apothecary*, something like that. The other—not sure what he called it—contains a clue in the first scene at the top. If you recall—"

"Hold on a second," he interrupted. "Okay," he said as he came back on. "I've got a photograph on my cell."

"See the woman in the vignette at the top left? She's wearing a brooch."

"Let me enlarge it. Yes, I see that."

"In the portrait Morell bought from Dad some years ago, Fernanda de Lobos is wearing that same brooch."

"Okay…meaning?"

"It's very likely that the brooch ties Fernanda to the composite. The couple in the first vignette are *peninsulares*, and yet the painter labeled their child a *mestiza*. Morell suspects the child might have been the product of a private pregnancy, meaning either the mother or the father was not the child's biological parent."

"You're saying Fernanda de Lobos, despite her aristocratic status, was a so-called casta?"

"That's what Morell suspects."

"And I suppose that *matters*?"

"According to him, it mattered a great deal. It would have affected her and possibly her descendants' legal right to inherit."

"So, now we get to it!" Olivera exclaimed. "The whole Bilyeu-De Lobos legacy, the plantation—"

"Yes, I suppose all of that would have been brought into question if Fernanda's ancestry—"

"A good reason to keep the paintings out of the public eye," he cut in.

"Yes, and a perfect setup for blackmail."

"I imagine the Bilyeus would have gone to great lengths—"

"Morell seems to think so."

"Yes, from what I've been able to gather, it certainly seems plausible."

"Morell said he'd be glad to continue researching all the vignettes."

"Well, yes, whatever he can come up with, but he may have already given us the key to this whole business." He paused.

"Sorry to have called so late, but I wanted to let you

know."

"Oh, no, I'm glad you called. When do you expect to get back to Hembree?"

"I imagine we'll leave tomorrow morning, though it's a shame it has to be such a quick trip."

"Hold on a second, please, ma'am. I'm getting another call."

"I'll let you go, Lieutenant. I'll be in touch as soon as we get back."

Chapter Thirty-Two

*Olivera's House*
*Wednesday, 10:35 p.m.*

When the phone call from Nadia Abboud in New Orleans came through, Olivera was just preparing to hit the sack. They quickly wrapped up their conversation to allow him to answer an incoming call. Seeing Springer's name on the screen, he had a hunch it was something important. "Hey, Springer, is that you?"

"Yeah, Chief. I hated to phone so late, but we got a problem. I just got a call from my niece. She was on her way home from the Magnolia, and as she was passing Larkspur, she heard some shots. You reckon we'd better drive over there?"

"You mean just now?" Olivera reached for his pants draped over the bedstead. "She heard shots just now?" He glanced down at his watch. "That's strange. Couldn't be hunters, not at this hour."

"I think we need to get over there, Chief."

He picked up his shirt. "Where are you?"

"Home, but I could swing by the station for the squad car, then be at your place in about ten."

"Okay, I'm getting dressed right now. And, Springer, grab some ammo. I hate to say it, but we may need it. I'll meet you out front."

Springer soon arrived, and Olivera got in. He set his

coffee cup in the holder between the seats and passed another cup to Springer.

"Thanks, Chief."

"Any idea what this is about? Your niece say anything?"

"She heard several shots. That's all."

"That's a good distance from here."

"Yeah, a couple of miles."

"I imagine by the time we get there—"

"Yeah," Springer cut in, "whatever it is will be over."

"By the way, I spoke with Nadia Abboud just now. She and Mosey are still in New Orleans."

"Find out anything?"

"Actually, I did." He took a sip of his coffee. "Those paintings may be the key to the whole deal."

"Not too surprising."

As they came to Little Smith Road, Springer stopped, looked both ways, then took off toward the outskirts of town.

"Morell, Dave's father, says it looks like Fernanda de Lobos—you remember her?—is the child in the first scene of the composite. She's just a toddler, but there's a textual inscription that suggests she is ethnically mixed."

"Implying?"

"That Hershel and Fernanda's descendants…that whole line of Bilyeus…shouldn't have been able to inherit."

"Dang!"

"Which explains why Arnold kept the paintings hidden. He couldn't get rid of them. They were too valuable. He'd used them to cover his gambling debts.

But he couldn't sell them, either, for fear of his ancestry coming out, which could have meant financial ruin for the family."

Springer, speeding along, eyes fixed on the road ahead, glanced over. "I follow you so far, Chief, but once Arnold and Ninon were dead, what possible differ'nce could it have made?"

"Good question. What difference *could* it have made and to whom?"

"All the Hembree Bilyeus are dead," Springer said. "We know that much."

"Yeah, they are, and the New Orleans Bilyeus wouldn't have been affected."

"I don't know, Chief. They inherited Larkspur from their cousin."

"Right." Olivera shook his head. "This is a legal nightmare if you ask me. I wonder what A. B. and DeGroat know about this. They were being targeted by Will Grayson. They must know something. They would have wanted to know their vulnerability. Actually, DeGroat being a lawyer—"

Springer broke in. "Reagan and me told you not to trust those two. I wouldn't trust either one of 'em."

"I guess I didn't, either, not in the beginning, but once they'd proved themselves innocent of Ninon's murder—"

"Just because they didn't kill Sister Clare, don't make them innocent in this business. If this is financial, that's a whole differ'nt ball of wax." Springer shook his head. "You got to ask yourself what they would do to protect that nice inheritance should somebody come along and try to ruin it for 'em."

"Even if Grayson was blackmailing them, as

DeGroat claims, he's dead now. Wouldn't that be the end of it?"

"He's dead, all right," Springer said, "but let me ask you somethin', Chief. How did Will, half-nuts and sick as he was, get mixed up in a blackmail scheme?"

"Money?" Olivera took a breath and let it out. "He must have needed money…for medical bills maybe. Or who knows?"

"But to carry out a scheme like that against the Bilyeus? You'd have to have your act together. And Will *did not*. Trust me."

"So, if not Grayson, who?"

"We should have been asking ourselves that all along." Springer gave him a quick glimpse. "Who put Will up to it?"

"Who you think?"

"I don't have any proof of this, mind you, but I think somebody from the old days, somebody close to Kit and Arnold."

"Like the Morris sisters?"

"I seriously doubt that. More like somebody from that old poker group."

"Well, that narrows it down considerably. They're all dead except, let's see…"

"McGinnis is dead," Springer said, "Morris, of course, Frye's dead. There's only one of 'em left, but nobody seems to know much about him."

"Raines's brother?"

Springer nodded. "He's the only one not accounted for. And since he doesn't live here, what's to say he wouldn't have hired somebody like Will to carry out his plan? But now that Will's dead, Raines is gonna have to pull somebody else in or do it himself."

"So, you think this Colton Raines is the brains behind the scheme?"

"Could be, and if he is, he might not stop with the paintings. I bet he's got his eye on Larkspur."

"I don't see that happening." He shook his head.

"If the stakes were high enough…"

"I think I see where you're going, Springer. You think he knows about this other business."

"If he knew about the paintings, he might have known about the dead child, though I have to admit that part's a little fuzzy."

"Not as fuzzy as it was."

"You find out something?"

"The infant died in the 1950s or 1960s, more or less, which falls within the timeframe of the poker game. Knowing what we know now, I have to wonder if the child wasn't *his*—Arnold's I mean. I'm not saying he killed the child, but he might not have wanted the world to know about it, especially if it looked casta."

"Well, Fernanda looked pretty Anglo to me."

"Anglo?" Olivera repeated. "That's the first time I've ever heard you use that word."

"You know what I mean, Chief. White."

"Yeah, she did," Olivera said, "at least in the painting she did. But even if she did look white, or Spanish, or whatever, her casta heritage might have showed up in later generations."

"That makes a pitiful kind of sense, don't it, Chief? Sort of crazy this obsession people have…"

Rambling through the facts of the case, they'd come to the turnoff to Larkspur. Olivera leaned forward and checked his gun. "Turn off the headlights before you pull in, Springer."

"The house is a good quarter mile off the road, Chief."

"I know, but I don't want them to see us coming."

Springer switched off the headlights and, slowing to a crawl, wound his way along the gravel road that led to the dirt road to the remodeled shotgun, the old overseer's cottage, now known as the Summer House. "I see a light ahead, Chief."

"Yeah, that's it. I'm thinking A. B. and DeGroat must have come back. I saw somebody pick them up at the Tavernette. Stop here. We don't want to get too close."

Springer turned off the motor and let the car glide to a stop behind the big pawpaw next to the old main house, now in ruins. The two got out, leaving the car doors open a crack. Olivera paused to listen. The place was quiet except for the sound of the wind, until suddenly, someone burst out of the front door of the shotgun. It was A. B. Bilyeu. Another man, whose movements seemed threatening, stepped out behind him. He was holding a gun on A. B., who turned and moved slowly backwards.

"Psst!" Olivera motioned to Springer and mouthed, "Where's DeGroat?"

Springer shrugged.

Olivera signaled Springer to go around to the back of the house, and after giving him enough time to reach his position, Olivera, with his weapon aimed, stealthily advanced toward the porch. When he was within a few yards of where they were standing, he shouted, "Hold it right there!"

The man, whose identity was a mystery, suddenly came to a halt.

"Drop the gun!" Olivera approached quickly.

"Hands above the head!"

Just then, Springer came through the door. "DeGroat's been shot, Chief."

"Bad?" Olivera, his gun still aimed, clambered up the steps.

"He's passed out, but he's got a pulse."

"Call the paramedics, Springer. I'll take care of this one." He pulled the man's hands behind him, cuffed him, and pushed him in the direction of the squad car. He called back to A. B. "A. B., you want to tell me what's going on?"

A. B. let go of the banister and collapsed onto the top step. "Raines," he gasped, hardly able to catch his breath, "he shot Cecil, and if you hadn't gotten here when you did…"

"Chief," Springer said, "The ambulance squad is on its way."

"Check on DeGroat, Springer. See if you can stop the bleeding. I'll take care of A. B." Olivera opened the backdoor of the squad car and, placing a hand on the suspect's head, pushed him in and closed the door. Hurrying back to the porch, "You okay?" he asked A. B.

"As soon as I catch my breath."

"Take it easy. Just sit there a minute."

While they waited for the paramedics, Olivera called McGinnis. "Were you asleep?"

"Not quite."

"We're at Larkspur. DeGroat's been shot, and we have a suspect in custody."

"Who, for God's sake?"

"I'm about to find out." He moved a few steps away from the porch. "A. B. is here. He's pretty shaken up. Soon as he calms down, I'm going to see what I can find out."

"Is DeGroat hurt badly?"

"Afraid so. The paramedics are on their way."

"You want me to come out?"

"Maybe. Let me see what I can find out first. I'll call you back."

Chapter Thirty-Three

*Delta Infirmary*
*Thursday, 2 a.m.*

Olivera sat outside Cecil DeGroat's hospital room
with McGinnis at his side. He checked his watch.
"Shouldn't be long. They told me I could speak with him
as soon as the anesthetic wears off."

"How's A. B.?" she asked.

"They've got him in a room. His blood pressure was
high. They're running some tests."

"Springer's with the suspect?"

"Yeah, and Reagan."

"Can I get you anything?" She started to get up.

"Why don't you go on home? There's nothing more
to do tonight."

"I think I will." She gathered up her belongings. "I'll
see you in the morning." She headed down the hall
toward the elevator.

The door to the room opened and a nurse in green
scrubs stepped out. "Lieutenant, he's awake, but try to
keep it short."

Olivera went in and stopped at the foot of DeGroat's
bed. He didn't recall having entered a hospital room,
though he'd been in the morgue countless times. The
décor was much like that of the morgue. The bedstead
and nightstand were made of the same heavy, dark wood

he'd noticed in other parts of the building. He remained standing, tapping his hat against his thigh, until DeGroat opened his eyes. "Mr. DeGroat, I'm sorry to have to do this"—he moved closer to the head of the bed—"but I need to ask you some questions."

DeGroat didn't speak, and when he moved, he winced. His right arm was bandaged.

"Mr. DeGroat, can you hear me?"

He winced again and opened his mouth. "Some water…" he mumbled.

Olivera filled a glass with water, then held it to DeGroat's lips. "I suppose it's okay for me to give you this."

He took a sip. "Thanks," he whispered.

Olivera set the glass back on the table and took a seat in the leather armchair next to the bed. "Can you talk?"

"I think so."

"Do you know the man who shot you?"

He slowly shook his head. "Not really."

"But you know who he is."

He nodded. "Hollis Raines."

"You said before that Will Grayson had tried to blackmail you, correct?"

He nodded again.

"Was Grayson working for Hollis Raines?"

"Not sure."

"It's my understanding that you drew your weapon first. Is that right?"

"Yes."

"But you didn't fire."

"No."

"Then Raines fired?"

"Yes."

"Did you provoke him in any way?"

He slowly shook his head.

"I'll need to speak to you again later," Olivera stood, "but I'm going to see if I can talk to your uncle now. I'll be back, but for now, get some rest. I expect that arm is going to be painful for a day or two."

DeGroat gave a moan, and Olivera left, closing the door softly behind him. "Nurse," he said as he approached the nurses station across from the room, "I need to speak to Mr. Bilyeu. Would that be possible?"

"They've given him a mild sedative." She raised her brow. "If he's asleep, I wouldn't bother him."

"Would you mind checking?"

She came from behind the counter, and he followed her to the end of the hall. She stepped into the darkened room, and he entered behind her. "Mr. Bilyeu, Lieutenant Olivera wants to speak to you, but I'm going to limit you to five minutes, understand?" She looked firmly at Olivera and then A. B., who, still dressed, was stretched out in a large recliner next to the bed.

A. B. flopped forward, holding onto the chair arms. "There's nothing wrong with me, I'm telling you."

"Your blood pressure is high," she said, "and the doctor is running some tests."

"I'm getting out of here soon as they let me," he insisted.

"You're spending the night with us, so you might as well get your clothes off and get in bed."

A. B. glared at the nurse, then Olivera. "What'd you let *him* in here for?"

Olivera frowned, having anticipated a little more appreciation, given he'd possibly saved the old guy's life.

"The lieutenant is going to ask you a few questions, and then I want you to get some rest, doctor's orders."

She placed a hospital gown on the bed and left.

"Sorry to bother you, A. B.," Olivera said, "but I would appreciate it if you could clear up a couple of things."

"Isn't it obvious?"

"Maybe."

"Hollis Raines—Colton Raines's son—showed up at the house. Didn't knock, just kicked in the door. Scared me to death. So, Cecil—he was in the kitchen—came through the door. I was in the front room on the sofa. I looked up at Cecil. He'd drawn his gun and was pointing at Raines. Then Raines pulled his gun and shot Cecil."

"Just like that? No threats, discussion, nothing?"

"There might have been if Cecil hadn't pulled his gun."

"You think Raines went there to harm you?"

"If not, what the devil was he doing there, kicking in the door in the middle of the night?"

"Your nephew says he doesn't really know Raines. Do you?"

"Oh, I know him, all right."

"You and Raines live in the same town, correct?"

A. B. nodded. "Yeah, but I was born there. He wasn't. He came to New Orleans with his daddy, years ago. Both of 'em…nothing but scoundrels. Been that way their whole lives."

"Why do you say that?"

"Colton set himself up as a businessman, but turned out he was working some oil scheme—or so I was told.

Never made an honest dime in his life. Then, he caught wind of some trouble with Arnold. Wrung some money out of him. Then when Arnold died, he started in on Emile."

"Emile?"

"Emile Bilyeu, my older brother. He took over Larkspur when Arnold died. And before Emile passed, he sort of put us in charge—me and Cecil. That's when we first learned…"

"When you first learned?" Olivera said.

A. B. shook his head. "About this whole mess." He rubbed his forehead.

"I think I know what you mean."

A. B.'s tired eyes rested on the cold terrazzo floor in front of him. "You've figured it out, have you?" He glanced up at Olivera.

"I believe so, but if you could, tell me if I have it right."

He sighed and nodded.

"Well, to begin with, Arnold Bilyeu had a hefty gambling debt, and he used some heirlooms, two paintings to be exact, to guarantee payment to Kit Morris, his friend and gambling buddy. Kit agreed not to sell the paintings. Said he'd hold them till a time when Arnold had the money to redeem them. But Colton Raines found out about the paintings, and more than that, the *significance* of the paintings for the Bilyeu family."

A. B.'s eyes narrowed.

"Colton Raines," Olivera continued, "being the sort of man he was, used the information against Arnold, and when Arnold died, against Emile, and when Emile died, against you."

A. B. nodded.

"And I suppose," Olivera paused for a moment, "as Colton got on in years, his son Hollis took over for him. Either Colton or Hollis must have brought Will Grayson in on the scheme."

A. B. nodded again.

"But when Will died, looks like Hollis came to Hembree himself, thinking he was ready to bring this long exhortation scheme to an end. He wanted Larkspur, and I guess he was tired of waiting."

A. B. raised his index finger, and Olivera stopped. "He didn't want Larkspur. He wanted *more money*. That's all they *ever* wanted."

"Or maybe to ruin the Bilyeu family reputation," Olivera countered.

Bilyeu chuckled. "Lieutenant, you're mighty innocent for a lawman." He chuckled again. "It was all about the money. They didn't give a plug nickel about *our* reputation, *their* reputation…just the money."

Olivera lifted his brow. "So, it wouldn't have mattered—"

"What?"

"I was just thinking about Arnold Bilyeu and what might have mattered to him. He was Colton Raines's target, his first target. We know Arnold was involved in a murder. The murder of Eugene Brown. But now I'm wondering if he might not have been involved somehow in a *second* murder. You wouldn't know anything about that, I suppose."

He frowned. "What murder?"

"Of a child."

"What child?" He pushed forward in his chair. "What child?" he repeated.

"I don't know what child, but just as we found

Arnold's paintings stashed in the cellar at Morris House, now we've come across a grave, a child's grave. The child died—or was killed—soon after birth, and he or she was buried in the woods next to the house. It occurs to me that just as Arnold had been allowed—"

"Allowed to what?"

"Well, Arnold had a secret. I'm referring to the paintings, which reveal certain ancestral *anomalies*, let us say."

A. B. chuckled again.

"You find this amusing?" Olivera said.

"In a twisted sort of way, yes, sir, I certainly do." A. B. took a breath, then sat bobbing his head.

"Would you mind explaining?"

"Lieutenant, surely you must be familiar with a lot of so-called castas yourself."

"Indeed."

"So why would a man like Arnold go to such lengths to cover up his *anomalies,* as you so delicately put it? Ha!"

"I've been given to understand that so-called castas weren't allowed to inherit."

"True, they weren't. But that rule went out with the Code Noir. Cecil and I inherited not from Arnold but Ninon. Ethnic purity is no longer a requisite—surely you know that. Why the Raineses thought they could put the screws to us is more than I can see."

"You may be right on that score but, should it come out that the Hembree Bilyeus weren't the purebreds they were thought to be—"

"Ha," Bilyeu said, "and just how many *purebreds* do you think you'd find in Hembree?"

"I haven't a clue."

"No, I expect you don't, but let me put it to you this way. How many people of pure Spanish blood do you think you'd find in any Latin American capital?"

"I don't know."

"Precious few is my guess."

"So," Olivera said, "you're saying that the Raineses were playing a losing game?"

"With us, indeed, they were."

Olivera thought for a moment, then stood. "I expect our five minutes is up. I appreciate your frankness, and I think we can continue this conversation when you're feeling better."

"I'm feeling just fine, Lieutenant, and if you'll send that nurse back in, I'm gonna see if I can get out of here tonight."

"Your nephew, I'm afraid, is stuck here for a couple of days."

"So?" Bilyeu said. "I've got a room at the Tavernette, and that's where I'm going if I can get somebody to call me a cab."

"I'm leaving now. I'd be glad to give you a lift, if the nurse—"

"Call her for me, Lieutenant."

Olivera, about to go for the nurse, stopped and looked back at A. B., who was sitting up in the recliner. "There's one thing I don't understand."

"What's that?"

"This afternoon, at the Tavernette, you didn't seem to know about the blackmail scheme. In fact, you seemed annoyed with your nephew for not telling you."

"I didn't know, not about Grayson's recent demands. Cecil has become somewhat protective of his old uncle. But I knew about Colton. I learned all about it

319

from Emile before he died."

Olivera thought for a moment, then opened the door and walked out into the hallway. He signaled the nurse, who looked annoyed but, even so, got up and came toward him.

Chapter Thirty-Four

*Police Station*
*Thursday, 3 a.m.*

Olivera kept his word to A. B. and dropped him off at the Tavernette, then drove back down Lee to the station, where Springer and Reagan sat drinking coffee and checking periodically on the detainees, Hollis Raines and Paul Krueger.

"First time we've had a full house in a while," Olivera said to the sergeants. He stopped at the coffee nook and filled his cup. "I'm trying to remember if I ate dinner. I don't think I did."

"There's some doughnuts left from this morning, Chief."

"No thanks, I think I'll get on with it, see if I can get a couple of hours of sleep at home before the night is over."

Springer stood, fishing the keys to the cells out of the top drawer of his desk. "He's waitin' for you, Chief."

"You get him booked?"

"Yep."

"Reagan," Olivera said, "thanks for coming in. You can go on home now."

Reagan got up from the chair next to Springer's desk. "I think I will, Lieutenant."

"Go ahead, we'll see you in the morning," Olivera

glanced at the wall clock, "which is about three, four hours from now."

Reagan winced, then, picking up his jacket, left through the back door.

Olivera made his way to the cell at the back, unlocked the door, and went in. The detainee was stretched out on the lower bunk, but as soon as Olivera had inserted the key in the lock, he sat up and reached for his sports jacket, which he'd hung over a chair. "Good evening, Lieutenant," he said in a low, slow voice, "or should I say good morning?"

Olivera, ignoring the question, switched on the recorder he'd taken from his pocket and placed it on the bunk. "Hollis Raines of New Orleans, Louisiana, correct?" He sat in the folding chair.

"That's right."

"So, Mr. Raines"—Olivera leaned forward—"how did you happen to come to Hembree?"

"I had business here."

"What kind of business?"

"I came to see A. B. Bilyeu and Cecil DeGroat."

"Did you let them know you were coming?"

"No."

"Your visit to Larkspur tonight was a little unorthodox for a business meeting, wouldn't you say?"

"I suppose."

"You seriously wounded Mr. DeGroat."

"That would have never happened if he hadn't drawn his gun. He threatened me. What was I to do? Stand there and let him shoot me?"

"You kicked his door in, did you not?" Olivera leaned back.

"I knocked, and they wouldn't answer, but I knew

they were in there."

Olivera inhaled and let the breath out slowly. "I suppose, then, you're saying this incident was *their* fault."

"Indeed it was, Lieutenant, indeed it was. I had no intention—"

"And yet you *did* arrive with a loaded gun."

"Of course, I did. I have a license to carry, and when I'm out in the boondocks—"

*Boondocks*. Indeed, they were, but somehow, coming out of Raines's mouth, it annoyed him. "Okay, let's get back to the reason for your meeting."

"My daddy, Colton Raines, had a little arrangement with the Bilyeus, first Arnold who, as you may know, passed on a few years back, and then with Emile, his cousin from New Orleans, who managed Larkspur for some time. When Emile died, there was nobody left to keep an eye on things except Emile's brother and nephew, A. B. and Cecil."

"What *arrangement* are you speaking of?"

"Well, when Mr. Kit Morris died, certain belongings should have passed on to me. That was the original arrangement, actually."

"And why was that?" Olivera said, clearly caught off-guard.

"Well, let's say in payment for service rendered."

"Service rendered? Could you be more specific?"

"From the time I was a kid, still living with my folks down the street from the Morrises, I helped at the poker games. Kit said I was a born mathematician, and most the time, he let me hold the bank. More often than not, I did small favors for the players, lit their cigars, filled up their glasses with whiskey or gin. I could always remember who preferred what. Or often they'd send me scrambling up the stairs with a message for the Morris sisters. Miss Eleanor and Miss Peggy never came down, but they'd send down snacks for the men."

"And you say Kit left the casta paintings to you? That's what we're talking about, I assume."

"He did."

"Was this put in a will?"

"I always thought there was a will, but there wasn't, and when Kit died, he hadn't told anybody where the paintings were. So I sort of gave up till some years ago, Daddy found out one day at the Royal Street Gallery in New Orleans that David Morell, the owner, was looking for the paintings Kit had."

"Did your father speak to Morell about that?"

"Not really, not directly. It wasn't till this week, after Will died, that we found out that the paintings had been discovered in the cellar."

"So, you didn't know about the alcove?"

"No."

"Interesting." Olivera got up from his chair and stood, glancing around. "About this property of Arnold's that you were to receive, the paintings, I mean. You or your father spoke to Emile about it after Arnold died?"

"Yes, actually it was Daddy who spoke to Emile, but he didn't get anywhere."

"And then you—or your father—spoke with A. B. and DeGroat?"

"That's right. I spoke to 'em, but it didn't do any good."

"Did you ever demand hush money from any of the Bilyeu family members?"

"Why would I do that? I just wanted what was mine.

That's all."

Olivera rubbed the back of his neck and sat back in the chair. "Well, Mr. Raines, what this boils down to is regardless of what sort of business you had with the Bilyeus, you apparently forcefully entered the Summer House and shot Mr. DeGroat, and therefore I am holding you on suspicion of illegal trespass and use of deadly force."

"But DeGroat pulled his gun first!"

"And according to the Castle Doctrine, he had a right to."

"I want to speak to a lawyer," he said, standing.

"Fine. Sergeant Springer has your cellphone?"

"He does."

"I'll send him in right away. But tell me this." He paused. "How did Will Grayson get mixed up in it? Apparently, he had nothing to gain. The man was sick, dying."

"I felt bad for Will. We were friends when we were kids. He was all alone after Kit died. I thought maybe he could exert some pressure on A. B. and DeGroat to come clean about the paintings."

"Were you aware of his meeting with DeGroat at Morris House?"

"Not specifically." He shook his head.

"And when you heard Grayson had died…"

"Yes, I suspected A. B. and DeGroat might have had something to do with it."

"But DeGroat claims he did not."

"I couldn't say one way or the other."

Olivera left the cell, locked it, and walked toward the front. "Springer"—he passed him the keys—"take Mr. Raines his cellphone and let him make a call. He wants to contact an attorney."

Springer opened the box holding the detainee's belongings and took out the cellphone. "Did he confess?"

"Far from it. And how this is going to be straightened out is more than I can see. It'll go to trial is my guess."

"You're kidding."

"I wish I were. A. B. says Colton and Hollis Raines were blackmailing them. Raines says he was just trying to get what was rightfully his. You want to place a bet?"

## Chapter Thirty-Five

*Police Station*
*Thursday, 10:00 a.m.*

At mid-morning on Thursday, Raines was still in custody and had placed a call to an attorney. Paul Krueger was about to be released on his own recognizance. Since no charges had been brought against Krueger, Olivera decided to let him go, but with a strong warning to stay away from Lauren Wilson and Mosey Frye. "One or both could still decide to press charges, so watch it," he counseled.

"You've got this all wrong, Lieutenant," Krueger said, apparently hoping to expunge whatever negative opinions Olivera might have formed. "I did *nothing*. It was no more than a harmless joke."

"No more harassment, Mr. Krueger, joke or no joke. Stay away from McAllister, the college, any place you might run into Dr. Wilson, even casually."

Krueger slung his backpack over one shoulder and headed for the front door, nodding to Ms. Hill as he passed her desk.

Olivera sighed and shook his head. "I'd be happy to see the last of that guy, but I'm afraid I'll have to get him back here for the trial."

Springer, who was reared back in his desk chair, eyes half closed, sat up straight and opened his eyes.

"What trial?"

"Oh, there'll be a trial, all right," Olivera said. "Too much to sort out in this other business although I suppose the lawyers might reach some sort of compromise."

"Raines and Bilyeu, you mean?"

"Can't tell for the life of me who's telling the truth."

"Or maybe *none* of them is telling the truth—you ever think about that, Chief?"

"You know what, Springer? I have a mind to drop in on Dr. Wilson. If either of us could figure this out, my bet would be on her."

"It would, would it?" Reagan chimed in as he reached Springer's desk, three coffees balanced between his fingers. He set the cups down, then handed one to Olivera. "Here you go, Lieutenant."

"Thanks, Reagan." Olivera took a sip, and instead of going to his cubicle, he remained leaning against Reagan's desk. He looked at Springer. "You haven't forgotten she's a profiler."

"Nope, hadn't forgotten that."

"She wasn't directly involved in the Ashby case, but she helped sort out some things at the end."

"True. So, what you gonna do, Chief, run it all by her?"

"I think I will." Usually, in such circumstances, Olivera would be heading to the morgue to run it by McGinnis, but this time he had a feeling that Wilson might pick up on something that hadn't caught the attention of either him or McGinnis. He pulled out his cell and tapped in her number. "Dr. Wilson—"

"Lieutenant?"

"Yes, Olivera here. Would you mind dropping by the station this morning? I wanted to run a couple of things by you and also to fill you in on what we've found out. Would that work for you?"

"Sure, Lieutenant. Let me throw some clothes on and I'll be right over."

"Appreciate it." He slipped his phone in his pocket and turned to Springer and Reagan. "She's coming in."

He moved to his cubicle and sat in his Executive, facing the evidence board. He had more to add to it, quite a bit, in fact, but hadn't had a chance, given the hustle of the last day. He took a few tabs out of his desk drawer and quickly labeled them, one for each incident—the discovery of the grave, the shooting at Larkspur, and his interviews with several people of interest—DeGroat, Bilyeu, and Raines. With thumbtacks, he attached the tabs to the board and sat back down to look, realizing he'd omitted the information Nadia had given him concerning Morell's thoughts on the paintings. If Fernanda de Lobos was, indeed, of mixed ancestry, as Morell conjectured, that might explain the information he'd received from Jessup and Ellison vis-à-vis baby Doe's remains. All the clues were beginning to form a kind of muddled whole, but what was disturbing him first and foremost was the contradictory information he'd received from A. B., DeGroat, and Hollis Raines. He was hoping Wilson could shed some light on that.

A few more minutes passed, and hearing someone come in at the front, he stepped to the door of his cubicle. "Dr. Wilson," he waved, "back here."

She walked toward him, pausing to speak to Springer and Reagan as she passed their desks.

Springer stood. "Can I get you anything, Dr. Wilson?"

"Thanks, Sergeant, but I'm fine."

"Come in, come in," Olivera said to Wilson.

She sat in the only available chair, the metal folding chair next to his desk.

"May I take your coat?"

"No, thanks." She slipped her hands in her coat pockets, a look of expectancy on her face.

"You're looking—" He stopped, uncertain how to finish that without saying the wrong thing.

"Happy?" she said.

He chuckled. "I guess I was going to say *chipper* but it didn't sound quite right."

"We aren't always sure what to say to each other these days, are we, Lieutenant?"

"No, we aren't." He sat back down. "I called you this morning, uh, for professional reasons—I mean I would like an opinion."

"I had a feeling you might."

He cleared his throat. "You see, after I left your place yesterday evening, something important happened. There was a confrontation between a couple of people of interest. The owners of Larkspur Plantation, A. B. Bilyeu and Cecil DeGroat, were out at the place about ten o'clock. Hollis Raines—the nephew of your neighbor Matthew, by the way—appeared at the door and when no one answered, kicked it in. So DeGroat pulled a gun on him but didn't shoot. Then Raines drew his gun and *did* shoot, wounding DeGroat."

"My lord!" She tensed up, a sudden blush passing over her cheeks.

"No one was seriously hurt, though," he hastened to add. "DeGroat sustained a pretty bad wound in the upper arm. He'll be all right in a couple of weeks."

"Well, that's good."

330

"A. B. was pretty shaken up, but refused to spend the night in the hospital," he said with a slight chuckle. "I dropped him at the Tavernette on my way home."

"Sounds like you had a busy night, Lieutenant."

"I did, indeed."

"What about the grave?" she asked. "Or is it too soon to know?"

"Actually, Jessup and Ellison were able to get quick results on a couple of points. They've dated the bones to the mid-twentieth century, more or less. They also suspect that the child was of mixed birth, and Dr. McGinnis believes, from her study of the bones, that the infant was quite young—a few days old, maybe—but not an aborted fetus or stillbirth. And one more thing. I heard from Nadia Abboud in New Orleans that the casta paintings are probably authentic Cardosos, and David Morell has noted a connection between the child pictured in one of the vignettes and the portrait of Fernanda de Lobos." Remembering that Wilson hadn't actually seen the paintings, he pulled out his cellphone and scrolled to the pictures he'd snapped. "This is what I'm referring to. He suspects that child"—he tapped the top corner of the composite—"who he believes to be Fernanda de Lobos and whom the painter labeled as *mestiza*, was born of a private pregnancy. So, the secret of the paintings seems to relate rather specifically to the Bilyeu-De Lobos ancestry."

She looked for a moment at the paintings. "And I suppose some families would want to keep such information under wraps." She handed him back the phone.

"That's what I thought, but after my interview with A. B., I'm not entirely sure. All along, I've suspected that some coverup might be at the heart of the incident, but now…"

"What did he say?"

"He said the Bilyeus, at least the ones living today, are not particularly concerned about such things. He says the whole idea of ethnic purity is a bit naïve, passé."

"That's interesting," she observed.

"I thought so too, but you and I aren't from here, are we?"

"So, if the desire to hide the paintings—"

"I'm hoping," he interrupted, "you can help me with that. You would think the interviews with the suspects might have cleared things up, given us some idea as to intention, culpability, but I'm more stumped than before." He shook his head. "Raines seemed every bit as earnest and reasonable as Bilyeu and DeGroat. As a profiler, I'm hoping you might be able to pick up on something."

"You want me to look for a *tell*, so to speak, something that will suggest who might be lying?"

"Yes," he nodded, "that's what I want."

She got up and paced toward the window at the back of the cubicle.

"Not much of a view, I'm afraid." He followed her with his eyes.

She stared out at the parking lot.

"Would you be able to help me out?"

She turned and faced him. "I'll do what I can, but it will have to be squeezed in."

"I understand. I know you're terribly busy, with the house and all."

"Tell me something. You said this Hollis Raines— and I'd like to hear a little more about him—kicked in the door?"

"That's right."

"Suggests a lot of anger, or at least some real aggression toward the Bilyeus. Did he know them well?" She came back toward the desk and sat in the folding chair.

"Not really. DeGroat, in fact, didn't know him at all. Only knew *of* him, he said."

"And Bilyeu?" she asked.

"Well, he claimed Hollis's father tried to blackmail his older brother Emile, who looked after Larkspur after Arnold died. I'm not entirely clear on that. I believe the alleged extortion might have begun with Colton, Hollis's father, then continued with Hollis and, more recently, Grayson. Colton is up in years. He was a member of the original poker group."

"And why exactly did they attempt—allegedly—to blackmail the Bilyeus?"

"That's not really clear, either. I assumed the plan was to use the paintings to expose family secrets. But after what A. B. said, I'm not sure there was any real interest on the part of the Bilyeus in covering any of it up. And besides that, Raines claims he wanted the paintings because they had been promised to him."

"Anything to support that claim?"

Olivera rubbed his chin. "Maybe, if Kit left a will, put apparently he didn't. I could check on that. I could ask Carlotta Humphrey. But if there had been a will, surely all that would have been worked out a long time ago."

"Maybe there *was* a will and it was destroyed."

"I guess." He sipped his coffee.

"More often than not, wills never get written down.

Hollis might have been told he would receive something but—"

"True. At any rate, Raines claims he *wasn't* blackmailing anyone, and of course he would, while Bilyeu and DeGroat claim he *was* blackmailing them and had also attempted to blackmail Emile before them. And one more thing. Colton was a member of the group, but Hollis was just a kid at the time, around ten. And Grayson was younger, too, about Hollis's age or younger."

"So, that really is interesting. As children hanging around a group of adults, they might have observed things, *known* things the adults never suspected they knew. "Little pitchers have big ears," my mom says.

"Hmm," Olivera murmured. "Yeah, I suppose so."

"But you think Raines's explanation was convincing?"

"I did, but maybe he'd already put together a story, knowing that at some point he might have to account for his actions."

"Just listening to you now, what really caught my attention was *what he did*. He came to Hembree without letting anyone know that he was coming, then, late at night, kicked in the door and shot DeGroat, despite little provocation."

"Well, DeGroat *did* pull a gun on him."

"But why would Raines shoot, rather quickly, I gather? Suggests a lack of control."

"Now that I'm hearing it all back from you, it does seem *out of character*, let's say. The man that Raines was trying to portray, at least in my presence, was not exactly the same Raines that trespassed at Larkspur."

"I don't suppose he knew anything about the grave,

did he? Or maybe he did, since he frequented Morris House at the time."

"That's right," he said, "but you know, I didn't ask Raines about the grave."

"Did you mention it to Bilyeu or DeGroat?"

"Bilyeu, not DeGroat. DeGroat was just coming out from under the anesthetic. I'll question him again today."

"What did Bilyeu say?"

"Nothing, but his reaction suggested he was hearing it for the first time."

"If I were you, Lieutenant, I would see what Raines can tell you about that. A ten-year-old boy is likely to have seen something, heard something."

"I will do that, right now, as a matter of fact. Would you care to watch?"

"Sure."

Olivera gathered his notes, including the gruesome photographs of the grave site, and picking up his cup, led the way to the interrogation room. Once everything was in place, he spoke to Springer. "I want to question Raines again."

"You think you can get him to talk without his lawyer here?"

"I don't know, but it's worth a try. Dr. Wilson has picked up on something." He looked in his pocket for his notepad and laid it on Springer's desk. "See if you can get the lawyer on the phone and let him know I would like to question Raines on a tangential matter. See if he can join us here as soon as possible."

Springer, looking at the pad, picked up the receiver and punched in the number. He spoke to the lawyer's secretary and, holding the phone to his chest, said, "His secretary says he's staying at the Tavernette. She'll give him a call and let us know."

The call came in quickly, and Raines's lawyer soon arrived at the station.

Olivera shook the man's hand. "I'm Lieutenant Olivera, and this is Dr. Lauren Wilson, forensic psychologist at Blanchard College."

"John Vickers. How do you do?" He shook Olivera's hand, then Wilson's. "Nice to make your acquaintance, ma'am. You're a professor, are you?"

"Yes, I'll be starting here this semester."

Vickers turned to Olivera. "If you don't mind, I'd like to get acquainted with Mr. Raines. I only recently received the call from his relative, Matthew Raines."

"Of course, how much time do you need?"

"Fifteen minutes, maybe less. What are the charges, Lieutenant?"

"No charges yet. But I'm holding him on suspicion of illegal trespass and use of deadly force. The man he shot, Cecil DeGroat, is at Delta Infirmary, and I've only been able to question him briefly."

"Mr. DeGroat hasn't pressed charges?"

"Not yet."

"Okay. Let me speak to my client, if you will."

Springer accompanied Mr. Vickers to Raines's cell, while Olivera and Wilson entered the small observation room. "Just before we begin, Springer will switch the light off, and you should be able to watch unseen."

"I didn't bring anything with me," she said. "If I could get some paper and a black ink pen."

"No problem. Let me ask Ms. Hill."

Olivera spoke to Ms. Hill and returned to the observation room with a legal pad and pen.

"Thanks," she said. "I'll pass along the document as

soon as I've had a chance to edit."

"Good. I wasn't expecting a formal report but—"

"Should I be called to testify, the court will want my original notes."

"Right." He stepped out of the room, and seeing Springer with Vickers and Raines heading toward the interrogation room, he peeked back in. "Looks like we're ready to start." He closed the door and entered the adjacent room behind Springer. "Mr. Raines, as Mr. Vickers may have explained, I would like to ask you a few questions on a matter that may or may not relate to your case."

"I understand."

"Okay, we'll be recording this"—he pressed the button to record—"so, let's begin. Lieutenant Gustavo Olivera interviewing Hollis Raines with his attorney, John Vickers, present. Mr. Raines"—he focused his attention on the suspect—"last night, actually this morning early, we spoke, and you gave me your version of the events that occurred on the night of Wednesday, January 6, at Larkspur Plantation. Some few hours earlier, Mr. Frank Ferguson, Jr. was thinning out the thicket next to the Morris house, which you're familiar with, correct?"

"Yes, I know the place," Raines answered.

"So, Ferguson was uprooting dead trees and in the process brought up a small gravestone entangled in the root ball of an elm." Olivera paused but continued to look closely at Raines, who seemed to be registering some sort of emotion, but he couldn't tell for sure. He had to wonder if Wilson was seeing what *he* was seeing. "A small casket was attached to the stone, and inside the casket, a human skeleton." He placed the pictures in front of Raines. "Forensic experts have dated the remains as mid-twentieth century more or less, which I believe corresponds to your time at Morris House, when you, as a young boy, had the run of the house and might have heard something or seen something related to the burial of the infant. Now, before you answer, I would like you to know that your cooperation in this matter would be appreciated. I would certainly be predisposed to encourage leniency, in the event…"

Raines appeared calm on the surface, his hands clasped and resting on the table. But something ever so slight about his demeanor seemed to have changed. He leaned over and whispered something in Vickers's ear. Then Vickers whispered something back, and Raines whispered to Vickers again. Once the exchange between client and lawyer had ended, Raines looked at Olivera and said, "Yes, I do know something, though I fully expected to go to my grave without ever revealing—"

"I will do my best," Olivera said, "to keep your revelation confidential if I possibly can."

"I have your word on that?" Raines asked.

Olivera nodded. "Yes, you have my word."

"I will tell you what I know, but I would want to protect the victim at all cost."

"You mean the deceased child?"

He shook his head. "The mother, who was little more than a child herself."

"One of the Morris sisters?"

"No, a girl who worked for the Morrises."

"You must have been close in age, you and the girl."

"Yes." Raines's voice broke. "She, uh, was a friend of ours."

"Your and Will's friend?"

Raines nodded.

"Answer for the recorder, please."

"She was our friend, yes," he said, then added, "but Will was younger, and she was a couple of years older than I."

"Can you tell me who the father was?"

"Arnold Bilyeu." With that revelation, his clasped hands visibly tightened.

"Do you know anything about the circumstances?"

"Rape…it had to have been. She was too young to give consent."

"And nothing was done?"

"I never heard anything specific. It was all very hush hush, given that Kit and his older sister felt, above all, they wanted to protect the girl. She stayed in the house while she was pregnant, and when the child died soon after it was born, they buried the body secretly. I was later told about that by Will Grayson. He knew the man who dug the grave and brought a stone for a marker."

"Did he say who that was?"

"Somebody from the Bilyeu place. I don't know his name."

"I have to wonder then," Olivera cleared his throat, "if you—or you and Grayson—were promised the casta paintings in return for your silence."

"That was probably the case, though as I said, Will was still a kid and wasn't really aware."

"You suspected then, when you were younger, that the adults concerned in this were aware of your knowledge of the situation. And," Olivera continued, "to keep you quiet, they offered you a future payoff of some kind?"

"Yes, that pretty much describes it."

"I also have to wonder if your alleged aggression toward Arnold Bilyeu's relatives might have been motivated in part by your feelings about Arnold, who you believed to have raped your friend."

Raines's eyes narrowed. "I won't deny that's a possibility, though it was my intention to get what was promised to me and nothing more."

"Have you ever spoken to Mr. DeGroat or Mr. A. B. Bilyeu about what you know or at least suspect concerning Arnold Bilyeu?"

He shook his head.

"Please answer for the recorder."

"No, I have not."

"And what about Mr. Emile Bilyeu?"

"No, but I suspected that he might have been aware."

"Could you say more about that?"

"I think he was aware of his cousin's reputation, let's say. I don't think Emile was particularly fond of Arnold, but he did seem to have an interest in preventing anything negative from being made public."

"And these paintings," Olivera said with exasperation in his voice, "why do you suppose they have been kept secret for all these decades? The Bilyeus—at least A. B. and DeGroat—don't seem to have a problem with their being made public."

"Simple, Lieutenant. Nobody knew where they were. Till this day, I haven't laid eyes on them. Neither had Will, God rest his soul."

"As soon as it's determined whom they belong to, perhaps…well…"

Once the interview had ended, Olivera and Wilson returned to his office to exchange reactions. "What do you think?" Olivera asked.

"Here are my observation notes—" She laid the legal pad on his desk. "—if you'd like to keep a copy. Actually, you keep the original, and I'd like a copy for my files."

"Certainly, but if you could stick around a while longer…?"

"Frank Ferguson will be at the house around noon to finish trimming the thicket. As long as he stays clear of the marked off area—"

"Sure, have him go ahead. Hopefully, we've seen the last of the revelations at Morris House."

"If I'd only known," she said with a slow shake of her head.

"You had a big hint. You bought the house from Mosey Frye."

"Lieutenant," she said with a grin, "that was unkind."

He laughed. "She's not going to be happy with me when she finds out I solved one without her."

"Well, credit where credit's due. If it hadn't been for Paul Krueger—"

"Oh, please, I'd rather share the spotlight with Mosey than that guy. I hope we've seen the last of him."

"I suspect you've scared him off." She grinned again.

"And in the meantime, Dr. Wilson, would you please get some modern locks on those doors and windows?"